P. G. Wodehouse was born in ⸻ ⸻ educated at Dulwich College. After working for the Hong Kong and Shanghai Bank for two years, he left to earn his living as a journalist and storywriter, writing the 'By the Way' column in the old *Globe*. He also contributed a series of school stories to a magazine for boys, the *Captain*, in one of which Psmith made his first appearance. Going to America before the First World War, he sold a serial to the *Saturday Evening Post*, and for the next twenty-five years almost all his books appeared first in this magazine. He was part author and writer of the lyrics of eighteen musical comedies including *Kissing Time*. He married in 1914 and in 1955 took American citizenship. He wrote over ninety books, and his work has won worldwide acclaim, having been translated into many languages. *The Times* hailed him as a 'comic genius recognized in his lifetime as a classic and an old master of farce'.

P. G. Wodehouse said, 'I believe there are two ways of writing novels. One is mine, making a sort of musical comedy without music and ignoring real life altogether; the other is going right deep down into life and not caring a damn . . .' He was created a Knight of the British Empire in the New Year's Honours List in 1975. In a BBC interview he said that he had no ambition left now that he had been knighted and there was a waxwork of him in Madame Tussaud's. He died on St Valentine's Day in 1975 at the age of ninety-three.

# P. G. WODEHOUSE

## *Lord Emsworth Acts for the Best*

### THE BLANDINGS SHORT STORIES

*With an Introduction by Frank Muir*

PENGUIN BOOKS

PENGUIN BOOKS

Published by the Penguin Group
Penguin Books Ltd, 27 Wrights Lane, London W8 5TZ, England
Penguin Putnam Inc., 375 Hudson Street, New York, New York 10014, USA
Penguin Books Australia Ltd, Ringwood, Victoria, Australia
Penguin Books Canada Ltd, 10 Alcorn Avenue, Toronto, Ontario, Canada M4V 3B2
Penguin Books India (P) Ltd, 11, Community Centre, Panchsheel Park, New Delhi – 110 017, India
Penguin Books (NZ) Ltd, Private Bag 102902, NSMC, Auckland, New Zealand
Penguin Books (South Africa) (Pty) Ltd, 5 Watkins Street, Denver Ext 4, Johannesburg 2094, South Africa

Penguin Books Ltd, Registered Offices: Harmondsworth, Middlesex, England

'The Custody of the Pumpkin', 'Lord Emsworth Acts for the Best', 'Pig-hoo-o-o-o-ey!',
'Company for Gertrude', 'The Go-getter' and 'Lord Emsworth and the Girl Friend'
previously published in *Blandings Castle* by Herbert Jenkins 1935 and by
Penguin Books 1954

'The Crime Wave at Blandings' previously published in *Lord Emsworth and Others*
by Herbert Jenkins 1937 and by Penguin Books 1966

'Birth of a Salesman' previously published in *Nothing Serious* by Herbert Jenkins 1950

'Sticky Wicket at Blandings' previously published in *Plum Pie* by Herbert Jenkins 1966

This collection first published in Penguin Books 1992
Reprinted in Penguin Classics 2001

1

Copyright 1935, 1937, 1950 by P. G. Wodehouse
Copyright © P. G. Wodehouse
Introduction copyright © Frank Muir, 1992
All rights reserved

The moral right of the author of the introduction has been asserted

Printed in England by Clays Ltd, St Ives plc

# CONTENTS

# INTRODUCTION

It was typical of P. G. Wodehouse and rather indicative. I went to see him at his house in Remensburg, Long Island, in the late 1960s, and when we were slumped on the patio after lunch and I tried to persuade him to visit England after being away from it for so many years, his reaction was:

Would I find Dulwich much changed?

I found difficulty in answering this. Not because it was an awkward question, which it was, but because I was suffering a great deal of personal agony at the time from a grossly overweight boxer-dog named Debbie who was sitting bolt upright in my lap. Debbie was one of the pack of stray dogs, each of them obese, partly limbless, foul breathed or in some other way socially unacceptable, who were enjoying the love and full feeding-bowls always available to them at the Wodehouse home.

P. G. Wodehouse, then aged eighty-four and looking back over some sixty-five years, knew perfectly well that Dulwich's Kardomah Café had almost certainly become a Pizza Palace, and the Seventh Day Pentecostal Mission a Discount Carpet Centre (Open All Day Sunday); but what he was asking me, of course, was how much, if anything, was left of that turn-of-the-century, comfortable, confident middle-class Dulwich ambience he had known as a schoolboy. And, more importantly, whether Dulwich College still provided the sporting and academic stimulations, and the friendships, which had given the young Plum not only the most carefree years of his life but also a firm base of achievement from which to launch himself gently (if one can launch oneself gently) into the career which was to make him, arguably, the greatest humorous writer Britain has produced.

Not that there can be much argument. Whether a reader finds Wodehouse, or anybody else, funny is a matter of personal taste – one man's guffaw is another person's groan, and women (including Wodehouse's official biographer, Lady Frances Donaldson) have tended to be more resistant to the attractions of Wodehouse's fictional world than men – but there are other qualities which go to make greatness in a writer, such as high standards over a long haul, craftsmanship and range.

In a working life of seventy-three years Plum (which he signed himself and liked to be called) wrote over a hundred novels and volumes of short stories, all of them, including the last novel published posthumously in 1977, of an extraordinarily consistent standard. He also wrote sixteen plays (usually with his friend Guy Bolton), the lyrics for twenty-eight musical comedies, for eighteen of which he also wrote or co-wrote the libretto (more libretti than W. S. Gilbert produced). And in between these he filled up the chinks with scriptwriting in Hollywood and with turning out short stories and magazine pieces for journals such as the *Saturday Evening Post* and *Punch*.

And greatness was emphatically thrust upon Plum by his fellow writers. Peter Quennell wrote in the early 1940s,

> Though not one non-literary reader in a thousand will lift his eyes from the page to consider Wodehouse as an artist, a fellow hack cannot fail to admire the extraordinary skill with which, judged by professional literary standards, he goes about his business. Every sentence has a job to do and – in spite of the air of lunatic irresponsibility which hangs around a Wodehouse novel – does it neatly and efficiently.'

In the middle 1930s Hilaire Belloc, his rich part-Belgian blood overwhelming for a while his cool part-English reticence, broadcast a rather embarrassingly fulsome tribute in which he proclaimed the shy Plum to be 'the best writer of our time! . . . the best living writer of English! . . . the head of my profession! . . .'

Other self-confessed Wodehousians included, and include, Her Majesty the Queen Mother; the Rt. Hon. Herbert Asquith; Professor Gilbert Murray; Arnold Bennett; Rudyard Kipling; Sir Arthur Conan Doyle; the novelist and playwright, Ian Hay; Auberon Waugh ('Wodehouse has been more read than any other English novelist by his fellow novelists'); Malcolm Muggeridge; Kingsley Amis; Bernard Levin (in *The Times* he likened Bertie Wooster's line, 'In my heliotrope pyjamas with the old-gold stripe' to one of the great speeches in *Macbeth*) and many, many more.

Evelyn Waugh pointed out one excellent reason for the profession's respect for Wodehouse: 'One has to regard a man as a Master who can produce on average three uniquely brilliant and quite original similes to every page.' For example:

> The unpleasant, acrid smell of burnt poetry.
>
> *Young Men in Spats* (1936)
> [This was Evelyn Waugh's favourite Wodehouse line]

> Into the face of the young man who sat on the terrace of the Hotel Magnifique at Cannes there had crept a look of furtive shame, the shifty, hangdog look which announces that an Englishman is about to talk French.
>
> *The Luck of the Bodkins* (1935)

> The drowsy stillness of the summer afternoon was shattered by what sounded to his strained senses like G. K. Chesterton falling on a sheet of tin.
>
> *Mr Mulliner Speaking* (1935)

> His whole aspect was that of a man who had been unexpectedly struck by lightning.
>
> *Eggs, Beans and Crumpets* (1940)

And not only Wodehouse's contemporary colleagues regarded him as the Master of Humorous Prose. So did younger writers. Douglas Adams, whose present-day novels (*The Hitch Hiker's Guide to the Galaxy*, for example) successfully combine comedy, science-fiction and fantasy, wrote in the *Guardian*:

> My first impression on encountering P. G. Wodehouse was that I didn't think I liked that sort of thing very much. I was about thirteen or fourteen and sitting in the lavatory in the house of some distantly related aunt or other. I was not in any hurry to emerge, since to do so would mean having to engage in conversation with my aunt again, so I cast around for something to occupy my time and found a book on the window sill. A Jeeves book. I read through the first page, and found it to be so far removed from everything I found exciting at the time, which was mostly The Beatles (still is, in fact) that it didn't interest me. Furthermore I couldn't work out what 'a moody e & b' was, and at the first mention of aunts I clapped the book shut and began to read the jokes in an old *Reader's Digest* instead. I was that desperate.
>
> It wasn't until about fifteen years later that I opened a Wodehouse

again. I was already earning my living as a comedy writer myself by then and suddenly realized, with goose-pimples rising all over me, that I was in the presence of a great master.

Since then I have devoured his work repeatedly and voraciously, not merely because he is a great comic writer, but because I think he is arguably the greatest musician of the English language I have ever encountered. He may not have anything to say about Real Life (he would hoot at the very idea) but art practised at that level doesn't have to be *about* anything . . .

A final, poignant affirmation of the peculiar pleasure which Plum's frivolous, beautifully made stories gave his fellow toilers in the vineyard came, via Evelyn Waugh, from the eminent Catholic theologian, author and translator of the Bible, Monsignor Ronald Knox. Towards the end of his biography of Monsignor Knox, Waugh noted: 'For the remaining years of his life, Ronnie applied himself to devotional reading and the works of P. G. Wodehouse.'

Plum was never a social joke-teller, a party prankster. In fact, there is little or no evidence that he ever 'cracked a joke' in company or tried to wring a smile with a pun; that sort of behaviour was simply not his style. He was tremendously affable but also unworldly and shy, and a great hater of parties, from which he was inclined to slip away unnoticed and take the Pekinese for a walk. He was wholly disinterested in politics and money. (He made a lot of money but it was handled by Ethel. All he needed for himself was a few dollars a week to buy his pipe tobacco.) Throughout his life, his only deep interests, apart from his work, were the American musical theatre, boxing and the public-school cricket results.

His father was a magistrate in Hong Kong and so Plum and his brothers were looked after in England by relations, including aunts – whom he got on with. He had a brilliant career at Dulwich College. He was no intellectual but he edited the school magazine, was in the Classical Sixth and wrote Latin and Greek verse as fluently as he wrote verse in English. He also sang in the choir and was a school prefect. All in all he sounds an appalling little tick, but not so. He was beefy and athletic, a good boxer (until bad eyesight put a stop to that) and a fine cricketer, and he was popular with all ranks in the school.

But Plum's real pleasure and satisfaction lay in writing. He discovered that he had a facility for writing stories and light, amusing verse and that there was nothing he preferred doing, day or night. He sold his first story while he was still at school. Later his father fixed him up with a lowly job in a city bank, but after two years Plum found that he was earning more by writing so he resigned and began his spectacular career as a professional humorist.

He liked America and first went there to see the great boxers in action (then, as now, most champs were American) but found that the *Saturday Evening Post* and others liked his stories and he could make a living there. He met and married a young widow, Ethel, who brought with her a daughter, Leonora. Plum so loved Leonora that he legally adopted her.

He began to make money. The musical shows he was writing with Guy Bolton and Jerome Kerne were successful and his stories were in demand. He found that stories about America and Americans did not come easily to him so he began writing about the sort of English characters for which America had no equivalent and which they found funny, i.e., chinless wonders, dotty old noblemen and butlers. Almost all his stories were first published in America, then in Britain in magazines such as the *Strand*, and then republished in book form on both sides of the Atlantic.

Plum was the consummate professional author. The ordinary business of life, for him, was a series of interruptions to writing. He would even sneak away from dinner-parties to nip upstairs and get in a thousand words. At one time he made a practice of sticking his pages to the walls of his room at eye level so that he could prowl along them and spot the parts that needed further attention.

He discovered golf. With his burly, athletic figure, bald head, and friendly blue eyes he might well have been the only man in the world who looked his best in plus fours. And with golf, of course, particularly its obsessional aspects, he had another subject to write about:

'After all, golf is only a game,' said Millicent.

Women say these things without thinking. It does not mean that there is any kink in their character. They simply do not realize what they are saying.

*The Clicking of Cuthbert* (1922)

The least thing upsets him on the links. He misses short putts because of the uproar of the butterflies in the adjoining meadows.

*The Clicking of Cuthbert* (1922)

Walter clasped her to his bosom, using the interlocking grip.

*A Few Quick Ones* (1959)

Plum began by writing school stories for boys' magazines such as the *Captain*. His characters grew up, as it were, with his invention of Rupert Psmith (pronounced Smith), a rich, monocled lad with an ironic turn of phrase. (He was modelled on Rupert D'Oyley Carte, an Eton schoolfriend of Wodehouse's cousin. Rupert D'Oyley Carte sported a monocle, embraced communism at Eton, addressed everybody as 'comrade' and, when asked by his housemaster how he was, replied: 'Sir, I grow thinnah and thinnah.')

After Psmith came Ukridge (pronounced yew-kridge), a burly, eccentric opportunist with great and hopeless schemes for getting rich quickly. The Ukridge stories are notable for their brilliant plots. Wodehouse was now getting very good indeed at story-telling but devising new plots was a constant nightmare to him. His technique was to invent a character like Psmith or Ukridge upon whom he could hang any number of plots – if he could think of them – which could then be made up into books.

In 1915 he had a go at writing about a conventional 'chinless wonder' whom he christened Bertie Wooster. He gave Bertie a man-servant named after a county cricketer of repute, Jeeves. Ten years later, when he decided to write some more Jeeves and Bertie stories, he realized the capabilities of the characters. He still left Bertie with only a pea-sized brain but made him use it to its full so that he was no longer a conventional 'silly-ass'. And he invested Jeeves with a mystical, brainy omnipotence. Most important of all, he made Bertie the narrator of the stories so that Plum could now, potentially at any rate, make every line of the story funny and not just the descriptions of action and the dialogue:

Jeeves entered – or perhaps one should say shimmered – into the room . . . tall and dark and impressive. He might have been one of the better class ambassadors or the youngish High Priest of some refined and dignified religion.

*Ring for Jeeves* (1953)

'Yes, sir,' said Jeeves in a low, cold voice, as if he had been bitten in the leg by a personal friend.

*Carry on, Jeeves* (1925)

'Very good,' I said coldly. 'In that case, tinkerty-tonk.' And I meant it to sting.

*Right Ho, Jeeves* (1934)

The period between the wars was Plum's most successful and rewarding. He became one of America's highest paid authors and he and Ethel moved between rented and bought houses in England, France and the USA, but increasingly in the USA where the work was. In 1934 they left England for good and only returned on rare visits.

In the 1920s Plum steadily added to his permanent cast of characters. We had, besides Jeeves and Bertie: Mr Mulliner in his chair at The Angler's Rest telling stories of his peculiar nephews; the Oldest Member at the golf club telling golf stories; there were the chinless wonders of the Drones Club; servants (sixty-three butlers come into various books); the clergy; and assorted extras given the name of whatever they habitually ate or drank, for example, Eggs, Beans, Brandy-and-Sodas and small ports. Many members of Wodehouse's repertory company were related or knew each other so they continually popped up in each other's stories, which gave much of Wodehouse's work an agreeable coherence; the reader feels amongst friends.

Of his stock of minor but important characters perhaps the most memorable are Bertie Wooster's awesome aunts. Plum disappointed the theorists who hoped to trace Plum's treatment of his aunts to an unhappy childhood at their hands, as experienced by such as Rudyard Kipling, but Plum firmly pointed out that the reason for his treatment of aunts was simply that because his stories required female villains and in comedy you cannot have nasty mothers, he made aunts the villains instead:

Aunt is calling Aunt like mastodons bellowing across primeval swamps.

*The Inimitable Jeeves* (1923)

It is bad to be trapped in a den of slavering aunts, lashing their tails and glaring at you out of their red eyes.

*The Mating Season* (1949)

The sort of house you look at and say to yourself, 'Somebody's aunt lives there.'

*Carry on, Jeeves* (1925)

Plum and Ethel paid a visit to England in 1939 for Plum to receive the honorary degree of Litt.D. from Oxford University. It was their last visit to England.

Plum's career, finances and friends were in the USA and in 1955, at the age of seventy-four, he became an American citizen and held dual nationality. In January 1975 the British Government, in an exceedingly rare moment when a burst of common sense coincided with awareness of literary genius in its bailiwick, honoured Plum at last with a knighthood. Sir Pelham Grenville Wodehouse KBE, aged ninety-three, was too frail to make the journey to London to be dubbed. The next month he went into hospital with a complicated respiratory problem. Typically, he took to bed with him the book he was currently working on so that being ill would not mean he would have to stop writing. A few days later, on 14 February 1975, he got out of bed to cross the room and died.

The book he was working on was a Blandings Castle novel, the final story in the series he had been writing for sixty-two years telling of the life of Clarence, ninth Earl of Emsworth, in his stately home, Blandings Castle, with his bossy sister Lady Constance, his horrid secretary, Mr Baxter the butler, Beach, his prize pig, Empress of Blandings and his unintelligent son, the Hon. Freddie Threepwood who came on visits and disturbed his father's peace and quiet:

'Frederick won't be staying long, will he?' Lord Emsworth asked, with a father's pathetic eagerness.

*Full Moon* (1947)

There seems to be a case for saying that the Blandings Castle stories are the most autobiographical of Plum's works. Certainly Plum put much of himself in the character of Lord Emsworth: the agony of having to dress up and waste time being social; the disinclination to argue (Plum once tried to arrange with Guy Bolton that should one of them be talked about insultingly the other would not argue but agree, and, if possible, add details); the dislike of facing the human race, singly or in bulk, at any time. And the sublime unworldliness, mind absent on higher matters, as demonstrated by Lord Emsworth talking to the steward at his club:

'Tell me, Adams, have I eaten my cheese?'
'Not yet, your Lordship. I was about to send the waiter for it.'

'Never mind. Tell him to bring the bill instead. I remember that I have an appointment. I must not be late.'

'Shall I take the fork, your Lordship?'

'The fork?'

'Your Lordship has inadvertently put a fork in your coat-pocket.'

Lord Emsworth felt in the pocket indicated, and, with the air of an inexpert conjuror whose trick has succeeded contrary to his expectations, produced a silver-plated fork.

*Something Fresh* (1915)


Lord Emsworth's life was organized for him by a strong-spirited woman, his sister Lady Constance; and so was Plum's, by his wife Ethel. Ethel was no ogre like Lady Constance but nevertheless she ran everything to do with the home, bought and sold their houses, arranged dinner parties and trips to casinos, took charge of the money and negotiated the Hollywood deals. Both Wodehouse and Lord Emsworth badly needed looking after.

Rudyard Kipling told the novelist and playwright Ian Hay that 'Lord Emsworth and the Girl Friend' was one of the most perfect short stories he had ever read. It is one of the few stories in which Plum allowed himself to mix a touch of sentiment with the humour, and I think it probable that the deep pleasure which the little girl in the story brings to Lord Emsworth might well be a tribute from Plum to his deeply loved step-daughter, Leonora, for the pleasure which she, in her short life, had brought him.

In 1977, two years after his death, Plum's last book was published to public and critical acclaim. The old magic had lasted the course. The book was named, appropriately: *Sunset at Blandings*.

FRANK MUIR

# THE CUSTODY OF THE PUMPKIN

The morning sunshine descended like an amber shower-bath on Blandings Castle, lighting up with a heartening glow its ivied walls, its rolling parks, its gardens, outhouses, and messuages, and such of its inhabitants as chanced at the moment to be taking the air. It fell on green lawns and wide terraces, on noble trees and bright flower-beds. It fell on the baggy trousers-seat of Angus McAllister, head-gardener to the ninth Earl of Emsworth, as he bent with dour Scottish determination to pluck a slug from its reverie beneath the leaf of a lettuce. It fell on the white flannels of the Hon. Freddie Threepwood, Lord Emsworth's second son, hurrying across the water-meadows. It also fell on Lord Emsworth himself and on Beach, his faithful butler. They were standing on the turret above the west wing, the former with his eye to a powerful telescope, the latter holding the hat which he had been sent to fetch.

'Beach,' said Lord Emsworth.

'M'lord?'

'I've been swindled. This dashed thing doesn't work.'

'Your lordship cannot see clearly?'

'I can't see at all, dash it. It's all black.'

The butler was an observant man.

'Perhaps if I were to remove the cap at the extremity of the instrument, m'lord, more satisfactory results might be obtained.'

'Eh? Cap? Is there a cap? So there is. Take it off, Beach.'

'Very good, m'lord.'

'Ah!' There was satisfaction in Lord Emsworth's voice. He twiddled and adjusted, and the satisfaction deepened. 'Yes, that's better. That's capital. Beach, I can see a cow.'

'Indeed, m'lord?'

'Down in the water-meadows. Remarkable. Might be two yards away. All right, Beach. Shan't want you any longer.'

'Your hat, m'lord?'

'Put it on my head.'

'Very good, m'lord.'

The butler, this kindly act performed, withdrew. Lord Emsworth continued gazing at the cow.

The ninth Earl of Emsworth was a fluffy-minded and amiable old gentleman with a fondness for new toys. Although the main interest of his life was his garden, he was always ready to try a side line, and the latest of these side lines was this telescope of his. Ordered from London in a burst of enthusiasm consequent upon the reading of an article on astronomy in a monthly magazine, it had been placed in position on the previous evening. What was now in progress was its trial trip.

Presently, the cow's audience-appeal began to wane. It was a fine cow, as cows go, but, like so many cows, it lacked sustained dramatic interest. Surfeited after a while by the spectacle of it chewing the cud and staring glassily at nothing, Lord Emsworth decided to swivel the apparatus round in the hope of picking up something a trifle more sensational. And he was just about to do so, when into the range of his vision there came the Hon. Freddie. White and shining, he tripped along over the turf like a Theocritan shepherd hastening to keep an appointment with a nymph, and a sudden frown marred the serenity of Lord Emsworth's brow. He generally frowned when he saw Freddie, for with the passage of the years that youth had become more and more of a problem to an anxious father.

Unlike the male codfish, which, suddenly finding itself the parent of three million five hundred thousand little codfish, cheerfully resolves to love them all, the British aristocracy is apt to look with a somewhat jaundiced eye on its younger sons. And Freddie Threepwood was one of those younger sons who rather invite the jaundiced eye. It seemed to the head of the family that there was no way of coping with the boy. If he was allowed to live in London, he piled up debts and got into mischief; and when you jerked him back into the purer surroundings of Blandings Castle, he just mooned about the place, moping broodingly. Hamlet's society at Elsinore must have had much the same effect on his stepfather as did that of Freddie Threepwood at Blandings on Lord Emsworth. And it is probable that what induced the latter to keep a telescopic eye on him at this moment was the fact that his demeanour was so mysteriously jaunty, his bearing so intriguingly free from its customary crushed misery. Some inner voice whispered to Lord Emsworth that this smiling, prancing youth was up to no good and would bear watching.

The inner voice was absolutely correct. Within thirty seconds its case had been proved up to the hilt. Scarcely had his lordship had time to wish, as he invariably wished on seeing his offspring, that Freddie had been something entirely different in manners, morals, and appearance, and had been the son of somebody else living a considerable distance away, when out of a small spinney near the end of the meadow there bounded a girl. And Freddie, after a cautious glance over his shoulder, immediately proceeded to fold this female in a warm embrace.

Lord Emsworth had seen enough. He tottered away from the telescope, a shattered man. One of his favourite dreams was of some nice, eligible girl, belonging to a good family, and possessing a bit of money of her own, coming along some day and taking Freddie off his hands; but that inner voice, more confident now than ever, told him that this was not she. Freddie would not sneak off in this furtive fashion to meet eligible girls, nor could he imagine any eligible girl, in her right senses, rushing into Freddie's arms in that enthusiastic way. No, there was only one explanation. In the cloistral seclusion of Blandings, far from the Metropolis with all its conveniences for that sort of thing, Freddie had managed to get himself entangled. Seething with anguish and fury, Lord Emsworth hurried down the stairs and out on to the terrace. Here he prowled like an elderly leopard waiting for feeding-time, until in due season there was a flicker of white among the trees that flanked the drive and a cheerful whistling announced the culprit's approach.

It was with a sour and hostile eye that Lord Emsworth watched his son draw near. He adjusted his pince-nez, and with their assistance was able to perceive that a fatuous smile of self-satisfaction illumined the young man's face, giving him the appearance of a beaming sheep. In the young man's buttonhole there shone a nosegay of simple meadow flowers, which, as he walked, he patted from time to time with a loving hand.

'Frederick!' bellowed his lordship.

The villain of the piece halted abruptly. Sunk in a roseate trance, he had not observed his father. But such was the sunniness of his mood that even this encounter could not damp him. He gambolled happily up.

'Hullo, guv'nor!' he carolled. He searched in his mind for a pleasant topic of conversation – always a matter of some little difficulty on these occasions. 'Lovely day, what?'

His lordship was not to be diverted into a discussion of the weather.

He drew a step nearer, looking like the man who smothered the young princes in the Tower.

'Frederick,' he demanded, 'who was that girl?'

The Hon. Freddie started convulsively. He appeared to be swallowing with difficulty something large and jagged.

'Girl?' he quavered. 'Girl? Girl, guv'nor?'

'That girl I saw you kissing ten minutes ago down in the water-meadows.'

'Oh!' said the Hon. Freddie. He paused. 'Oh, ah!' He paused again. 'Oh, ah, yes! I've been meaning to tell you about that, guv'nor.'

'You have, have you?'

'All perfectly correct, you know. Oh, yes, indeed! All most absolutely correct-o! Nothing fishy, I mean to say, or anything like that. She's my fiancée.'

A sharp howl escaped Lord Emsworth, as if one of the bees humming in the lavender-beds had taken time off to sting him in the neck.

'Who is she?' he boomed. 'Who is this woman?'

'Her name's Donaldson.'

'Who is she?'

'Aggie Donaldson. Aggie's short for Niagara. Her people spent their honeymoon at the Falls, she tells me. She's American and all that. Rummy names they give kids in America,' proceeded Freddie, with hollow chattiness. 'I mean to say! Niagara! I ask you!'

'Who is she?'

'She's most awfully bright, you know. Full of beans. You'll love her.'

'Who is she?'

'And can play the saxophone.'

'Who,' demanded Lord Emsworth for the sixth time, 'is she? And where did you meet her?'

Freddie coughed. The information, he perceived, could no longer be withheld, and he was keenly alive to the fact that it scarcely fell into the class of tidings of great joy.

'Well, as a matter of fact, guv'nor, she's a sort of cousin of Angus McAllister's. She's come over to England for a visit, don't you know, and is staying with the old boy. That's how I happened to run across her.'

Lord Emsworth's eyes bulged and he gargled faintly. He had had many unpleasant visions of his son's future, but they had never included one of him walking down the aisle with a sort of cousin of his head-gardener.

'Oh!' he said. 'Oh, indeed?'

'That's the strength of it, guv'nor.'

Lord Emsworth threw his arms up, as if calling on Heaven to witness a good man's persecution, and shot off along the terrace at a rapid trot. Having ranged the grounds for some minutes, he ran his quarry to earth at the entrance to the yew alley.

The head-gardener turned at the sound of his footsteps, He was a sturdy man of medium height, with eyebrows that would have fitted a bigger forehead. These, added to a red and wiry beard, gave him a formidable and uncompromising expression. Honesty Angus McAllister's face had in full measure, and also intelligence; but it was a bit short on sweetness and light.

'McAllister,' said his lordship, plunging without preamble into the matter of his discourse. 'That girl. You must send her away.'

A look of bewilderment clouded such of Mr McAllister's features as were not concealed behind his beard and eyebrows.

'Gurrul?'

'That girl who is staying with you. She must go!'

'Gae where?'

Lord Emsworth was not in the mood to be finicky about details.

'Anywhere,' he said. 'I won't have her here a day longer.'

'Why?' inquired Mr McAllister, who liked to thresh these things out.

'Never mind why. You must send her away immediately.'

Mr McAllister mentioned an insuperable objection.

'She's payin' me twa poon' a week,' he said simply.

Lord Emsworth did not grind his teeth, for he was not given to that form of displaying emotion; but he leaped some ten inches into the air and dropped his pince-nez. And, though normally a fair-minded and reasonable man, well aware that modern earls must think twice before pulling the feudal stuff on their employees, he took on the forthright truculence of a large landowner of the early Norman period ticking off a serf.

'Listen, McAllister! Listen to me! Either you send that girl away today or you can go yourself. I mean it!'

A curious expression came into Angus McAllister's face – always excepting the occupied territories. It was the look of a man who has not forgotten Bannockburn, a man conscious of belonging to the country of William Wallace and Robert the Bruce. He made Scotch noises at the back of his throat.

'Y'r lorrudsheep will accept ma notis,' he said, with formal dignity.

'I'll pay you a month's wages in lieu of notice and you will leave this afternoon,' retorted Lord Emsworth with spirit.

'Mphm!' said Mr McAllister.

Lord Emsworth left the battlefield with a feeling of pure exhilaration, still in the grip of the animal fury of conflict. No twinge of remorse did he feel at the thought that Angus McAllister had served him faithfully for ten years. Nor did it cross his mind that he might miss McAllister.

But that night, as he sat smoking his after-dinner cigarette, Reason, so violently expelled, came stealing timidly back to her throne, and a cold hand seemed suddenly placed upon his heart.

With Angus McAllister gone, how would the pumpkin fare?

The importance of this pumpkin in the Earl of Emsworth's life requires, perhaps, a word of explanation. Every ancient family in England has some little gap in its scroll of honour, and that of Lord Emsworth was no exception. For generations back his ancestors had been doing notable deeds; they had sent out from Blandings Castle statesmen and warriors, governors and leaders of the people: but they had not – in the opinion of the present holder of the title – achieved a full hand. However splendid the family record might appear at first sight, the fact remained that no Earl of Emsworth had ever won a first prize for pumpkins at the Shrewsbury Show. For roses, yes. For tulips, true. For spring onions, granted. But not for pumpkins; and Lord Emsworth felt it deeply.

For many a summer past he had been striving indefatigably to remove this blot on the family escutcheon, only to see his hopes go tumbling down. But this year at last victory had seemed in sight, for there had been vouchsafed to Blandings a competitor of such amazing parts that his lordship, who had watched it grow practically from a pip, could not envisage failure. Surely, he told himself as he gazed on its golden roundness, even Sir Gregory Parsloe-Parsloe, of Matching-ham Hall, winner for three successive years, would never be able to produce anything to challenge this superb vegetable.

And it was this supreme pumpkin whose welfare he feared he had jeopardized by dismissing Angus McAllister. For Angus was its official trainer. He understood the pumpkin. Indeed, in his reserved Scottish way, he even seemed to love it. With Angus gone, what would the harvest be?

Such were the meditations of Lord Emsworth as he reviewed the position of affairs. And though, as the days went by, he tried to tell himself that Angus McAllister was not the only man in the world who understood pumpkins, and that he had every confidence, the most complete and unswerving confidence, in Robert Barker, recently Angus's second-in-command, now promoted to the post of head-gardener and custodian of the Blandings Hope, he knew that this was but shallow bravado. When you are a pumpkin owner with a big winner in your stable, you judge men by hard standards, and every day it became plainer that Robert Barker was only a makeshift. Within a week Lord Emsworth was pining for Angus McAllister.

It might be purely imagination, but to his excited fancy the pumpkin seemed to be pining for Angus too. It appeared to be drooping and losing weight. Lord Emsworth could not rid himself of the horrible idea that it was shrinking. And on the tenth night after McAllister's departure he dreamed a strange dream. He had gone with King George to show his Gracious Majesty the pumpkin, promising him the treat of a lifetime; and, when they arrived, there in the corner of the frame was a shrivelled thing the size of a pea. He woke, sweating, with his Sovereign's disappointed screams ringing in his ears; and Pride gave its last quiver and collapsed. To reinstate Angus would be a surrender, but it must be done.

'Beach,' he said that morning at breakfast, 'do you happen to – er – to have McAllister's address?'

'Yes, your lordship,' replied the butler. 'He is in London, residing at number eleven Buxton Crescent.'

'Buxton Crescent? Never heard of it.'

'It is, I fancy, your lordship, a boarding-house or some such establishment off the Cromwell Road. McAllister was accustomed to make it his headquarters whenever he visited the Metropolis on account of its handiness for Kensington Gardens. He liked,' said Beach with respectful reproach, for Angus had been a friend of his for nine years, 'to be near the flowers, your lordship.'

Two telegrams, passing through it in the course of the next twelve hours, caused some gossip at the post office of the little town of Market Blandings.

The first ran:

MCALLISTER,
11 BUXTON CRESCENT
CROMWELL ROAD
LONDON

RETURN IMMEDIATELY – EMSWORTH

The second:

LORD EMSWORTH
BLANDINGS CASTLE
SHROPSHIRE

I WILL NOT – MCALLISTER

Lord Emsworth had one of those minds capable of accommodating but one thought at a time – if that; and the possibility that Angus McAllister might decline to return had not occurred to him. It was difficult to adjust himself to this new problem, but he managed it at last. Before nightfall he had made up his mind. Robert Barker, that broken reed, could remain in charge for another day or so, and meanwhile he would go up to London and engage a real head-gardener, the finest head-gardener that money could buy.

It was the opinion of Dr Johnson that there is in London all that life can afford. A man, he held, who is tired of London is tired of life itself. Lord Emsworth, had he been aware of this statement, would have contested it warmly. He hated London. He loathed its crowds, its smells, its noises; its omnibuses, its taxis, and its hard pavements. And, in addition to all its other defects, the miserable town did not seem able to produce a single decent head-gardener. He went from agency to agency, interviewing candidates, and not one of them came within a mile of meeting his requirements. He disliked their faces, he distrusted their references. It was a harsh thing to say of any man, but he was dashed if the best of them was even as good as Robert Barker.

It was, therefore, in a black and soured mood that his lordship, having lunched frugally at the Senior Conservative Club on the third day of his visit, stood on the steps in the sunshine, wondering how on earth he was to get through the afternoon. He had spent the morning rejecting head-gardeners, and the next batch was not due until the morrow. And what – besides rejecting head-gardeners – was there for a man of reasonable tastes to do with his time in this hopeless town?

And then there came into his mind a remark which Beach the butler had made at the breakfast-table about flowers in Kensington Gardens. He could go to Kensington Gardens and look at the flowers.

He was about to hail a taxicab from the rank down the street when there suddenly emerged from the Hotel Magnificent over the way a young man. This young man proceeded to cross the road, and, as he drew near, it seemed to Lord Emsworth that there was about his appearance something oddly familiar. He stared for a long instant before he could believe his eyes, then with a wordless cry bounded down the steps just as the other started to mount them.

'Oh, hullo, guv'nor!' ejaculated the Hon. Freddie, plainly startled.

'What – what are you doing here?' demanded Lord Emsworth.

He spoke with heat, and justly so. London, as the result of several spirited escapades which still rankled in the mind of a father who had had to foot the bills, was forbidden ground to Freddie.

The young man was plainly not at his ease. He had the air of one who is being pushed towards dangerous machinery in which he is loath to become entangled. He shuffled his feet for a moment, then raised his left shoe and rubbed the back of his right calf with it.

'The fact is, guv'nor –'

'You know you are forbidden to come to London.'

'Absolutely, guv'nor, but the fact is –'

'And why anybody but an imbecile should want to come to London when he could be at Blandings –'

'I know, guv'nor, but the fact is –' Here Freddie, having replaced his wandering foot on the pavement, raised the other, and rubbed the back of his left calf. 'I wanted to see you,' he said. 'Yes. Particularly wanted to see you.'

This was not strictly accurate. The last thing in the world which the Hon. Freddie wanted was to see his parent. He had come to the Senior Conservative Club to leave a carefully written note. Having delivered which, it had been his intention to bolt like a rabbit. This unforeseen meeting had upset his plans.

'To see me?' said Lord Emsworth. 'Why?'

'Got – er – something to tell you. Bit of news.'

'I trust it is of sufficient importance to justify your coming to London against my express wishes.'

'Oh, yes. Oh, yes, yes-yes. Oh, rather. It's dashed important. Yes – not to put too fine a point upon it – most dashed important. I say, guv'nor, are you in fairly good form to stand a bit of a shock?'

A ghastly thought rushed into Lord Emsworth's mind. Freddie's mysterious arrival – his strange manner – his odd hesitation and uneasiness – could it mean –? He clutched the young man's arm feverishly.

'Frederick! Speak! Tell me! Have the cats got at it?'

It was a fixed idea of Lord Emsworth, which no argument would have induced him to abandon, that cats had the power to work some dreadful mischief on his pumpkin and were continually lying in wait for the opportunity of doing so; and his behaviour on the occasion when one of the fast sporting set from the stables, wandering into the kitchen garden and finding him gazing at the Blandings Hope, had rubbed itself sociably against his leg, lingered long in that animal's memory.

Freddie stared.

'Cats? Why? Where? Which? What cats?'

'Frederick! Is anything wrong with the pumpkin?'

In a crass and materialistic world there must inevitably be a scattered few here and there in whom pumpkins touch no chord. The Hon. Freddie Threepwood was one of these. He was accustomed to speak in mockery of all pumpkins, and had even gone so far as to allude to the Hope of Blandings as 'Percy'. His father's anxiety, therefore, merely caused him to giggle.

'Not that I know of,' he said.

'Then what do you mean?' thundered Lord Emsworth, stung by the giggle. 'What do you mean, sir, by coming here and alarming me – scaring me out of my wits, by Gad! – with your nonsense about giving me shocks?'

The Hon. Freddie looked carefully at his fermenting parent. His fingers, sliding into his pocket, closed on the note which nestled there. He drew it forth.

'Look here, guv'nor,' he said nervously. 'I think the best thing would be for you to read this. Meant to leave it for you with the hall-porter. It's – well, you just cast your eye over it. Goodbye, guv'nor. Got to see a man.'

And, thrusting the note into his father's hand, the Hon. Freddie turned and was gone. Lord Emsworth, perplexed and annoyed, watched him skim up the road and leap into a cab. He seethed impotently. Practically any behaviour on the part of his son Frederick had the power to irritate him, but it was when he was vague and mysterious and incoherent that the young man irritated him most.

He looked at the letter in his hand, turned it over, felt it. Then – for it had suddenly occurred to him that if he wished to ascertain its contents he had better read it – he tore open the envelope.

The note was brief, but full of good reading matter.

DEAR GUV'NOR,

Awfully sorry and all that, but couldn't hold out any longer. I've popped up to London in the two-seater and Aggie and I were spliced this morning. There looked like being a bit of a hitch at one time, but Aggie's guv'nor, who has come over from America, managed to wangle it all right by getting a special licence or something of that order. A most capable Johnny. He's coming to see you. He wants to have a good long talk with you about the whole binge. Lush him up hospitably and all that, would you mind, because he's a really sound egg, and you'll like him.

Well, cheerio:                                        Your affectionate son,

FREDDIE

P.S. – You won't mind if I freeze on to the two-seater for the nonce, what? It may come in useful for the honeymoon.

The Senior Conservative Club is a solid and massive building, but, as Lord Emsworth raised his eyes dumbly from the perusal of this letter, it seemed to him that it was performing a kind of whirling dance. The whole of the immediate neighbourhood, indeed, appeared to be shimmying in the middle of a thick mist. He was profoundly stirred. It is not too much to say that he was shaken to the core of his being. No father enjoys being flouted and defied by his own son; nor is it reasonable to expect a man to take a cheery view of life who is faced with the prospect of supporting for the remainder of his years a younger son, a younger son's wife, and possibly younger grand-children.

For an appreciable space of time he stood in the middle of the pavement, rooted to the spot. Passers-by bumped into him or grumblingly made detours to avoid a collision. Dogs sniffed at his ankles. Seedy-looking individuals tried to arrest his attention in order to speak of their financial affairs. Lord Emsworth heeded none of them. He remained where he was, gaping like a fish, until suddenly his faculties seemed to return to him.

An imperative need for flowers and green trees swept upon Lord Emsworth. The noise of the traffic and the heat of the sun on the stone pavement were afflicting him like a nightmare. He signalled energetically to a passing cab.

'Kensington Gardens,' he said, and sank back on the cushioned seat.

Something dimly resembling peace crept into his lordship's soul as he paid off his cab and entered the cool shade of the gardens. Even from the road he had caught a glimpse of stimulating reds and yellows; and as he ambled up the asphalt path and plunged round the corner the flower-beds burst upon his sight in all their consoling glory.

'Ah!' breathed Lord Emsworth rapturously, and came to a halt before a glowing carpet of tulips. A man of official aspect, wearing a peaked cap and a uniform, stopped as he heard the exclamation and looked at him with approval and even affection.

'Nice weather we're 'avin',' he observed.

Lord Emsworth did not reply. He had not heard. There is that about a well-set-out bed of flowers which acts on men who love their gardens like a drug, and he was in a sort of trance. Already he had completely forgotten where he was, and seemed to himself to be back in his paradise of Blandings. He drew a step nearer to the flower-bed, pointing like a setter.

The official-looking man's approval deepened. This man with the peaked cap was the park-keeper, who held the rights of the high, the low, and the middle justice over that section of the gardens. He, too, loved these flower-beds, and he seemed to see in Lord Emsworth a kindred soul. The general public was too apt to pass by, engrossed in its own affairs, and this often wounded the park-keeper. In Lord Emsworth he thought that he recognized one of the right sort.

'Nice –' he began.

He broke off with a sharp cry. If he had not seen it with his own eyes, he would not have believed it. But, alas, there was no possibility of a mistake. With a ghastly shock he realized that he had been deceived in this attractive stranger. Decently, if untidily, dressed; clean; respectable to the outward eye; the stranger was in reality a dangerous criminal, the blackest type of evil-doer on the park-keeper's index. He was a Kensington Gardens flower-picker.

For, even as he uttered the word 'Nice', the man had stepped lightly over the low railing, had shambled across the strip of turf, and before you could say 'weather' was busy on his dark work. In the brief instant in which the park-keeper's vocal cords refused to obey him, he was two tulips ahead of the game and reaching out to scoop in a third.

'Hi!!!' roared the park-keeper, suddenly finding speech. ''I there!!!'

Lord Emsworth turned with a start.

'Bless my soul!' he murmured reproachfully.

He was in full possession of his senses now, such as they were, and understood the enormity of his conduct. He shuffled back on to the asphalt, contrite.

'My dear fellow —' he began remorsefully.

The park-keeper began to speak rapidly and at length. From time to time Lord Emsworth moved his lips and made deprecating gestures, but he could not stem the flood. Louder and more rhetorical grew the park-keeper and denser and more interested the rapidly assembling crowd of spectators. And then through the stream of words another voice spoke.

'Wot's all this?'

The Force had materialized in the shape of a large, solid constable.

The park-keeper seemed to understand that he had been superseded. He still spoke, but no longer like a father rebuking an erring son. His attitude now was more that of an elder brother appealing for justice against a delinquent junior. In a moving passage he stated his case.

''E Says,' observed the constable judicially, speaking slowly and in capitals, as if addressing an untutored foreigner, ''E Says You Was Pickin' The Flowers.'

'I saw 'im. I was standin' as close as I am to you.'

''E Saw You,' interpreted the constable. ''E Was Standing At Your Side.'

Lord Emsworth was feeling weak and bewildered. Without a thought of annoying or doing harm to anybody, he seemed to have unchained the fearful passions of a French Revolution; and there came over him a sense of how unjust it was that this sort of thing should be happening to him, of all people – a man already staggering beneath the troubles of a Job.

'I'll 'ave to ask you for your name and address,' said the constable, more briskly. A stubby pencil popped for an instant into his stern mouth and hovered, well and truly moistened, over the virgin page of his notebook – that dreadful notebook before which taxi-drivers shrink and hardened bus-conductors quail.

'I – I – why, my dear fellow – I mean, officer – I am the Earl of Emsworth.'

Much has been written of the psychology of crowds, designed to show how extraordinary and inexplicable it is, but most of such writing is exaggeration. A crowd generally behaves in a perfectly natural and intelligible fashion. When, for instance, it sees a man in a badly fitting tweed suit and a hat he ought to be ashamed of getting put through it for pinching flowers in the Park, and the man says he is an earl, it laughs. This crowd laughed.

'Ho?' The constable did not stoop to join in the merriment of the rabble, but his lip twitched sardonically. 'Have you a card, your lordship?'

Nobody intimate with Lord Emsworth would have asked such a foolish question. His card-case was the thing he always lost second when visiting London – immediately after losing his umbrella.

'I – er – I'm afraid –'

'R!' said the constable. And the crowd uttered another happy, hyena-like laugh, so intensely galling that his lordship raised his bowed head and found enough spirit to cast an indignant glance. And, as he did so, the hunted look faded from his eyes.

'McAllister!' he cried.

Two new arrivals had just joined the throng, and, being of rugged and knobbly physique, had already shoved themselves through to the ringside seats. One was a tall, handsome, smooth-faced gentleman of authoritative appearance, who, if he had not worn rimless glasses, would have looked like a Roman emperor. The other was a shorter, sturdier man with a bristly red beard.

'McAllister!' moaned his lordship piteously. 'McAllister, my dear fellow, do please tell this man who I am.'

After what had passed between himself and his late employer, a lesser man than Angus McAllister might have seen in Lord Emsworth's predicament merely a judgement. A man of little magnanimity would have felt that here was where he got a bit of his own back.

Not so this splendid Glaswegian.

'Aye,' he said. 'Yon's Lorrud Emsworruth.'

'Who are you?' inquired the constable searchingly.

'I used to be head-gardener at the cassel.'

'Exactly,' bleated Lord Emsworth. 'Precisely. My head-gardener.'

The constable was shaken. Lord Emsworth might not look like an earl, but there was no getting away from the fact that Angus McAllister was supremely head-gardeneresque. A staunch admirer of the aristocracy, the constable perceived that zeal had caused him to make a bit of a bloomer.

In this crisis, however, he comported himself with masterly tact. He scowled blackly upon the interested throng.

'Pass along there, please. Pass along,' he commanded austerely. 'Ought to know better than block up a public thoroughfare like this. Pass along!'

He moved off, shepherding the crowd before him. The Roman emperor with the rimless glasses advanced upon Lord Emsworth, extending a large hand.

'Pleased to meet you at last,' he said. 'My name is Donaldson, Lord Emsworth.'

For a moment the name conveyed nothing to his lordship. Then its significance hit him, and he drew himself up with hauteur.

'You'll excuse us, Angus,' said Mr Donaldson. 'High time you and I had a little chat, Lord Emsworth.'

Lord Emsworth was about to speak, when he caught the other's eye. It was a strong, keen, level grey eye, with a curious forcefulness about it that made him feel strangely inferior. There is every reason to suppose that Mr Donaldson had subscribed for years to those personality courses advertised in the magazines which guarantee to impart to the pupil who takes ten correspondence lessons the ability to look the boss in the eye and make him wilt. Mr Donaldson looked Lord Emsworth in the eye, and Lord Emsworth wilted.

'How do you do?' he said weakly.

'Now listen, Lord Emsworth,' proceeded Mr Donaldson. 'No sense in having hard feelings between members of a family. I take it you've heard by this that your boy and my girl have gone ahead and fixed it up? Personally, I'm delighted. That boy is a fine young fellow.'

Lord Emsworth blinked.

'You are speaking of my son Frederick?' he said incredulously.

'Of your son Frederick. Now, at the moment, no doubt, you are feeling a trifle sore. I don't blame you. You have every right to be sorer than a gumboil. But you must remember – young blood, eh? It will, I am convinced, be a lasting grief to that splendid young man –'

'You are still speaking of my son Frederick?'

'Of Frederick, yes. It will, I say, be a lasting grief to him if he feels he has incurred your resentment. You must forgive him, Lord Emsworth. He must have your support.'

'I suppose he'll have to have it, dash it!' said his lordship unhappily. 'Can't let the boy starve.'

Mr Donaldson's hand swept round in a wide, grand gesture.

'Don't you worry about that. I'll look after that end of it. I am not a rich man –'

'Ah!' said Lord Emsworth rather bleakly. There had been something about the largeness of the other's manner which had led him to entertain hopes.

'I doubt,' continued Mr Donaldson frankly, for he was a man who believed in frankness in these matters, 'if, all told, I have as much as ten million dollars in the world.'

Lord Emsworth swayed like a sapling in the breeze.

'Ten million? Ten million? Did you say you had ten million dollars?'

'Between nine and ten, I suppose. Not more. You must remember,' said Mr Donaldson, with a touch of apology, 'that conditions have changed very much in America of late. We have been through a tough time, a mighty tough time. Many of my friends have been harder hit than I have. But things are coming back. Yes, sir, they're coming right back. I am a firm believer in President Roosevelt and the New Deal. Under the New Deal, the American dog is beginning to eat more biscuits. That, I should have mentioned, is my line. I am Donaldson's Dog-Biscuits.'

'Donaldson's Dog-Biscuits? Indeed? Really! Fancy that!'

'You have heard of Donaldson's Dog-Biscuits?' asked their proprietor eagerly.

'Never,' said Lord Emsworth cordially.

'Oh! Well, that's who I am. And, as I say, the business is beginning to pick up nicely after the slump. All over the country our salesmen are reporting that the American dog is once more becoming biscuit-conscious. And so I am in a position, with your approval, to offer Frederick a steady and possibly a lucrative job. I propose, always with your consent, of course, to send him over to Long Island City to start

16

learning the business. I have no doubt that he will in time prove a most valuable asset to the firm.'

Lord Emsworth could conceive of no way in which Freddie could be of value to a dog-biscuit firm, except possibly as a taster; but he refrained from damping the other's enthusiasm by saying so. In any case, the thought of the young man actually earning his living, and doing so three thousand miles from Blandings Castle, would probably have held him dumb.

'He seems full of keenness. But, in my opinion, to be able to give of his best and push the Donaldson biscuit as it should be pushed, he must feel that he has your moral support, Lord Emsworth – his father's moral support.'

'Yes, yes, yes,' said Lord Emsworth heartily. A feeling of positive adoration for Mr Donaldson was thrilling him. The getting rid of Freddie, which he himself had been unable to achieve in twenty-six years, this godlike dog-biscuit manufacturer had accomplished in less than a week. What a man! felt Lord Emsworth. 'Oh, yes, yes, yes!' he said. 'Yes, indeed. Most decidedly.'

'They sail on Wednesday.'

'Capital!'

'Early in the morning.'

'Splendid!'

'I may give them a friendly message from you? A forgiving, fatherly message?'

'Certainly, certainly, certainly. Inform Frederick that he has my best wishes.'

'I will.'

'Mention that I shall watch his future progress with considerable interest.'

'Exactly.'

'Say that I hope he will work hard and make a name for himself.'

'Just so.'

'And,' concluded Lord Emsworth, speaking with a paternal earnestness well in keeping with this solemn moment, 'tell him – er – not to hurry home.'

He pressed Mr Donaldson's hand with feelings too deep for further speech. Then he galloped swiftly to where Angus McAllister stood brooding over the tulip bed.

'McAllister!'

The head-gardener's beard waggled grimly. He looked at his late employer with cold eyes. It is never difficult to distinguish between a Scotsman with a grievance and a ray of sunshine, and Lord Emsworth, gazing upon the dour man, was able to see at a glance into which category Angus McAllister fell. His tongue seemed to cleave to his palate, but he forced himself to speak.

'McAllister . . . I wish . . . I wonder . . .'

'Weel?'

'I wonder . . . I wish . . . What I want to say,' faltered Lord Emsworth humbly, 'is, have you accepted another situation yet?'

'I am conseederin' twa.'

'Come back to me!' pleaded his lordship, his voice breaking. 'Robert Barker is worse than useless. Come back to me!'

Angus McAllister gazed woodenly at the tulips.

'A' weel –' he said at length.

'You will?' cried Lord Emsworth joyfully. 'Splendid! Capital! Excellent!'

'A' didna say I wud.'

'I thought you said "I will",' said his lordship, dashed.

'I didna say "A' weel"; I said "A' weel",' said Mr McAllister stiffly. 'Meanin' mebbe I might, mebbe not.'

Lord Emsworth laid a trembling hand upon his shoulder.

'McAllister, I will raise your salary.'

The beard twitched.

'Dash it, I'll double it.'

The eyebrows flickered.

'McAllister . . . Angus . . .' said Lord Emsworth in a low voice. 'Come back! The pumpkin needs you.'

In an age of rush and hurry like that of today, an age in which there are innumerable calls on the time of everyone, it is possible that here and there throughout the ranks of those who have read this chronicle there may be one or two who for various reasons found themselves unable to attend the last Agricultural Show at Shrewsbury. For these a few words must be added.

Sir Gregory Parsloe-Parsloe, of Matchingham Hall, was there, of course, but it would not have escaped the notice of a close observer that his mien lacked something of the haughty arrogance which had characterized it in other years. From time to time, as he paced the tent devoted to the exhibition of vegetables, he might have been seen to bite his lip, and his eye had something of that brooding look which Napoleon's must have worn at Waterloo.

But there was the right stuff in Sir Gregory. He was a gentleman and a sportsman. In the Parsloe tradition there was nothing small or mean. Halfway down the tent he stopped, and with a quick, manly gesture thrust out his hand.

'Congratulate you, Emsworth,' he said huskily.

Lord Emsworth looked up with a start. He had been deep in his thoughts.

'Eh? Oh, thanks. Thanks, my dear fellow, thanks, thanks. Thank you very much.' He hesitated. 'Er – can't both win, eh?'

Sir Gregory puzzled it out and saw that he was right.

'No,' he said. 'No. See what you mean. Can't both win. No getting round that.'

He nodded and walked on, with who knows what vultures gnawing at his broad bosom. And Lord Emsworth – with Angus McAllister, who had been a silent, beard-waggling witness of the scene, at his side – turned once more to stare reverently at that which lay on the strawy bottom of one of the largest packing-cases ever seen in Shrewsbury town.

A card had been attached to the exterior of the packing-case. It bore the simple legend:

## PUMPKINS. FIRST PRIZE

The housekeeper's room at Blandings Castle, G.H.Q. of the domestic staff that ministered to the needs of the Earl of Emsworth, was in normal circumstances a pleasant and cheerful apartment. It caught the afternoon sun; and the paper which covered its walls had been conceived in a jovial spirit by someone who held that the human eye, resting on ninety-seven simultaneous pink birds perched upon ninety-seven blue rose-bushes, could not but be agreeably stimulated and refreshed. Yet, with the entry of Beach, the butler, it was as though there had crept into its atmosphere a chill dreariness; and Mrs Twemlow, the housekeeper, laying down her knitting, gazed at him in alarm.

'Whatever is the matter, Mr Beach?'

The butler stared moodily out of the window. His face was drawn and he breathed heavily, as a man will who is suffering from a combination of strong emotion and adenoids. A ray of sunshine, which had been advancing jauntily along the carpet, caught sight of his face and slunk out, abashed.

'I have come to a decision, Mrs Twemlow.'

'What about?'

'Ever since his lordship started to grow it I have seen the writing on the wall plainer and plainer, and now I have made up my mind. The moment his lordship returns from London, I tender my resignation. Eighteen years have I served in his lordship's household, commencing as underfootman and rising to my present position, but now the end has come.'

'You don't mean you're going just because his lordship has grown a beard?'

'It is the only way, Mrs Twemlow. That beard is weakening his lordship's position throughout the entire countryside. Are you aware that at the recent Sunday school treat I heard cries of "Beaver!"?'

'No!'

'Yes! And this spirit of mockery and disrespect will spread. And, what is more, that beard is alienating the best elements in the County. I saw Sir Gregory Parsloe-Parsloe look very sharp at it when he dined with us last Friday.'

'It is not a handsome beard,' admitted the housekeeper.

'It is not. And his lordship must be informed. As long as I remain in his lordship's service, it is impossible for me to speak. So I shall tender my resignation. Once that is done, my lips will no longer be sealed. Is that buttered toast under that dish, Mrs Twemlow?'

'Yes, Mr Beach. Take a slice. It will cheer you up.'

'Cheer me up!' said the butler, with a hollow laugh that sounded like a knell.

It was fortunate that Lord Emsworth, seated at the time of this conversation in the smoking-room of the Senior Conservative Club in London, had no suspicion of the supreme calamity that was about to fall upon him; for there was already much upon his mind.

In the last few days, indeed, everything seemed to have gone wrong. Angus McAllister, his head-gardener, had reported an alarming invasion of greenfly among the roses. A favourite and respected cow, strongly fancied for the Milk-Giving Jerseys event at the forthcoming Cattle Show, had contracted a mysterious ailment which was baffling the skill of the local vet. And on top of all this a telegram had arrived from his lordship's younger son, the Hon. Frederick Threepwood, announcing that he was back in England and desirous of seeing his father immediately.

This, felt Lord Emsworth, as he stared bleakly before him at the little groups of happy Senior Conservatives, was the most unkindest cut of all. What on earth was Freddie doing in England? Eight months before he had married the only daughter of Donaldson's Dog-Biscuits, of Long Island City, in the United States of America; and in Long Island City he ought now to have been, sedulously promoting the dog-biscuit industry's best interests. Instead of which, here he was in London – and, according to his telegram, in trouble.

Lord Emsworth passed a hand over his chin, to assist thought, and was vaguely annoyed by some obstacle that intruded itself in the path of his fingers. Concentrating his faculties, such as they were, on this obstacle, he discovered it to be his beard. It irritated him. Hitherto, in moments of stress, he had always derived comfort from the feel of a clean-shaven chin. He felt now as if he were rubbing his hand over seaweed; and most unjustly – for it was certainly not that young man's fault that he had decided to grow a beard – he became aware of an added sense of grievance against the Hon. Freddie.

It was at this moment that he perceived his child approaching him across the smoking-room floor.

'Hullo, guv'nor!' said Freddie.

'Well, Frederick?' said Lord Emsworth.

There followed a silence. Freddie was remembering that he had not met his father since the day when he had slipped into the latter's hand a note announcing his marriage to a girl whom Lord Emsworth had never seen – except once, through a telescope, when he, Freddie, was kissing her in the grounds of Blandings Castle. Lord Emsworth, on his side, was brooding on that phrase 'in trouble', which had formed so significant a part of his son's telegram. For fifteen years he had been reluctantly helping Freddie out of trouble; and now, when it had seemed that he was off his hands for ever, the thing had started all over again.

'Do sit down,' he said testily.

Freddie had been standing on one leg, and his constrained attitude annoyed Lord Emsworth.

'Right-ho,' said Freddie, taking a chair. 'I say, guv'nor, since when the foliage?'

'What?'

'The beard. I hardly recognized you.'

Another spasm of irritation shot through his lordship.

'Never mind my beard!'

'I don't if you don't,' said Freddie agreeably. 'It was dashed good of you, guv'nor, to come bounding up to town so promptly.'

'I came because your telegram said that you were in trouble.'

'British,' said Freddie approvingly. 'Very British.'

'Though what trouble you can be in I cannot imagine. It is surely not money again?'

'Oh, no. Not money. If that had been all, I would have applied to the good old pop-in-law. Old Donaldson's an ace. He thinks the world of me.'

'Indeed? I met Mr Donaldson only once, but he struck me as a man of sound judgement.'

'That's what I say. He thinks I'm a wonder. If it were simply a question of needing a bit of the ready, I could touch him like a shot. But it isn't money that's the trouble. It's Aggie. My wife, you know.'

'Well?'

'She's left me.'

'Left you!'

'Absolutely flat. Buzzed off, and the note pinned to the pin-cushion.

She's now at the Savoy and won't let me come near her; and I'm at a service-flat in King Street, eating my jolly old heart out, if you know what I mean.'

Lord Emsworth uttered a deep sigh. He gazed drearily at his son, marvelling that it should be in the power of any young man, even a specialist like Freddie, so consistently to make a mess of his affairs. By what amounted to a miracle this offspring of his had contrived to lure a millionaire's daughter into marrying him; and now, it seemed, he had let her get away. Years before, when a boy, and romantic as most boys are, his lordship had sometimes regretted that the Emsworths, though an ancient clan, did not possess a Family Curse. How little he had suspected that he was shortly about to become the father of it.

'The fault,' he said tonelessly, 'was, I suppose, yours?'

'In a way, yes. But –'

'What precisely occurred?'

'Well, it was like this, guv'nor. You know how keen I've always been on the movies. Going to every picture I could manage, and so forth. Well, one night, as I was lying awake, I suddenly got the idea for a scenario of my own. And dashed good it was, too. It was about a poor man who had an accident, and the coves at the hospital said that an operation was the only thing that could save his life. But they wouldn't operate without five hundred dollars down in advance, and he hadn't got five hundred dollars. So his wife got hold of a millionaire.'

'What,' inquired Lord Emsworth, 'is all this drivel?'

'Drivel, guv'nor?' said Freddie, wounded. 'I'm only telling you my scenario.'

'I have no wish to hear it. What I am anxious to learn from you – in as few words as possible – is the reason for the breach between your wife and yourself.'

'Well, I'm telling you. It all started with the scenario. When I'd written it, I naturally wanted to sell it to somebody; and just about then Pauline Petite came East and took a house at Great Neck, and a pal of mine introduced me to her.'

'Who is Pauline Petite?'

'Good heavens, guv'nor!' Freddie stared, amazed. 'You don't mean to sit there and tell me you've never heard of Pauline Petite! The movie star. Didn't you see "Passion's Slaves"?'

'I did not.'

'Nor "Silken Fetters"?'

'Never.'

'Nor "Purple Passion"? Nor "Bonds of Gold"? Nor "Seduction"? Great Scott, guv'nor, you haven't lived!'

'What about this woman?'

'Well, a pal introduced me to her, you see, and I started to pave the way to getting her interested in this scenario of mine. Because, if she liked it, of course it meant everything. Well, this involved seeing a good deal of her, you understand, and one night Jane Yorke happened to come on us having a bite together at an inn.'

'Good God!'

'Oh, it was all perfectly respectable, guv'nor. All strictly on the up-and-up. Purely a business relationship. But the trouble was I had kept the thing from Aggie because I wanted to surprise her. I wanted to be able to come to her with the scenario accepted and tell her I wasn't such a fool as I looked.'

'Any woman capable of believing that –'

'And most unfortunately I had said that I had to go to Chicago that night on business. So, what with one thing and another – Well, as I said just now, she's at the Savoy and I'm –'

'Who is Jane Yorke?'

A scowl marred Freddie's smooth features.

'A pill, guv'nor. One of the worst. A Jebusite and Amalekite. If it hadn't been for her, I believe I could have fixed the thing. But she got hold of Aggie and whisked her away and poisoned her mind. This woman, guv'nor, has got a brother in the background, and she wanted Aggie to marry the brother. And my belief is that she is trying to induce Aggie to pop over to Paris and get a divorce, so as to give the blighted brother another look in, dash him! So now, guv'nor, is the time for action. Now is the moment to rally round as never before. I rely on you.'

'Me? What on earth do you expect me to do?'

'Why, go to her and plead with her. They do it in the movies. I've seen thousands of pictures where the white-haired old father –'

'Stuff and nonsense!' said Lord Emsworth, stung to the quick – for, like so many well-preserved men of ripe years, he was under the impression that he was merely slightly brindled. 'You have made your bed, and you must stew in it.'

'Eh?'

'I mean, you must stew in your own juice. You have brought this trouble on yourself by your own idiotic behaviour, and you must bear the consequences.'

'You mean you won't go and plead!'

'No.'

'You mean yes?'

'I mean no.'

'Not plead?' said Freddie, desiring to get this thing clear.

'I refuse to allow myself to be drawn into the matter.'

'You won't even give her a ring on the telephone?'

'I will not.'

'Oh, come, guv'nor. Be a sport. Her suite's Number Sixty-seven. You can get her in a second and state my case, all for the cost of twopence. Have a pop at it.'

'No.'

Freddie rose with set face.

'Very well,' he said tensely. 'Then I may as well tell you, guv'nor, that my life is as good as over. The future holds nothing for me. I am a spent egg. If Aggie goes to Paris and gets that divorce, I shall retire to some quiet spot and there pass the few remaining years of my existence, a blighted wreck. Goodbye, guv'nor.'

'Goodbye.'

'Honk-honk!' said Freddie moodily.

As a general rule, Lord Emsworth was an early and a sound sleeper, one of the few qualities which he shared with Napoleon Bonaparte being the ability to slumber the moment his head touched the pillow. But that night, weighed down with his troubles, he sought unconsciousness in vain. And somewhere in the small hours of the morning he sat up in bed, quaking. A sudden grisly thought had occurred to him.

Freddie had stated that, in the event of his wife obtaining a divorce, he proposed to retire for the rest of his life to some quiet spot. Suppose by 'quiet spot' he meant Blandings Castle! The possibility shook Lord Emsworth like an ague. Freddie had visited Blandings for extended periods before, and it was his lordship's considered opinion that the boy was a worse menace to the happy life of rural England than botts, greenfly, or foot-and-mouth disease. The prospect of having him at Blandings indefinitely affected Lord Emsworth like a blow on the base of the skull.

An entirely new line of thought was now opened. Had he in the recent interview, he asked himself, been as kind as he should have been? Had he not been a little harsh? Had he been just a shade lacking in sympathy? Had he played quite the part a father ought to have played?

The answers to the questions, in the order stated, were as follows: No. Yes. Yes. And No.

Waking after a belated sleep and sipping his early tea, Lord Emsworth found himself full of a new resolve. He had changed his mind. It was his intention now to go to this daughter-in-law of his and plead with her as no father-in-law had ever pleaded yet.

A man who has had a disturbed night is not at his best on the following morning. Until after luncheon Lord Emsworth felt much too heavy-headed to do himself justice as a pleader. But a visit to the flowers at Kensington Gardens, followed by a capital chop and half a bottle of claret at the Regent Grill, put him into excellent shape. The heaviness had vanished, and he felt alert and quick-witted.

So much so that, on arriving at the Savoy Hotel, he behaved with a cunning of which he had never hitherto suspected himself capable. On the very verge of giving his name to the desk-clerk, he paused. It might well be, he reflected, that this daughter-in-law of his, including the entire Emsworth family in her feud, would, did she hear that he was waiting below, nip the whole programme in the bud by refusing to see him. Better, he decided, not to risk it. Moving away from the desk, he headed for the lift, and presently found himself outside the door of Suite Sixty-seven.

He tapped on the door. There was no answer. He tapped again, and, once more receiving no reply, felt a little non-plussed. He was not a very farseeing man, and the possibility that his daughter-in-law might not be at home had not occurred to him. He was about to go away when, peering at the door, he perceived that it was ajar. He pushed it open; and, ambling in, found himself in a cosy sitting-room, crowded, as feminine sitting-rooms are apt to be, with flowers of every description.

Flowers were always a magnet to Lord Emsworth, and for some happy minutes he pottered from vase to vase, sniffing.

It was after he had sniffed for perhaps the twentieth time that the impression came to him that the room contained a curious echo. It was almost as though, each time he sniffed, some other person sniffed too.

And yet the place was apparently empty. To submit the acoustics to a final test, his lordship sniffed once more. But this time the sound that followed was of a more sinister character. It sounded to Lord Emsworth exactly like a snarl.

It was a snarl. Chancing to glance floorwards, he became immediately aware, in close juxtaposition to his ankles, of what appeared at first sight to be a lady's muff. But, this being one of his bright afternoons, he realized in the next instant that it was no muff but a toy dog of the kind which women are only too prone to leave lying about their sitting-rooms.

'God bless my soul!' exclaimed Lord Emsworth, piously commending his safety to Heaven, as so many of his rugged ancestors had done in rather similar circumstances on the battlefields of the Middle Ages.

He backed uneasily. The dog followed him. It appeared to have no legs, but to move by faith alone.

'Go away, sir!' said Lord Emsworth.

He hated small dogs. They nipped you. Take your eye off them, and they had you by the ankle before you knew where you were. Discovering that his manoeuvres had brought him to a door, he decided to take cover. He opened the door and slipped through. Blood will tell. An Emsworth had taken cover at Agincourt.

He was now in a bedroom, and, judging by the look of things, likely to remain there for some time. The woolly dog, foiled by superior intelligence, was now making no attempt to conceal its chagrin. It had cast off all pretence of armed neutrality and was yapping with a hideous intensity and shrillness. And ever and anon it scratched with baffled fury at the lower panels.

'Go away, sir!' thundered his lordship.

'Who's there?'

Lord Emsworth leaped like a jumping bean. So convinced had he been of the emptiness of this suite of rooms that the voice, speaking where no voice should have been, crashed into his nerve centres like a shell.

'Who is there?'

The mystery, which had begun to assume an aspect of the supernatural, was solved. On the other side of the room was a door, and it was from behind this that the voice had spoken. It occurred to Lord Emsworth that it was merely part of the general malignity of Fate that he should have selected for a formal father-in-lawful call the moment when his daughter-in-law was taking a bath.

He approached the door, and spoke soothingly.

'Pray do not be alarmed, my dear.'

'Who are you? What are you doing in my room?'

'There is no cause for alarm —'

He broke off abruptly, for his words had suddenly been proved fundamentally untrue. There was very vital cause for alarm. The door of the bedroom had opened, and the muff-like dog, shrilling hate, was scuttling in its peculiar legless manner straight for his ankles.

Peril brings out unsuspected qualities in every man. Lord Emsworth was not a professional acrobat, but the leap he gave in this crisis would have justified his being mistaken for one. He floated through the air like a homing bird. From where he had been standing the bed was a considerable distance away, but he reached it with inches to spare, and stood there, quivering. Below him, the woolly dog raged like the ocean at the base of a cliff.

It was at this point that his lordship became aware of a young woman standing in the doorway through which he had just passed.

About this young woman there were many points which would have found little favour in the eyes of a critic of feminine charm. She was too short, too square, and too solid. She had a much too determined chin. And her hair was of an unpleasing gingery hue. But the thing Lord Emsworth liked least about her was the pistol she was pointing at his head.

A plaintive voice filtered through the bathroom door.

'Who's there?'

'It's a man,' said the girl behind the gun.

'I know it's a man. He spoke to me. Who is he?'

'I don't know. A nasty-looking fellow. I saw him hanging about the passage outside your door, and I got my gun and came along. Come on out.'

'I can't. I'm all wet.'

It is not easy for a man who is standing on a bed with his hands up to achieve dignity, but Lord Emsworth did the best he could.

'My dear madam!'

'What are you doing here?'

'I found the door ajar —'

'And walked in to see if there were any jewel-cases ajar, too. I think,' added the young woman, raising her voice so as to make herself audible to the unseen bather, 'it's Dopey Smith.'

'Who?'

'Dopey Smith. The fellow the cops said tried for your jewels in New York. He must have followed you over here.'

'I am not Dopey Smith, madam,' cried his lordship. 'I am the Earl of Emsworth.'

'You are?'

'Yes, I am.'

'Yes, you are!'

'I came to see my daughter-in-law.'

'Well, here she is.'

The bathroom door opened, and there emerged a charming figure draped in a kimono. Even in that tense moment Lord Emsworth was conscious of a bewildered astonishment that such a girl could ever have stooped to mate with his son Frederick.

'Who did you say he was?' she asked, recommending herself still more strongly to his lordship's esteem by scooping up the woolly dog and holding it securely in her arms.

'He says he's the Earl of Emsworth.'

'I am the Earl of Emsworth.'

The girl in the kimono looked keenly at him as he descended from the bed.

'You know, Jane,' she said, a note of uncertainty in her voice, 'it might be. He looks very like Freddie.'

The appalling slur on his personal appearance held Lord Emsworth dumb. Like other men, he had had black moments when his looks had not altogether satisfied him, but he had never supposed that he had a face like Freddie's.

The girl with the pistol uttered a stupefying whoop.

'Jiminy Christmas!' she cried. 'Don't you see?'

'See what?'

'Why, it *is* Freddie. Disguised. Trying to get at you this way. It's just the sort of movie stunt he would think clever. Take them off, Ralph Vandeleur – I know you!'

She reached out a clutching hand, seized his lordship's beard in a vice-like grip, and tugged with all the force of a modern girl, trained from infancy at hockey, tennis, and Swedish exercises.

It had not occurred to Lord Emsworth a moment before that anything could possibly tend to make his situation more uncomfortable than it already was. He saw now that he had been mistaken in this view. Agony beyond his liveliest dreams flamed through his shrinking frame.

The girl regarded him with a somewhat baffled look.

'H'm!' she said disappointedly. 'It seems to be real. Unless,' she continued, on a more optimistic note, 'he's fixed it on with specially strong fish-glue or something. I'd better try again.'

'No, don't,' said his lordship's daughter-in-law. 'It isn't Freddie. I would have recognized him at once.'

'Then he's a crook, after all. Kindly step into that cupboard, George, while I phone for the constabulary.'

Lord Emsworth danced a few steps.

'I will not step into cupboards. I insist on being heard. I don't know who this woman is –'

'My name's Jane Yorke, if you're curious.'

'Ah! The woman who poisons my son's wife's mind against him! I know all about you.' He turned to the girl in the kimono. 'Yesterday my son Frederick implored me by telegram to come to London. I saw him at my club. Stop that dog barking!'

'Why shouldn't he bark?' said Miss Yorke. 'He's in his own home.'

'He told me,' proceeded Lord Emsworth, raising his voice, 'that there had been a little misunderstanding between you –'

'Little misunderstanding is good,' said Miss Yorke.

'He dined with that woman for a purpose.'

'And directly I saw them,' said Miss Yorke, 'I knew what the purpose was.'

The Hon. Mrs Threepwood looked at her friend, wavering.

'I believe it's true,' she said, 'and he really is Lord Emsworth. He seems to know all that happened. How could he know if Freddie hadn't told him?'

'If this fellow is a crook from the other side, of course he would know. The thing was in *Broadway Whispers* and *Town Gossip*, wasn't it?'

'All the same –'

The telephone bell rang sharply.

'I assure you –' began Lord Emsworth.

'Right!' said the unpleasant Miss Yorke, at the receiver. 'Send him right up.' She regarded his lordship with a brightly triumphant eye. 'You're out of luck, my friend,' she said. 'Lord Emsworth has just arrived, and he's on his way up now.'

There are certain situations in which the human brain may be excused for reeling. Lord Emsworth's did not so much reel as perform a kind of dance, as if it were in danger of coming unstuck. Always a dreamy and absent-minded man, unequal to the rough hurly-burly of life, he had passed this afternoon through an ordeal which might well have unsettled the most practical. And this extraordinary announcement, coming on top of all he had been through, was too much for him. He tottered into the sitting-room and sank into a chair. It seemed to him that he was living in a nightmare.

And certainly in the figure that entered a few moments later there was nothing whatever to correct this impression. It might have stepped straight into anybody's nightmare and felt perfectly at home right from the start.

The figure was that of a tall, thin man with white hair and a long and flowing beard of the same venerable hue. Strange as it seemed that a person of such appearance should not have been shot on sight early in his career, he obviously had reached an extremely advanced age. He was either a man of about a hundred and fifty who was rather young for his years or a man of about a hundred and ten who had been aged by trouble.

'My dear child!' piped the figure in a weak, quavering voice.

'Freddie!' cried the girl in the kimono.

'Oh, dash it!' said the figure.

There was a pause, broken by a sort of gasping moan from Lord Emsworth. More and more every minute his lordship was feeling the strain.

'Good God, guv'nor!' said the figure, sighting him.

His wife pointed at Lord Emsworth.

'Freddie, is that your father?'

'Oh, yes. Rather. Of course. Absolutely. But he said he wasn't coming.'

'I changed my mind,' said Lord Emsworth in a low, stricken voice.

'I told you so, Jane,' said the girl. 'I thought he was Lord Emsworth all the time. Surely you can see the likeness now?'

A kind of wail escaped his lordship.

'Do I look like that?' he said brokenly. He gazed at his son once more and shut his eyes.

'Well,' said Miss Yorke, in her detestable managing way, turning her forceful personality on the newcomer, 'now that you are here, Freddie Threepwood, looking like Father Christmas, what's the idea? Aggie told you never to come near her again.'

A young man of his natural limpness of character might well have retired in disorder before this attack, but Love had apparently made Frederick Threepwood a man of steel. Removing his beard and eyebrows, he directed a withering glance at Miss Yorke.

'I don't want to talk to you,' he said. 'You're a serpent in the bosom. I mean a snake in the grass.'

'Oh, am I?'

'Yes, you are. You poisoned Aggie's mind against me. If it hadn't been for you, I could have got her alone and told her my story as man to man.'

'Well, let's hear it now. You've had plenty of time to rehearse it.'

Freddie turned to his wife with a sweeping gesture.

'I –' He paused. 'I say, Aggie, old thing, you look perfectly topping in that kimono.'

'Stick to the point,' said Miss Yorke.

'That is the point,' said Mrs Freddie, not without a certain softness. 'But if you think I look perfectly topping, why do you go running around with movie-actresses with carroty hair?'

'Red-gold,' suggested Freddie deferentially.

'Carroty!'

'Carroty it is. You're absolutely right. I never liked it all along.'

'Then why were you dining with it?'

'Yes, why?' inquired Miss Yorke.

'I wish you wouldn't butt in,' said Freddie petulantly. 'I'm not talking to you.'

'You might just as well, for all the good it's going to do you.'

'Be quiet, Jane. Well, Freddie?'

'Aggie,' said the Hon. Freddie, 'it was this way.'

'Never believe a man who starts a story like that,' said Miss Yorke.

'Do please be quiet, Jane. Yes, Freddie?'

'I was trying to sell that carroty female a scenario, and I was keeping it from you because I wanted it to be a surprise.'

'Freddie darling! Was that really it?'

'You don't mean to say –' began Miss Yorke incredulously.

'Absolutely it. And, in order to keep in with the woman – whom, I may as well tell you, I disliked rather heartily from the start – I had to lush her up a trifle from time to time.'

'Of course.'

'You have to with these people.'

'Naturally.'

'Makes all the difference in the world if you push a bit of food into them preparatory to talking business.'

'All the difference in the world.'

Miss Yorke, who seemed temporarily to have lost her breath, recovered it.

'You don't mean to tell me,' she cried, turning in a kind of wild despair to the injured wife, 'that you really believe this apple sauce?'

'Of course she does,' said Freddie. 'Don't you, precious?'

'Of course I do, sweetie-pie.'

'And, what's more,' said Freddie, pulling from his breast-pocket a buff-coloured slip of paper with the air of one who draws from his sleeve that extra ace which makes all the difference in a keenly contested game, 'I can prove it. Here's a cable that came this morning from the Super-Ultra-Art Film Company, offering me a thousand solid dollars for the scenario. So another time, you, will you kindly refrain from judging your – er – fellows by the beastly light of your own – ah – foul imagination?'

'Yes,' said his wife, 'I must say, Jane, that you have made as much mischief as anyone ever did. I wish in future you would stop interfering in other people's concerns.'

'Spoken,' said Freddie, 'with vim and not a little terse good sense. And I may add –'

'If you ask me,' said Miss Yorke, 'I think it's a fake.'

'What's a fake?'

'That cable.'

'What do you mean, a fake?' cried Freddie indignantly. 'Read it for yourself.'

'It's quite easy to get cables cabled you by cabling a friend in New York to cable them.'

'I don't get that,' said Freddie, puzzled.

'I do,' said his wife; and there shone in her eyes the light that shines only in the eyes of wives who, having swallowed their husband's story, resent destructive criticism from outsiders. 'And I never want to see you again, Jane Yorke.'

'Same here,' agreed Freddie. 'In Turkey they'd shove a girl like that in a sack and drop her in the Bosphorus.'

'I might as well go,' said Miss Yorke.

'And don't come back,' said Freddie. 'The door is behind you.'

The species of trance which had held Lord Emsworth in its grip during the preceding conversational exchanges was wearing off. And now, perceiving that Miss Yorke was apparently as unpopular with the rest of the company as with himself, he came gradually to life again. His recovery was hastened by the slamming of the door and the spectacle of his son Frederick clasping in his arms a wife who, his lordship had never forgotten, was the daughter of probably the only millionaire in existence who had that delightful willingness to take Freddie off his hands which was, in Lord Emsworth's eyes, the noblest quality a millionaire could possess.

He sat up and blinked feebly. Though much better, he was still weak.

'What was your scenario about, sweetness?' asked Mrs Freddie.

'I'll tell you, angel-face. Or should we stir up the guv'nor? He seems a bit under the weather.'

'Better leave him to rest for awhile. That woman Jane Yorke upset him.'

'She would upset anybody. If there's one person I bar, it's the blister who comes between man and wife. Not right, I mean, coming between man and wife. My scenario's about a man and wife. This fellow, you understand, is a poor cove – no money, if you see what I mean – and he has an accident, and the hospital blokes say they won't operate unless he can chip in with five hundred dollars down in advance. But where to get it? You see the situation?'

'Oh, yes.'

'Strong, what?'

'Awfully strong.'

'Well, it's nothing to how strong it gets later on. The cove's wife gets hold of a millionaire bloke and vamps him and lures him to the flat and gets him to promise he'll cough up the cash. Meanwhile, cutbacks of the doctor at the hospital on the phone. And she laughing merrily so as not to let the millionaire bloke guess that her heart is aching. I forgot to tell you the cove had to be operated on immediately or he would hand in his dinner-pail. Dramatic, eh?'

'Frightfully.'

'Well, then the millionaire bloke demands his price. I thought of calling it "A Woman's Price".'

'Splendid.'

'And now comes the blow-out. They go into the bedroom and – Oh, hullo, guv'nor! Feeling better?'

Lord Emsworth had risen. He was tottering a little as he approached them, but his mind was at rest.

'Much better, thank you.'

'You know my wife, what?'

'Oh, Lord Emsworth,' said Mrs Freddie, 'I'm so dreadfully sorry. I wouldn't have had anything like this happen for the world. But –'

Lord Emsworth patted her hand paternally. Once more he was overcome with astonishment that his son Frederick should have been able to win the heart of a girl so beautiful, so sympathetic, so extraordinarily rich.

'The fault was entirely mine, my dear child. But –' He paused. Something was plainly troubling him. 'Tell me, when Frederick was wearing that beard – when Frederick was – was – when he was wearing that beard, did he really look like me?'

'Oh, yes. Very like.'

'Thank you, my dear. That was all I wanted to know. I will leave you now. You will wish to be alone. You must come down to Blandings, my dear child, at the very earliest opportunity.'

He walked thoughtfully from the room.

'Does this hotel,' he inquired of the man who took him down in the lift, 'contain a barber's shop?'

'Yes, sir.'

'I wonder if you would direct me to it?' said his lordship.

Lord Emsworth sat in his library at Blandings Castle, drinking that last restful whisky and soda of the day. Through the open window came the scent of flowers and the little noises of the summer night.

He should have been completely at rest, for much had happened since his return to sweeten life for him. Angus McAllister had reported that the greenfly were yielding to treatment with whale-oil solution; and the stricken cow had taken a sudden turn for the better, and at last advices was sitting up and taking nourishment with something of the old appetite. Moreover, as he stroked his shaven chin, his lordship felt a better, lighter man, as if some burden had fallen from him.

And yet, as he sat there, a frown was on his forehead.

He rang the bell.

'M'lord?'

Lord Emsworth looked at his faithful butler with appreciation. Deuce of a long time Beach had been at the castle, and would, no doubt, be there for many a year to come. A good fellow. Lord Emsworth had liked the way the man's eyes had lighted up on his return, as if the sight of his employer had removed a great weight from his mind.

'Oh, Beach,' said his lordship, 'kindly put in a trunk-call to London on the telephone.'

'Very good, m'lord.'

'Get through to Suite Number Sixty-seven at the Savoy Hotel, and speak to Mr Frederick.'

'Yes, your lordship.'

'Say that I particularly wish to know how that scenario of his ended.'

'Scenario, your lordship?'

'Scenario.'

'Very good, m'lord.'

Lord Emsworth returned to his reverie. Time passed. The butler returned.

'I have spoken to Mr Frederick, your lordship.'

'Yes?'

'He instructed me to give your lordship his best wishes, and to tell you that, when the millionaire and Mr Cove's wife entered the bedroom, there was a black jaguar tied to the foot of the bed.'

'A jaguar?'

'A jaguar, your lordship. Mrs Cove stated that it was there to protect her honour, whereupon the millionaire, touched by this, gave her the money, and they sang the Theme Song as a duet. Mr Cove made a satisfactory recovery after his operation, your lordship.'

'Ah!' said Lord Emsworth, expelling a deep breath. 'Thank you, Beach, that is all.'

# PIG-HOO-O-O-O-EY!

Thanks to the publicity given to the matter by *The Bridgnorth, Shifnal, and Albrighton Argus* (with which is incorporated *The Wheat-Growers' Intelligencer and Stock Breeders' Gazetteer*), the whole world today knows that the silver medal in the Fat Pigs class at the eighty-seventh annual Shropshire Agricultural Show was won by the Earl of Emsworth's black Berkshire sow, Empress of Blandings.

Very few people, however, are aware how near that splendid animal came to missing the coveted honour.

Now it can be told.

This brief chapter of Secret History may be said to have begun on the night of the eighteenth of July, when George Cyril Wellbeloved (twenty-nine), pig-man in the employ of Lord Emsworth, was arrested by Police-Constable Evans of Market Blandings for being drunk and disorderly in the tap-room of the Goat and Feathers. On July the nineteenth, after first offering to apologize, then explaining that it had been his birthday, and finally attempting to prove an alibi, George Cyril was very properly jugged for fourteen days without the option of a fine.

On July the twentieth, Empress of Blandings, always hitherto a hearty and even a boisterous feeder, for the first time on record declined all nourishment. And on the morning of July the twenty-first, the veterinary surgeon called in to diagnose and deal with this strange asceticism, was compelled to confess to Lord Emsworth that the thing was beyond his professional skill.

Let us just see, before proceeding, that we have got these dates correct:

July 18. – Birthday Orgy of Cyril Wellbeloved.
July 19. – Incarceration of Ditto.
July 20. – Pig Lays off the Vitamins.
July 21. – Veterinary Surgeon Baffled.
Right.

The effect of the veterinary surgeon's announcement on Lord Emsworth was overwhelming. As a rule, the wear and tear of our complex modern life left this vague and amiable peer unscathed. So long as he had sunshine, regular meals, and complete freedom from the society of his younger son Frederick, he was placidly happy. But there were chinks in his armour, and one of these had been pierced this morning. Dazed by the news he had received, he stood at the window of the great library of Blandings Castle, looking out with unseeing eyes.

As he stood there, the door opened. Lord Emsworth turned; and having blinked once or twice, as was his habit when confronted suddenly with anything, recognized in the handsome and imperious-looking woman who had entered, his sister, Lady Constance Keeble. Her demeanour, like his own, betrayed the deepest agitation.

'Clarence,' she cried, 'an awful thing has happened!'

Lord Emsworth nodded dully.

'I know. He's just told me.'

'What! Has he been here?'

'Only this moment left.'

'Why did you let him go? You must have known I would want to see him.'

'What good would that have done?'

'I could at least have assured him of my sympathy,' said Lady Constance stiffly.

'Yes, I suppose you could,' said Lord Emsworth, having considered the point. 'Not that he deserves any sympathy. The man's an ass.'

'Nothing of the kind. A most intelligent young man, as young men go.'

'Young? Would you call him young? Fifty, I should have said, if a day.'

'Are you out of your senses? Heacham fifty?'

'Not Heacham. Smithers.'

As frequently happened to her when in conversation with her brother, Lady Constance experienced a swimming sensation in the head.

'Will you kindly tell me, Clarence, in a few simple words, what you imagine we are talking about?'

'I'm talking about Smithers. Empress of Blandings is refusing her food, and Smithers says he can't do anything about it. And he calls himself a vet!'

'Then you haven't heard? Clarence, a dreadful thing has happened. Angela has broken off her engagement to Heacham.'

'And the Agricultural Show on Wednesday week!'

'What on earth has that got to do with it?' demanded Lady Constance, feeling a recurrence of the swimming sensation.

'What has it got to do with it?' said Lord Emsworth warmly. 'My champion sow, with less than ten days to prepare herself for a most searching examination in competition with all the finest pigs in the county, starts refusing her food —'

'Will you stop maundering on about your insufferable pig and give your attention to something that really matters? I tell you that Angela — your niece Angela — has broken off her engagement to Lord Heacham and expresses her intention of marrying that hopeless ne'er-do-well, James Belford.'

'The son of old Belford, the parson?'

'Yes.'

'She can't. He's in America.'

'He is not in America. He is in London.'

'No,' said Lord Emsworth, shaking his head sagely. 'You're wrong. I remember meeting his father two years ago out on the road by Meeker's twenty-acre field, and he distinctly told me the boy was sailing for America next day. He must be there by this time.'

'Can't you understand? He's come back.'

'Oh? Come back? I see. Come *back*?'

'You know there was once a silly sentimental sort of affair between him and Angela; but a year after he left she became engaged to Heacham and I thought the whole thing was over and done with. And now it seems that she met this young man Belford when she was in London last week, and it has started all over again. She tells me she has written to Heacham and broken the engagement.'

There was a silence. Brother and sister remained for a space plunged in thought. Lord Emsworth was the first to speak.

'We've tried acorns,' he said. 'We've tried skim milk. And we've tried potato-peel. But, no, she won't touch them.'

Conscious of two eyes raising blisters on his sensitive skin, he came to himself with a start.

'Absurd! Ridiculous! Preposterous!' he said, hurriedly. 'Breaking the engagement? Pooh! Tush! What nonsense! I'll have a word with that young man. If he thinks he can go about the place playing fast and loose with my niece and jilting her without so much as a —'

'Clarence!'

Lord Emsworth blinked. Something appeared to be wrong, but he could not imagine what. It seemed to him that in his last speech he had struck just the right note – strong, forceful, dignified.

'Eh?'

'It is Angela who has broken the engagement.'

'Oh, Angela?'

'She is infatuated with this man Belford. And the point is, what are we to do about it?'

Lord Emsworth reflected.

'Take a strong line,' he said firmly. 'Stand no nonsense. Don't send 'em a wedding-present.'

There is no doubt that, given time, Lady Constance would have found and uttered some adequately corrosive comment on this imbecile suggestion; but even as she was swelling preparatory to giving tongue, the door opened and a girl came in.

She was a pretty girl, with fair hair and blue eyes which in their softer moments probably reminded all sorts of people of twin lagoons slumbering beneath a southern sky. This, however, was not one of those moments. To Lord Emsworth, as they met his, they looked like something out of an oxy-acetylene blow-pipe; and, as far as he was capable of being disturbed by anything that was not his younger son Frederick, he was disturbed. Angela, it seemed to him, was upset about something; and he was sorry. He liked Angela.

To ease a tense situation, he said:

'Angela, my dear, do you know anything about pigs?'

The girl laughed. One of those sharp, bitter laughs which are so unpleasant just after breakfast.

'Yes, I do. You're one.'

'Me?'

'Yes, you. Aunt Constance says that, if I marry Jimmy, you won't let me have my money.'

'Money? Money?' Lord Emsworth was mildly puzzled. 'What money? You never lent me any money.'

Lady Constance's feelings found vent in a sound like an overheated radiator.

'I believe this absent-mindedness of yours is nothing but a ridiculous pose, Clarence. You know perfectly well that when poor Jane died she left you Angela's trustee.'

'And I can't touch my money without your consent till I'm twenty-five.'

'Well, how old are you?'

'Twenty-one.'

'Then what are you worrying about?' asked Lord Emsworth, surprised. 'No need to worry about it for another four years. God bless my soul, the money is quite safe. It is in excellent securities.'

Angela stamped her foot. An unladylike action, no doubt, but how much better than kicking an uncle with it, as her lower nature prompted.

'I have told Angela,' explained Lady Constance, 'that, while we naturally cannot force her to marry Lord Heacham, we can at least keep her money from being squandered by this wastrel on whom she proposes to throw herself away.'

'He isn't a wastrel. He's got quite enough money to marry me on, but he wants some capital to buy a partnership in a –'

'He is a wastrel. Wasn't he sent abroad because –'

'That was two years ago. And since then –'

'My dear Angela, you may argue until –'

'I'm not arguing. I'm simply saying that I'm going to marry Jimmy, if we both have to starve in the gutter.'

'What gutter?' asked his lordship, wrenching his errant mind away from thoughts of acorns.

'Any gutter.'

'Now, please listen to me, Angela.'

It seemed to Lord Emsworth that there was a frightful amount of conversation going on. He had the sensation of having become a mere bit of flotsam upon a tossing sea of female voices. Both his sister and his niece appeared to have much to say, and they were saying it simultaneously and fortissimo. He looked wistfully at the door.

It was smoothly done. A twist of the handle, and he was where beyond those voices there was peace. Galloping gaily down the stairs, he charged out into the sunshine.

His gaiety was not long-lived. Free at last to concentrate itself on the really serious issues of life, his mind grew sombre and grim. Once more there descended upon him the cloud which had been oppressing his soul before all this Heacham-Angela-Belford business began. Each step that took him nearer to the sty where the ailing Empress resided seemed a heavier step than the last. He reached the sty; and, draping himself over the rails, peered moodily at the vast expanse of pig within.

For, even though she had been doing a bit of dieting of late, Empress of Blandings was far from being an ill-nourished animal. She resembled a captive balloon with ears and a tail, and was as nearly circular as a pig can be without bursting. Nevertheless, Lord Emsworth, as he regarded her, mourned and would not be comforted. A few more square meals under her belt, and no pig in all Shropshire could have held its head up in the Empress's presence. And now, just for lack of those few meals, the supreme animal would probably be relegated to the mean obscurity of an 'Honourably Mentioned'. It was bitter, bitter.

He became aware that somebody was speaking to him; and, turning, perceived a solemn young man in riding breeches.

'I say,' said the young man.

Lord Emsworth, though he would have preferred solitude, was relieved to find that the intruder was at least one of his own sex. Women are apt to stray off into side-issues, but men are practical and can be relied on to stick to the fundamentals. Besides, young Heacham probably kept pigs himself and might have a useful hint or two up his sleeve.

'I say, I've just ridden over to see if there was anything I could do about this fearful business.'

'Uncommonly kind and thoughtful of you, my dear fellow,' said Lord Emsworth, touched. 'I fear things look very black.'

'It's an absolute mystery to me.'

'To me, too.'

'I mean to say, she was all right last week.'

'She was all right as late as the day before yesterday.'

'Seemed quite cheery and chirpy and all that.'

'Entirely so.'

'And then this happens – out of a blue sky, as you might say.'

'Exactly. It is insoluble. We have done everything possible to tempt her appetite.'

'Her appetite? Is Angela ill?'

'Angela? No, I fancy not. She seemed perfectly well a few minutes ago.'

'You've seen her this morning, then? Did she say anything about this fearful business?'

'No. She was speaking about some money.'

'It's all so dashed unexpected.'

'Like a bolt from the blue,' agreed Lord Emsworth.

'Such a thing has never happened before. I fear the worst. According to the Wolff-Lehmann feeding standards, a pig, if in health, should consume daily nourishment amounting to fifty-seven thousand eight hundred calories, these to consist of proteins four pounds five ounces, carbohydrates twenty-five pounds –'

'What has that got to do with Angela?'

'Angela?'

'I came to find out why Angela has broken off our engagement.'

Lord Emsworth marshalled his thoughts. He had a misty idea that he had heard something mentioned about that. It came back to him.

'Ah, yes, of course. She has broken off the engagement, hasn't she? I believe it is because she is in love with someone else. Yes, now that I recollect, that was distinctly stated. The whole thing comes back to me quite clearly. Angela has decided to marry someone else. I knew there was some satisfactory explanation. Tell me, my dear fellow, what are your views on linseed meal?'

'What do you mean, linseed meal?'

'Why, linseed meal,' said Lord Emsworth, not being able to find a better definition. 'As a food for pigs.'

'Oh, curse all pigs!'

'What!' There was a sort of astounded horror in Lord Emsworth's voice. He had never been particularly fond of young Heacham, for he was not a man who took much to his juniors, but he had not supposed him capable of anarchistic sentiments like this. 'What did you say?'

'I said, "Curse all pigs!" You keep talking about pigs. I'm not interested in pigs. I don't want to discuss pigs. Blast and damn every pig in existence!'

Lord Emsworth watched him, as he strode away, with an emotion that was partly indignation and partly relief – indignation that a landowner and a fellow son of Shropshire could have brought himself to utter such words, and relief that one capable of such utterance was not going to marry into his family. He had always in his woollen-headed way been very fond of his niece Angela, and it was nice to think that the child had such solid good sense and so much cool discernment. Many girls of her age would have been carried away by the glamour of young Heacham's position and wealth; but she, divining with an intuition beyond her years that he was unsound on the subject of pigs, had drawn back while there was still time and refused to marry him.

A pleasant glow suffused Lord Emsworth's bosom, to be frozen out a few moments later as he perceived his sister Constance bearing down upon him. Lady Constance was a beautiful woman, but there were times when the charm of her face was marred by a rather curious expression; and from nursery days onward his lordship had learned that this expression meant trouble. She was wearing it now.

'Clarence,' she said, 'I have had enough of this nonsense of Angela and young Belford. The thing cannot be allowed to go drifting on. You must catch the two o'clock train to London.'

'What! Why?'

'You must see this man Belford and tell him that, if Angela insists on marrying him, she will not have a penny for four years. I shall be greatly surprised if that piece of information does not put an end to the whole business.'

Lord Emsworth scratched meditatively at the Empress's tank-like back. A mutinous expression was on his mild face.

'Don't see why she shouldn't marry the fellow,' he mumbled.

'Marry James Belford?'

'I don't see why not. Seems fond of him and all that.'

'You never have had a grain of sense in your head, Clarence. Angela is going to marry Heacham.'

'Can't stand that man. All wrong about pigs.'

'Clarence, I don't wish to have any more discussion and argument. You will go to London on the two o'clock train. You will see Mr Belford. And you will tell him about Angela's money. Is that quite clear?'

'Oh, all right,' said his lordship moodily. 'All right, all right, all right.'

The emotions of the Earl of Emsworth, as he sat next day facing his luncheon-guest, James Bartholomew Belford, across a table in the main dining-room of the Senior Conservative Club, were not of the liveliest and most agreeable. It was bad enough to be in London at all on such a day of golden sunshine. To be charged, while there, with the task of blighting the romance of two young people for whom he entertained a warm regard was unpleasant to a degree.

For, now that he had given the matter thought, Lord Emsworth recalled that he had always liked this boy Belford. A pleasant lad, with, he remembered now, a healthy fondness for that rural existence which so appealed to himself. By no means the sort of fellow who, in the very presence and hearing of Empress of Blandings, would have spoken disparagingly and with oaths of pigs as a class. It occurred to Lord Emsworth, as it has occurred to so many people, that the distribution of money in this world is all wrong. Why should a man like pig-despising Heacham have a rent roll that ran into the tens of thousands, while this very deserving youngster had nothing?

These thoughts not only saddened Lord Emsworth – they embarrassed him. He hated unpleasantness, and it was suddenly borne in upon him that, after he had broken the news that Angela's bit of capital was locked up and not likely to get loose, conversation with his young friend during the remainder of lunch would tend to be somewhat difficult.

He made up his mind to postpone the revelation. During the meal, he decided, he would chat pleasantly of this and that; and then, later, while bidding his guest goodbye, he would spring the thing on him suddenly and dive back into the recesses of the club.

Considerably cheered at having solved a delicate problem with such adroitness, he started to prattle.

'The gardens at Blandings,' he said, 'are looking particularly attractive this summer. My head-gardener, Angus McAllister, is a man with whom I do not always find myself seeing eye to eye, notably in the matter of hollyhocks, on which I consider his views subversive to a degree; but there is no denying that he understands roses. The rose garden –'

'How well I remember that rose garden,' said James Belford, sighing slightly and helping himself to brussels sprouts. 'It was there that Angela and I used to meet on summer evenings.'

Lord Emsworth blinked. This was not an encouraging start, but the Emsworths were a fighting clan. He had another try.

'I have seldom seen such a blaze of colour as was to be witnessed there during the month of June. Both McAllister and I adopted a very strong policy with the slugs and plant lice, with the result that the place was a mass of flourishing Damasks and Ayrshires and –'

'Properly to appreciate roses,' said James Belford, 'you want to see them as a setting for a girl like Angela. With her fair hair gleaming against the green leaves she makes a rose garden seem a veritable Paradise.'

'No doubt,' said Lord Emsworth. 'No doubt. I am glad you liked my rose garden. At Blandings, of course, we have the natural advantage of loamy soil, rich in plant food and humus; but, as I often say to McAllister, and on this point we have never had the slightest disagreement, loamy soil by itself is not enough. You must have manure. If every autumn a liberal mulch of stable manure is spread upon the beds and the coarser parts removed in the spring before the annual forking –'

'Angela tells me,' said James Belford, 'that you have forbidden our marriage.'

Lord Emsworth choked dismally over his chicken. Directness of this kind, he told himself with a pang of self-pity, was the sort of thing young Englishmen picked up in America. Diplomatic circumlocution flourished only in a more leisurely civilization, and in those energetic and forceful surroundings you learned to Talk Quick and Do It Now, and all sorts of uncomfortable things.

'Er – well, yes, now you mention it, I believe some informal decision of that nature was arrived at. You see, my dear fellow, my sister Constance feels rather strongly –'

'I understand. I suppose she thinks I'm a sort of prodigal.'

'No, no, my dear fellow. She never said that. Wastrel was the term she employed.'

'Well, perhaps I did start out in business on those lines. But you can take it from me that when you find yourself employed on a farm in Nebraska belonging to an apple-jack-nourished patriarch with strong views on work and a good vocabulary, you soon develop a certain liveliness.'

'Are you employed on a farm?'

'I was employed on a farm.'

'Pigs?' said Lord Emsworth in a low, eager voice.

'Among other things.'

Lord Emsworth gulped. His fingers clutched at the table-cloth.

'Then perhaps, my dear fellow, you can give me some advice. For the last two days my prize sow, Empress of Blandings, has declined all nourishment. And the Agricultural Show is on Wednesday week. I am distracted with anxiety.'

James Belford frowned thoughtfully.

'What does your pig-man say about it?'

'My pig-man was sent to prison two days ago. Two days!' For the first time the significance of the coincidence struck him. 'You don't think that can have anything to do with the animal's loss of appetite?'

'Certainly. I imagine she is missing him and pining away because he isn't there.'

Lord Emsworth was surprised. He had only a distant acquaintance with George Cyril Wellbeloved, but from what he had seen of him he had not credited him with this fatal allure.

'She probably misses his afternoon call.'

Again his lordship found himself perplexed. He had had no notion that pigs were such sticklers for the formalities of social life.

'His call?'

'He must have had some special call that he used when he wanted her to come to dinner. One of the first things you learn on a farm is hog-calling. Pigs are temperamental. Omit to call them, and they'll starve rather than put on the nose-bag. Call them right, and they will follow you to the ends of the earth with their mouths watering.'

'God bless my soul! Fancy that.'

'A fact, I assure you. These calls vary in different parts of America. In Wisconsin, for example, the words "Poig, Poig, Poig" bring home – in both the literal and the figurative sense – the bacon. In Illinois, I believe they call "Burp, Burp, Burp", while in Iowa the phrase "Kus, Kus, Kus" is preferred. Proceeding to Minnesota, we find "Peega, Peega, Peega" or, alternatively, "Oink, Oink, Oink", whereas in Milwaukee, so largely inhabited by those of German descent, you will hear the good old Teuton "Komm Schweine, Komm Schweine". Oh, yes, there are all sorts of pig-calls, from the Massachusetts "Phew, Phew, Phew" to the "Loo-ey, Loo-ey, Loo-ey" of Ohio, not counting various local devices such as beating on tin cans with axes or rattling pebbles in a suit-case. I knew a man out in Nebraska who used to call his pigs by tapping on the edge of the trough with his wooden leg.'

'Did he, indeed?'

'But a most unfortunate thing happened. One evening, hearing a woodpecker at the top of a tree, they started shinning up it; and when the man came out he found them all lying there in a circle with their necks broken.'

'This is no time for joking,' said Lord Emsworth, pained.

'I'm not joking. Solid fact. Ask anybody out there.'

Lord Emsworth placed a hand to his throbbing forehead.

'But if there is this wide variety, we have no means of knowing which call Wellbeloved . . .'

'Ah,' said James Belford, 'but wait. I haven't told you all. There is a master-word.'

'A what?'

'Most people don't know it, but I had it straight from the lips of Fred Patzel, the hog-calling champion of the Western States. What a man! I've known him to bring pork chops leaping from their plates. He informed me that, no matter whether an animal has been trained to answer to the Illinois "Burp" or the Minnesota "Oink", it will always give immediate service in response to this magic combination of syllables. It is to the pig world what the Masonic grip is to the human. "Oink" in Illinois or "Burp" in Minnesota, and the animal merely raises its eyebrows and stares coldly. But go to either state and call "Pig-hoo-oo-ey!" . . .'

The expression on Lord Emsworth's face was that of a drowning man who sees a lifeline.

'Is that the master-word of which you spoke?'

'That's it.'

'Pig –!'

'– hoo-oo-ey.'

'Pig-hoo-o-ey!'

'You haven't got it quite right. The first syllable should be short and staccato, the second long and rising into a falsetto, high but true.'

'Pig-hoo-o-o-ey.'

'Pig-hoo-o-o-ey.'

'Pig-hoo-o-o-ey!' yodelled Lord Emsworth, flinging his head back and giving tongue in a high, penetrating tenor which caused ninety-three Senior Conservatives, lunching in the vicinity, to congeal into living statues of alarm and disapproval.

'More body to the "hoo",' advised James Belford.

'Pig-hoo-o-o-ey!'

The Senior Conservative Club is one of the few places in London where lunchers are not accustomed to getting music with their meals. White-whiskered financiers gazed bleakly at bald-headed politicians, as if asking silently what was to be done about this. Bald-headed politicians stared back at white-whiskered financiers, replying in the language of the eye that they did not know. The general sentiment prevailing was a vague determination to write to the Committee about it.

'Pig-hoo-o-o-ey!' carolled Lord Emsworth. And, as he did so, his eye fell on the clock over the mantelpiece. Its hands pointed to twenty minutes to two.

He started convulsively. The best train in the day for Market Blandings was the one which left Paddington station at two sharp. After that there was nothing till the five-five.

He was not a man who often thought; but, when he did, to think was with him to act. A moment later he was scudding over the carpet, making for the door that led to the broad staircase.

Throughout the room which he had left, the decision to write in strong terms to the Committee was now universal; but from the mind, such as it was, of Lord Emsworth the past, with the single exception of the word 'Pig-hoo-o-o-o-ey!', had been completely blotted.

Whispering the magic syllables, he sped to the cloakroom and retrieved his hat. Murmuring them over and over again, he sprang into a cab. He was still repeating them as the train moved out of the station; and he would doubtless have gone on repeating them all the way to Market Blandings had he not, as was his invariable practice when travelling by rail, fallen asleep after the first ten minutes of the journey.

The stopping of the train at Swindon Junction woke him with a start. He sat up, wondering, after his usual fashion on these occasions, who and where he was. Memory returned to him, but a memory that was, alas, incomplete. He remembered his name. He remembered that he was on his way home from a visit to London. But what it was that you said to a pig when inviting it to drop in for a bite of dinner he had completely forgotten.


It was the opinion of Lady Constance Keeble, expressed verbally during dinner in the brief intervals when they were alone, and by means of silent telepathy when Beach, the butler, was adding his dignified presence to the proceedings, that her brother Clarence, in his expedition to London to put matters plainly to James Belford, had made an outstanding idiot of himself.

There had been no need whatever to invite the man Belford to lunch; but, having invited him to lunch, to leave him sitting, without having clearly stated that Angela would have no money for four years, was the act of a congenital imbecile. Lady Constance had been aware ever since their childhood days that her brother had about as much sense as a —

Here Beach entered, superintending the bringing-in of the savoury, and she had been obliged to suspend her remarks.

This sort of conversation is never agreeable to a sensitive man, and his lordship had removed himself from the danger zone as soon as he could manage it. He was now seated in the library, sipping port and straining a brain which Nature had never intended for hard exercise in an effort to bring back that word of magic of which his unfortunate habit of sleeping in trains had robbed him.

'Pig —'

He could remember as far as that; but of what avail was a single syllable? Besides, weak as his memory was, he could recall that the whole gist or nub of the thing lay in the syllable that followed. The 'pig' was a mere preliminary.

Lord Emsworth finished his port and got up. He felt restless, stifled. The summer night seemed to call to him like some silver-voiced swineherd calling to his pig. Possibly, he thought, a breath of fresh air might stimulate his brain-cells. He wandered downstairs; and, having dug a shocking old slouch hat out of the cupboard where he hid it to keep his sister Constance from impounding and burning it, he strode heavily out into the garden.

He was pottering aimlessly to and fro in the parts adjacent to the rear of the castle when there appeared in his path a slender female form. He recognized it without pleasure. Any unbiased judge would have said that his niece Angela, standing there in the soft, pale light, looked like some dainty spirit of the Moon. Lord Emsworth was not an unbiased judge. To him Angela merely looked like Trouble. The march of civilization has given the modern girl a vocabulary and an ability to use it which her grandmother never had. Lord Emsworth would not have minded meeting Angela's grandmother a bit.

'Is that you, my dear?' he said nervously.

'Yes.'

'I didn't see you at dinner.'

'I didn't want any dinner. The food would have choked me. I can't eat.'

'It's precisely the same with my pig,' said his lordship. 'Young Belford tells me —'

Into Angela's queenly disdain there flashed a sudden animation.

'Have you seen Jimmy? What did he say?'

'That's just what I can't remember. It began with the word "Pig" —'

'But after he had finished talking about you, I mean. Didn't he say anything about coming down here?'

'Not that I remember.'

'I expect you weren't listening. You've got a very annoying habit, Uncle Clarence,' said Angela maternally, 'of switching your mind off and just going blah when people are talking to you. It gets you very much disliked on all sides. Didn't Jimmy say anything about me?'

'I fancy so. Yes, I am nearly sure he did.'

'Well, what?'

'I cannot remember.'

There was a sharp clicking noise in the darkness. It was caused by Angela's upper front teeth meeting her lower front teeth; and was followed by a sort of wordless exclamation. It seemed only too plain that the love and respect which a niece should have for an uncle were in the present instance at a very low ebb.

'I wish you wouldn't do that,' said Lord Emsworth plaintively.

'Do what?'

'Make clicking noises at me.'

'I will make clicking noises at you. You know perfectly well, Uncle Clarence, that you are behaving like a bohunkus.'

'A what?'

'A bohunkus,' explained his niece coldly, 'is a very inferior sort of worm. Not the kind of worm that you see on lawns, which you can respect, but a really degraded species.'

'I wish you would go in, my dear,' said Lord Emsworth. 'The night air may give you a chill.'

'I won't go in. I came out here to look at the moon and think of Jimmy. What are you doing out here, if it comes to that?'

'I came here to think. I am greatly exercised about my pig, Empress of Blandings. For two days she has refused her food, and young Belford says she will not eat until she hears the proper call or cry. He very kindly taught it to me, but unfortunately I have forgotten it.'

'I wonder you had the nerve to ask Jimmy to teach you pig-calls, considering the way you're treating him.'

'But –'

'Like a leper, or something. And all I can say is that, if you remember this call of his, and it makes the Empress eat, you ought to be ashamed of yourself if you still refuse to let me marry him.'

'My dear,' said Lord Emsworth earnestly, 'if through young Belford's instrumentality Empress of Blandings is induced to take nourishment once more there is nothing I will refuse him – nothing.'

'Honour bright?'

'I give you my solemn word.'

'You won't let Aunt Constance bully you out of it?'

Lord Emsworth drew himself up.

'Certainly not,' he said proudly. 'I am always ready to listen to your Aunt Constance's views, but there are certain matters where I claim the right to act according to my own judgement.' He paused and stood musing. 'It began with the word "Pig –"'

From somewhere near at hand music made itself heard. The servants' hall, its day's labours ended, was refreshing itself with the house-keeper's gramophone. To Lord Emsworth the strains were merely an additional annoyance. He was not fond of music. It reminded him of his younger son Frederick, a flat but persevering songster both in and out of the bath.

'Yes, I can distinctly recall as much as that. Pig – Pig –'

'WHO –'

Lord Emsworth leaped in the air. It was as if an electric shock had been applied to his person.

'WHO stole my heart away?' howled the gramophone. 'WHO –?'

The peace of the summer night was shattered by a triumphant shout. 'Pig-HOO-o-o-o-ey!'

A window opened. A large, bald head appeared. A dignified voice spoke.

'Who is there? Who is making that noise?'

'Beach!' cried Lord Emsworth. 'Come out here at once.'

'Very good, your lordship.'

And presently the beautiful night was made still more lovely by the added attraction of the butler's presence.

'Beach, listen to this.'

'Very good, your lordship.'

'Pig-hoo-o-o-o-ey!'

'Very good, your lordship.'

'Now you do it.'

'I, your lordship?'

'Yes. It's a way you call pigs.'

'I do not call pigs, your lordship,' said the butler coldly.

'What do you want Beach to do it for?' asked Angela.

'Two heads are better than one. If we both learn it, it will not matter should I forget it again.'

'By Jove, yes! Come on, Beach. Push it over the thorax,' urged the girl eagerly. 'You don't know it, but this is a matter of life and death. At-a-boy, Beach! Inflate the lungs and go to it.'

It had been the butler's intention, prefacing his remarks with the statement that he had been in service at the castle for eighteen years, to explain frigidly to Lord Emsworth that it was not his place to stand in the moonlight practising pig-calls. If, he would have gone on to add, his lordship saw the matter from a different angle, then it was his, Beach's, painful duty to tender his resignation, to become effective one month from that day.

But the intervention of Angela made this impossible to a man of chivalry and heart. A paternal fondness for the girl, dating from the days when he had stooped to enacting – and very convincingly, too, for his was a figure that lent itself to the impersonation – the role of a hippopotamus for her childish amusement, checked the words he would have uttered. She was looking at him with bright eyes, and even the rendering of pig-noises seemed a small sacrifice to make for her sake.

'Very good, your lordship,' he said in a low voice, his face pale and set in the moonlight. 'I shall endeavour to give satisfaction. I would merely advance the suggestion, your lordship, that we move a few steps farther away from the vicinity of the servants' hall. If I were to be overheard by any of the lower domestics, it would weaken my position as a disciplinary force.'

'What chumps we are!' cried Angela, inspired. 'The place to do it is outside the Empress's sty. Then, if it works, we'll see it working.'

Lord Emsworth found this a little abstruse, but after a moment he got it.

'Angela,' he said, 'you are a very intelligent girl. Where you get your brains from, I don't know. Not from my side of the family.'

The bijou residence of the Empress of Blandings looked very snug and attractive in the moonlight. But beneath even the beautiful things of life there is always an underlying sadness. This was supplied in the present instance by a long, low trough, only too plainly full to the brim of succulent mash and acorns. The fast, obviously, was still in progress.

The sty stood some considerable distance from the castle walls, so that there had been ample opportunity for Lord Emsworth to rehearse his little company during the journey. By the time they had ranged themselves against the rails, his two assistants were letter-perfect.

'Now,' said his lordship.

There floated out upon the summer night a strange composite sound that sent the birds roosting in the trees above shooting off their perches like rockets. Angela's clear soprano rang out like the voice of the village blacksmith's daughter. Lord Emsworth contributed a reedy tenor. And the bass notes of Beach probably did more to startle the birds than any other one item in the programme.

They paused and listened. Inside the Empress's boudoir there sounded the movement of a heavy body. There was an inquiring grunt. The next moment the sacking that covered the doorway was pushed aside, and the noble animal emerged.

'Now!' said Lord Emsworth again.

Once more that musical cry shattered the silence of the night. But it brought no responsive movement from Empress of Blandings. She stood there motionless, her nose elevated, her ears hanging down, her eyes everywhere but on the trough where, by rights, she should now have been digging in and getting hers. A chill disappointment crept over Lord Emsworth, to be succeeded by a gust of petulant anger.

'I might have known it,' he said bitterly. 'That young scoundrel was deceiving me. He was playing a joke on me.'

'He wasn't,' cried Angela indignantly. 'Was he, Beach?'

'Not knowing the circumstances, miss, I cannot venture an opinion.'

'Well, why has it no effect, then?' demanded Lord Emsworth.

'You can't expect it to work right away. We've got her stirred up, haven't we? She's thinking it over, isn't she? Once more will do the trick. Ready, Beach?'

'Quite ready, miss.'

'Then when I say three. And this time, Uncle Clarence, do please for goodness' sake not yowl like you did before. It was enough to put any pig off. Let it come out quite easily and gracefully. Now, then. One, two – three!'

The echoes died away. And as they did so a voice spoke.

'Community singing?'

'Jimmy!' cried Angela, whisking round.

'Hullo, Angela. Hullo, Lord Emsworth. Hullo, Beach.'

'Good evening, sir. Happy to see you once more.'

'Thanks. I'm spending a few days at the Vicarage with my father. I got down here by the five-five.'

Lord Emsworth cut peevishly in upon these civilities.

'Young man,' he said, 'what do you mean by telling me that my pig would respond to that cry? It does nothing of the kind.'

'You can't have done it right.'

'I did it precisely as you instructed me. I have had, moreover, the assistance of Beach here and my niece Angela —'

'Let's hear a sample.'

Lord Emsworth cleared his throat.

'Pig-hoo-o-o-o-ey!'

James Belford shook his head.

'Nothing like it,' he said. 'You want to begin the "Hoo" in a low minor of two quarter notes in four-four time. From this build gradually to a higher note, until at last the voice is soaring in full crescendo, reaching F sharp on the natural scale and dwelling for two retarded half-notes, then breaking into a shower of accidental grace-notes.'

'God bless my soul!' said Lord Emsworth, appalled. 'I shall never be able to do it.'

'Jimmy will do it for you,' said Angela. 'Now that he's engaged to me, he'll be one of the family and always popping about here. He can do it every day till the show is over.'

James Belford nodded.

'I think that would be the wisest plan. It is doubtful if an amateur could ever produce real results. You need a voice that has been trained on the open prairie and that has gathered richness and strength from competing with tornadoes. You need a manly, sunburned, wind-scorched voice with a suggestion in it of the crackling of corn husks and the whisper of evening breezes in the fodder. Like this!'

Resting his hands on the rail before him, James Belford swelled before their eyes like a young balloon. The muscles on his cheekbones stood out, his forehead became corrugated, his ears seemed to shimmer. Then, at the very height of the tension, he let it go like, as the poet beautifully puts it, the sound of a great Amen.

'Pig-HOOOOO-OOO-OOO-O-O-ey!'

They looked at him, awed. Slowly, fading off across hill and dale, the vast bellow died away. And suddenly, as it died, another, softer sound succeeded it. A sort of gulpy, gurgly, plobby, squishy, woffle-some sound, like a thousand eager men drinking soup in a foreign restaurant. And, as he heard it, Lord Emsworth uttered a cry of rapture.

The Empress was feeding.

# COMPANY FOR GERTRUDE

The Hon. Freddie Threepwood, married to the charming daughter of Donaldson's Dog-Biscuits of Long Island City, N.Y., and sent home by his father-in-law to stimulate the sale of the firm's products in England, naturally thought right away of his aunt Georgiana. There, he reasoned, was a woman who positively ate dog-biscuits. She had owned, when he was last in the country, a matter of four Pekes, two Poms, a Yorkshire terrier, five Sealyhams, a Borzoi, and an Airedale: and if that didn't constitute a promising market for Donaldson's Dog-Joy ('Get your dog thinking the Donaldson way'), he would like to know what did. The Alcester connexion ought, he considered, to be good for at least ten of the half-crown cellophane-sealed packets a week.

A day or so after his arrival, accordingly, he hastened round to Upper Brook Street to make a sales-talk: and it was as he was coming rather pensively out of the house at the conclusion of the interview that he ran into Beefy Bingham, who had been up at Oxford with him. Several years had passed since the other, then a third-year Blood and Trial Eights man, had bicycled along tow-paths saying rude things through a megaphone about Freddie's stomach, but he recognized him instantly. And this in spite of the fact that the passage of time appeared to have turned old Beefers into a clergyman. For the colossal frame of this Bingham was now clad in sober black, and he was wearing one of those collars which are kept in position without studs, purely by the exercise of will-power.

'Beefers!' cried Freddie, his slight gloom vanishing in the pleasure of this happy reunion.

The Rev. Rupert Bingham, though he returned his greeting with cordiality, was far from exuberant. He seemed subdued, gloomy, as if he had discovered schism among his flock. His voice, when he spoke, was the voice of a man with a secret sorrow.

'Oh, hullo, Freddie. I haven't seen you for years. Keeping pretty fit!'

'As a fiddle, Beefers, old man, as a fiddle. And you?'

'Oh, I'm all right,' said the Rev. Rupert, still with that same strange gloom. 'What were you doing in that house?'

'Trying to sell dog-biscuits.'

'Do you sell dog-biscuits?'

'I do when people have sense enough to see that Donaldson's Dog-Joy stands alone. But could I make my fat-headed aunt see that? No, Beefers, not though I talked for an hour and sprayed her with printed matter like a –'

'Your aunt? I didn't know Lady Alcester was your aunt.'

'Didn't you, Beefers? I thought it was all over London.'

'Did she tell you about me?'

'What about you? Great Scott! Are you the impoverished bloke who wants to marry Gertrude?'

'Yes.'

'Well, I'm dashed.'

'I love her, Freddie,' said the Rev. Rupert Bingham. 'I love her as no man . . .'

'Rather. Quite. Absolutely. I know. All the usual stuff. And she loves you, what?'

'Yes. And now they've gone and sent her off to Blandings, to be out of my way.'

'Low. Very low. But why are you impoverished? What about tithes? I always understood you birds made a pot out of tithes.'

'There aren't any tithes where I am.'

'No tithes?'

'None.'

'H'm. Not so hot. Well, what are you going to do about it, Beefers?'

'I thought of calling on your aunt, and trying to reason with her.'

Freddie took his old friend's arm sympathetically and drew him away.

'No earthly good, old man. If a woman won't buy Donaldson's Dog-Joy, it means she has some sort of mental kink and it's no use trying to reason with her. We must think of some other procedure. So Gertrude is at Blandings, is she? She would be. The family seem to look on the place as a sort of Bastille. Whenever the young of the species make a floater like falling in love with the wrong man, they are always shot off to Blandings to recover. The guv'nor has often complained about it bitterly. Now, let me think.'

They passed into Park Street. Some workmen were busy tearing up the paving with pneumatic drills, but the whirring of Freddie's brain made the sound almost inaudible.

'I've got it,' he said at length, his features relaxing from the terrific strain. 'And it's a dashed lucky thing for you, my lad, that I went last night to see that super-film, "Young Hearts Adrift", featuring Rosalie Norton and Otto Byng. Beefers, old man, you're legging it straight down to Blandings this very afternoon.'

'What!'

'By the first train after lunch. I've got the whole thing planned out. In this super-film, "Young Hearts Adrift", a poor but deserving young man was in love with the daughter of rich and haughty parents, and they took her away to the country so that she could forget, and a few days later a mysterious stranger turned up at the place and ingratiated himself with the parents and said he wanted to marry their daughter, and they gave their consent, and the wedding took place, and then he tore off his whiskers and it was Jim!'

'Yes, but . . .'

'Don't argue. The thing's settled. My aunt needs a sharp lesson. You would think a woman would be only too glad to put business in the way of her nearest and dearest, especially when shown samples and offered a fortnight's free trial. But no! She insists on sticking to Peterson's Pup-Food, a wholly inferior product – lacking, I happen to know, in many of the essential vitamins – and from now on, old boy, I am heart and soul in your cause.'

'Whiskers?' said the Rev. Rupert doubtfully.

'You won't have to wear any whiskers. My guv'nor's never seen you. Or has he?'

'No, I've not met Lord Emsworth.'

'Very well, then.'

'But what good will it do me, ingratiating myself, as you call it, with your father? He's only Gertrude's uncle.'

'What good? My dear chap, are you aware that the guv'nor owns the countryside for miles around? He has all sorts of livings up his sleeve – livings simply dripping with tithes – and can distribute them to whoever he likes. I know, because at one time there was an idea of making me a parson. But I would have none of it.'

The Rev. Rupert's face cleared.

'Freddie, there's something in this.'

'You bet there's something in it.'

'But how can I ingratiate myself with your father?'

'Perfectly easy. Cluster round him. Hang on his every word. Interest

yourself in his pursuits. Do him little services. Help him out of chairs
. . . Why, great Scott, I'd undertake to ingratiate myself with Stalin if I
gave my mind to it. Pop off and pack the old toothbrush, and I'll go
and get the guv'nor on the phone.'

At about the time when this pregnant conversation was taking place in
London, W. I, far away in distant Shropshire Clarence, ninth Earl of
Emsworth, sat brooding in the library of Blandings Castle. Fate,
usually indulgent to this dreamy peer, had suddenly turned nasty and
smitten him a grievous blow beneath the belt.

They say Great Britain is still a first-class power, doing well and
winning respect from the nations: and, if so, it is, of course, extremely
gratifying. But what of the future? That was what Lord Emsworth was
asking himself. Could this happy state of things last? He thought not.
Without wishing to be pessimistic, he was dashed if he saw how a
country containing men like Sir Gregory Parsloe-Parsloe of Matchingham Hall could hope to survive.

Strong? No doubt. Bitter? Granted. But not, we think, too strong,
not – in the circumstances – unduly bitter. Consider the facts.

When, shortly after the triumph of Lord Emsworth's pre-eminent
sow, Empress of Blandings, in the Fat Pigs Class at the eighty-seventh
annual Shropshire Agricultural Show, George Cyril Wellbeloved, his
lordship's pig-man, had expressed a desire to hand in his portfolio and
seek employment elsewhere, the amiable peer, though naturally grieved,
felt no sense of outrage. He put the thing down to the old roving spirit
of the Wellbeloveds. George Cyril, he assumed, wearying of Shropshire, wished to try a change of air in some southern or eastern county.
A nuisance, undoubtedly, for the man, when sober, was beyond
question a force in the piggery. He had charm and personality. Pigs
liked him. Still, if he wanted to resign office, there was nothing to be
done about it.

But when, not a week later, word was brought to Lord Emsworth
that, so far from having migrated to Sussex or Norfolk or Kent or
somewhere, the fellow was actually just round the corner in the
neighbouring village of Much Matchingham, serving under the banner
of Sir Gregory Parsloe-Parsloe of Matchingham Hall, the scales fell
from his eyes. He realized that black treachery had been at work.
George Cyril Wellbeloved had sold himself for gold, and Sir Gregory
Parsloe-Parsloe, hitherto looked upon as a high-minded friend and

fellow Justice of the Peace, stood revealed as that lowest of created things, a lurer-away of other people's pig-men.

And there was nothing one could do about it.

Monstrous!

But true.

So deeply was Lord Emsworth occupied with the consideration of this appalling state of affairs that it was only when the knock upon the door was repeated that it reached his consciousness.

'Come in,' he said hollowly.

He hoped it was not his niece Gertrude. A gloomy young woman. He could hardly stand Gertrude's society just now.

It was not Gertrude. It was Beach, the butler.

'Mr Frederick wishes to speak to your lordship on the telephone.'

An additional layer of greyness fell over Lord Emsworth's spirit as he toddled down the great staircase to the telephone closet in the hall. It was his experience that almost any communication from Freddie indicated trouble.

But there was nothing in his son's voice as it floated over the wire to suggest that all was not well.

'Hullo, guv'nor.'

'Well, Frederick?'

'How's everything at Blandings?'

Lord Emsworth was not the man to exhibit the vultures gnawing at his heart to a babbler like the Hon. Freddie. He replied, though it hurt him to do so, that everything at Blandings was excellent.

'Good-oh!' said Freddie. 'Is the old dosshouse very full up at the moment?'

'If,' replied his lordship, 'you are alluding to Blandings Castle, there is nobody at present staying here except myself and your cousin Gertrude. Why?' he added in quick alarm. 'Were you thinking of coming down?'

'Good God, no!' cried his son with equal horror. 'I mean to say, I'd love it, of course, but just now I'm too busy with Dog-Joy.'

'Who is Popjoy?'

'Popjoy? Popjoy? Oh, ah, yes. He's a pal of mine and, as you've plenty of room, I want you to put him up for a bit. Nice chap. You'll like him. Right-ho, then, I'll ship him off on the three-fifteen.'

Lord Emsworth's face had assumed an expression which made it fortunate for his son that television was not yet in operation on the telephone systems of England: and he had just recovered enough breath for the delivery of a blistering refusal to have any friend of Freddie's within fifty miles of the place when the other spoke again.

'He'll be company for Gertrude.'

And at these words a remarkable change came over Lord Emsworth. His face untwisted itself. The basilisk glare died out of his eyes.

'God bless my soul! That's true!' he exclaimed. 'That's certainly true. So he will. The three-fifteen, did you say? I will send the car to Market Blandings to meet it.'

Company for Gertrude? A pleasing thought. A fragrant, refreshing, stimulating thought. Somebody to take Gertrude off his hands occasionally was what he had been praying for ever since his sister Georgiana had dumped her down on him.

One of the chief drawbacks to entertaining in your home a girl who has been crossed in love is that she is extremely apt to go about the place doing good. All that life holds for her now is the opportunity of being kind to others, and she intends to be kind if it chokes them. For two weeks Lord Emsworth's beautiful young niece had been moving to and fro through the castle with a drawn face, doing good right and left: and his lordship, being handiest, had had to bear the brunt of it. It was with the first real smile he had smiled that day that he came out of the telephone-cupboard and found the object of his thoughts entering the hall in front of him.

'Well, well, well, my dear,' he said cheerily. 'And what have you been doing?'

There was no answering smile on his niece's face. Indeed, looking at her, you could see that this was a girl who had forgotten how to smile. She suggested something symbolic out of Maeterlinck.

'I have been tidying your study, Uncle Clarence,' she replied listlessly. 'It was in a dreadful mess.'

Lord Emsworth winced as a man of set habits will who has been remiss enough to let a Little Mother get at his study while his back is turned, but he continued bravely on the cheerful note.

'I have been talking to Frederick on the telephone.'

'Yes?' Gertrude sighed, and a bleak wind seemed to blow through the hall. 'Your tie's crooked, Uncle Clarence.'

'I like it crooked,' said his lordship, backing. 'I have a piece of news for you. A friend of Frederick's is coming down here tonight for a visit. His name, I understand, is Popjoy. So you will have some young society at last.'

'I don't want young society.'

'Oh, come, my dear.'

She looked at him thoughtfully with large, sombre eyes. Another sigh escaped her.

'It must be wonderful to be as old as you are, Uncle Clarence.'

'Eh?' said his lordship, starting.

'To feel that there is such a short, short step to the quiet tomb, to the ineffable peace of the grave. To me, life seems to stretch out endlessly, like a long, dusty desert. Twenty-three! That's all I am. Only twenty-three. And all our family live to sixty.'

'What do you mean, sixty?' demanded his lordship, with the warmth of a man who would be that next birthday. 'My poor father was seventy-seven when he was killed in the hunting-field. My uncle Robert lived till nearly ninety. My cousin Claude was eighty-four when he broke his neck trying to jump a five-barred gate. My mother's brother, Alistair . . .'

'Don't!' said the girl with a little shudder. 'Don't! It makes it all seem so awful and hopeless.'

Yes, that was Gertrude: and in Lord Emsworth's opinion she needed company.

The reactions of Lord Emsworth to the young man Popjoy, when he encountered him for the first time in the drawing-room shortly before dinner, were in the beginning wholly favourable. His son's friend was an extraordinarily large and powerful person with a frank, open, ingenuous face about the colour of the inside of a salmon, and he seemed a little nervous. That, however, was in his favour. It was, his lordship felt, a pleasant surprise to find in one of the younger generation so novel an emotion as diffidence.

He condoned, therefore, the other's trick of laughing hysterically even when the subject under discussion was the not irresistibly ludicrous one of greenfly in the rose-garden. He excused him for appearing to find something outstandingly comic in the statement that the glass was going up. And when, springing to his feet at the entrance of Gertrude, the young man performed some complicated steps in conjunction with a table covered with china and photograph-frames, he joined in the mirth which the feat provoked not only from the visitor but actually from Gertrude herself.

Yes, amazing though it might seem, his niece Gertrude, on seeing this young Popjoy, had suddenly burst into a peal of happy laughter. The gloom of the last two weeks appeared to be gone. She laughed. The young man laughed.

They proceeded down to dinner in a perfect gale of merriment, rather like a chorus of revellers exiting after a concerted number in an old-fashioned comic opera.

And at dinner the young man had spilt his soup, broken a wine-glass and almost taken another spectacular toss when leaping up at the end of the meal to open the door. At which Gertrude had laughed, and the young man had laughed, and his lordship had laughed – though not, perhaps, quite so heartily as the young folks, for that wine-glass had been one of a set which he valued.

However, weighing profit and loss as he sipped his port, Lord Emsworth considered that the ledger worked out on the right side. True, he had taken into his home what appeared to be a half-witted acrobat: but then any friend of his son Frederick was bound to be weak in the head, and, after all, the great thing was that Gertrude seemed to appreciate the newcomer's society. He looked forward contentedly to a succession of sunshine days of peace, perfect peace with loved ones far away; days when he would be able to work in his garden without the fear, which had been haunting him for the last two weeks, of finding his niece drooping wanly at his side and asking him if he was wise to stand about in the hot sun. She had company now that would occupy her elsewhere.

His lordship's opinion of his guest's mental deficiencies was strengthened late that night when, hearing footsteps on the terrace, he poked his head out and found him standing beneath his window, blowing kisses at it.

At the sight of his host he appeared somewhat confused.

'Lovely evening,' he said, with his usual hyenaesque laugh. 'I – er – thought . . . or, rather . . . that is to say . . . Ha, ha, ha!'

'Is anything the matter?'

'No, no! No! No, thanks, no! No! No, no! I – er – ho, ho, ho! – just came out for a stroll, ha, ha!'

Lord Emsworth returned to his bed a little thoughtfully. Perhaps some premonition of what was to come afflicted his subconscious mind, for, as he slipped between the sheets, he shivered. But gradually, as he dozed off, his equanimity became restored.

Looking at the thing in the right spirit, it might have been worse.

After all, he felt, the mists of sleep beginning to exert their usual beneficent influence, he might have been entertaining at Blandings Castle one of his nephews, or one of his sisters, or even – though this was morbid – his younger son Frederick.

In matters where shades of feeling are involved, it is not always easy for the historian to be as definite as he could wish. He wants to keep the record straight, and yet he cannot take any one particular moment of time, pin it down for the scrutiny of Posterity and say, 'This was the moment when Lord Emsworth for the first time found himself wishing that his guest would tumble out of an upper window and break his neck.' To his lordship it seemed that this had been from the beginning his constant day-dream, but such was not the case. When, on the second morning of the other's visit, the luncheon-gong had found them chatting in the library and the young man, bounding up, had extended a hand like a ham and, placing it beneath his host's arm, gently helped him to rise, Lord Emsworth had been quite pleased by the courteous attention.

But when the fellow did the same thing day after day, night after night, every time he caught him sitting; when he offered him an arm to help him across floors; when he assisted him up stairs, along corridors, down paths, out of rooms and into raincoats; when he snatched objects from his hands to carry them himself; when he came galloping out of the house on dewy evenings laden down with rugs, mufflers, hats and, on one occasion, positively a blasted respirator . . . why, then Lord Emsworth's proud spirit rebelled. He was a tough old gentleman and, like most tough old gentlemen, did not enjoy having his juniors look on him as something pathetically helpless that crawled the earth waiting for the end.

It had been bad enough when Gertrude was being the Little Mother. This was infinitely worse. Apparently having conceived for him one of those unreasoning, overwhelming devotions, this young Popjoy stuck closer than a brother; and for the first time Lord Emsworth began to appreciate what must have been the feelings of that Mary who aroused a similar attachment in the bosom of her lamb. It was as if he had been an Oldest Inhabitant fallen into the midst of a troop of Boy Scouts, all doing Good Deeds simultaneously, and he resented it with an indescribable bitterness. One can best illustrate his frame of mind by saying that, during the last phase, if he had been called upon to choose between his guest and Sir Gregory Parsloe-Parsloe as a companion for a summer ramble through the woods, he would have chosen Sir Gregory.

And then, on top of all this, there occurred the episode of the step-ladder.

The Hon. Freddie Threepwood, who had decided to run down and see how matters were developing, learned the details of this rather unfortunate occurrence from his cousin Gertrude. She met him at Market Blandings Station, and he could see there was something on her mind. She had not become positively Maeterlinckian again, but there was sorrow in her beautiful eyes: and Freddie, rightly holding that with a brainy egg like himself directing her destinies they should have contained only joy and sunshine, was disturbed by this.

'Don't tell me the binge has sprung a leak,' he said anxiously.

Gertrude sighed.

'Well, yes and no.'

'What do you mean, yes and no? Properly worked, the thing can't fail. This points to negligence somewhere. Has old Beefers been ingratiating himself?'

'Yes.'

'Hanging on the guv'nor's every word? Interesting himself in his pursuits? Doing him little services? And been at it two weeks? Good heavens! By now the guv' nor should be looking on him as a prize pig. Why isn't he?'

'I didn't say he wasn't. Till this afternoon I rather think he was. At any rate, Rupert says he often found Uncle Clarence staring at him in a sort of lingering, rather yearning way. But when that thing happened this afternoon, I'm afraid he wasn't very pleased.'

'What thing?'

'That step-ladder business. It was like this. Rupert and I sort of went for a walk after lunch, and by the time I had persuaded him that he ought to go and find Uncle Clarence and ingratiate himself with him, Uncle Clarence had disappeared. So Rupert hunted about for a long time and at last heard a snipping noise and found him miles away standing on a step-ladder, sort of pruning some kind of tree with a pair of shears. So Rupert said, "Oh, there you are!" And Uncle Clarence said, Yes, there he was, and Rupert said, "Ought you to tire yourself? Won't you let me do that for you?"'

'The right note,' said Freddie approvingly. 'Assiduity. Zeal. Well?'

'Well, Uncle Clarence said, "No, thank you!" – and Rupert thinks it was "Thank you" – and Rupert stood there for a bit, sort of talking, and then he suddenly remembered and told Uncle Clarence that you had just phoned that you were coming down this evening, and I think Uncle Clarence must have got a touch of cramp or something, because he gave a kind of sudden sharp groan, Rupert says, and sort of quivered all over. This made the steps wobble, of course, so Rupert dashed forward to steady them, and he doesn't know how it happened, but they suddenly seemed to sort of shut up like a pair of scissors, and the next thing he knew Uncle Clarence was sitting on the grass, not seeming to like it much, Rupert says. He had ricked his ankle a bit and shaken himself up a bit, and altogether, Rupert says, he wasn't fearfully sunny. Rupert says he thinks he may have lost ground a little.'

Freddie pondered with knit brows. He was feeling something of the chagrin of a general who, after sweating himself to a shadow planning a great campaign, finds his troops unequal to carrying it out.

'It's such a pity it should have happened. One of the vicars near here has just been told by the doctor that he's got to go off to the south of France, and the living is in Uncle Clarence's gift. If only Rupert could have had that, we could have got married. However, he's bought Uncle Clarence some lotion.'

Freddie started. A more cheerful expression came into his sternly careworn face.

'Lotion?'

'For his ankle.'

'He couldn't have done better,' said Freddie warmly. 'Apart from showing the contrite heart, he has given the guv'nor medicine, and medicine to the guv'nor is what catnip is to the cat. Above all things he dearly loves a little bit of amateur doctoring. As a rule he tries it on somebody else – two years ago he gave one of the housemaids some patent ointment for chilblains and she went screaming about the house – but, no doubt, now that the emergency has occurred, he will be equally agreeable to treating himself. Old Beefers has made the right move.'

In predicting that Lord Emsworth would appreciate the gift of lotion, Freddie had spoken with an unerring knowledge of his father's character. The master of Blandings was one of those fluffy-minded old gentlemen who are happiest when experimenting with strange drugs. In a less censorious age he would have been a Borgia. It was not until he had retired to bed that he discovered the paper-wrapped bottle on the table by his side. Then he remembered that the pest Popjoy had mumbled something at dinner about buying him something or other for his injured ankle. He tore off the paper and examined the contents of the bottle with a lively satisfaction. The liquid was a dingy grey and sloshed pleasantly when you shook it. The name on the label – Blake's Balsam – was new to him, and that in itself was a recommendation.

His ankle had long since ceased to pain him, and to some men this might have seemed an argument against smearing it with balsam; but not to Lord Emsworth. He decanted a liberal dose into the palm of his hand. He sniffed it. It had a strong, robust, bracing sort of smell. He spent the next five minutes thoughtfully rubbing it in. Then he put the light out and went to sleep.

It is a truism to say that in the world as it is at present constituted few things have more far-reaching consequences than the accident of birth. Lord Emsworth had probably suspected this. He was now to receive direct proof. If he had been born a horse instead of the heir to an earldom, that lotion would have been just right for him. It was for horses, though the Rev. Rupert Bingham had omitted to note the fact, that Blake had planned his balsam; and anyone enjoying even a superficial acquaintance with horses and earls knows that an important difference between them is that the latter have the more sensitive skins. Waking at a quarter to two from dreams of being burned at the stake by Red Indians, Lord Emsworth found himself suffering acute pain in the right leg.

He was a little surprised. He had not supposed that that fall from the ladder had injured him so badly. However, being a good amateur doctor, he bore up bravely and took immediate steps to cope with the trouble. Having shaken the bottle till it foamed at the mouth, he rubbed in some more lotion. It occurred to him that the previous application might have been too sketchy, so this time he did it thoroughly. He rubbed and kneaded for some twenty minutes. Then he tried to go to sleep.

Nature has made some men quicker thinkers than others. Lord Emsworth's was one of those leisurely brains. It was not till nearly four o'clock that the truth came home to him. When it did, he was just on the point of applying a fifth coating of the balsam to his leg. He stopped abruptly, replaced the cork, and, jumping out of bed, hobbled to the cold-water tap and put as much of himself under it as he could manage.

The relief was perceptible, but transitory. At five he was out again, and once more at half-past. At a quarter to six, succeeding in falling asleep, he enjoyed a slumber, somewhat disturbed by the intermittent biting of sharks, which lasted till a few minutes past eight. Then he woke as if an alarm clock had rung, and realized that further sleep was out of the question.

He rose from his bed and peered out of the window. It was a beautiful morning. There had been rain in the night and a world that looked as if it had just come back from the cleaner's sparkled under a beaming sun. Cedars cast long shadows over the smooth green lawns. Rooks cawed soothingly: thrushes bubbled in their liquid and musical way: and the air was full of a summer humming. Among those present of the insect world, Lord Emsworth noticed several prominent gnats.

Beyond the terrace, glittering through the trees, gleamed the waters of the lake. They seemed to call to him like a bugle. Although he had neglected the practice of late, there was nothing Lord Emsworth enjoyed more than a before-breakfast dip: and today anything in the nature of water had a particularly powerful appeal for him. The pain in his ankle had subsided by now to a dull throbbing, and it seemed to him that a swim might remove it altogether. Putting on a dressing-gown and slippers, he took his bathing-suit from its drawer and went downstairs.

The beauties of a really fine English summer day are so numerous that it is excusable in a man if he fails immediately to notice them all. Only when the sharp agony of the first plunge had passed and he was floating out in mid-water did Lord Emsworth realize that in some extraordinary way he had overlooked what was beyond dispute the best thing that this perfect morning had to offer him. Gazing from his bedroom window, he had observed the sun, the shadows, the birds, the trees, and the insects, but he had omitted to appreciate the fact that nowhere in this magic world that stretched before him was there a trace of his young guest, Popjoy. For the first time in two weeks he appeared to be utterly alone and free from him.

Floating on his back and gazing up into the turquoise sky, Lord Emsworth thrilled at the thought. He kicked sportively in a spasm of pure happiness. But this, he felt, was not enough. It failed to express his full happiness. To the ecstasy of this golden moment only music – that mystic language of the soul – could really do justice. The next instant there had cut quiveringly into the summer stillness that hung over the gardens of Blandings Castle a sudden sharp wail that seemed to tell of a human being in mortal distress. It was the voice of Lord Emsworth, raised in song.

It was a gruesome sound, calculated to startle the stoutest: and two bees, buzzing among the lavender, stopped as one bee and looked at each other with raised eyebrows. Nor were they alone affected. Snails withdrew into their shells: a squirrel doing callisthenics on the cedar nearly fell off its branch: and – moving a step up in the animal kingdom – the Rev. Rupert Bingham, standing behind the rhododendron bushes and wondering how long it would be before the girl he loved came to keep her tryst, started violently, dropped his cigarette and, tearing off his coat, rushed to the water's edge.

Out in the middle of the lake, Lord Emsworth's transports continued undiminished. His dancing feet kicked up a flurry of foam. His short-sighted, but sparkling, eyes stared into the blue. His voice rose to a pulsing scream.

'Love me,' sang Lord Emsworth, 'and the wo-o-o-o-rld is – ah – mi-yun!'

'It's all right,' said a voice in his ear. 'Keep cool. Keep quite cool.'

The effect of a voice speaking suddenly, as it were out of the void, is always, even in these days of wireless, disconcerting to a man. Had he been on dry land Lord Emsworth would have jumped. Being in ten feet of water, he went under as if a hand had pushed him. He experienced a momentary feeling of suffocation, and then a hand gripped him painfully by the fleshy part of the arm and he was on the surface again, spluttering.

'Keep quite cool,' murmured the voice. 'There's no danger.'

And now he recognized whose voice it was.

There is a point beyond which the human brain loses its kinship with the Infinite and becomes a mere seething mass of deleterious passions. Malays, when pushed past this point, take down the old *kris* from its hook and go out and start carving up the neighbours. Women have hysterics. Earls, if Lord Emsworth may be taken as a sample, haul back their right fists and swing them as violently as their age and physique will permit. For two long weeks Lord Emsworth had been enduring this pestilential young man with outward nonchalance, but the strain had told. Suppressed emotions are always the most dangerous. Little by little, day by day, he had been slowly turning into a human volcano, and this final outrage blew the lid off him.

He raged with a sense of intolerable injury. Was it not enough that this porous plaster of a young man should adhere to him on shore? Must he even pursue him out into the waste of waters and come fooling about and pawing at him when he was enjoying the best swim he had had that summer? In all their long and honourable history no member of his ancient family had ever so far forgotten the sacred obligations of hospitality as to plug a guest in the eye. But then they had never had guests like this. With a sharp, passionate snort, Lord Emsworth extracted his right hand from the foam, clenched it, drew it back and let it go.

He could have made no more imprudent move. If there was one thing the Rev. Rupert Bingham, who in his time had swum for Oxford, knew, it was what to do when drowning men struggled. Something that might have been a very hard and knobbly leg of mutton smote Lord Emsworth violently behind the ear: the sun was turned off at the main: the stars came out, many of them of a singular brightness: there was a sound of rushing waters: and he knew no more.

When Lord Emsworth came to himself, he was lying in bed. And, as it seemed a very good place to be, he remained there. His head ached abominably, but he scarcely noticed this, so occupied was he with the thoughts which surged inside it. He mused on the young man Popjoy: he meditated on Sir Gregory Parsloe-Parsloe: and wondered from time to time which he disliked the more. It was a problem almost too nice for human solution. Here, on the one hand, you had a man who pestered you for two weeks and wound up by nearly murdering you as you bathed, but who did not steal pig-men: there, on the other, one who stole pig-men but stopped short of actual assault on the person. Who could hope to hold the scales between such a pair?

He had just remembered the lotion and was wondering if this might not be considered the deciding factor in this contest for the position of the world's premier blot, when the door opened and the Hon. Freddie Threepwood insinuated himself into the room.

'Hullo, guv'nor.'

'Well, Frederick?'

'How are you feeling?'

'Extremely ill.'

'Might have been worse, you know.'

'Bah!'

'Watery grave and all that.'

'Tchah!' said Lord Emsworth.

There was a pause. Freddie, wandering about the room, picked up and fidgeted with a chair, a vase, a hair-brush, a comb, and a box of matches: then, retracing his steps, fidgeted with them all over again in the reverse order. Finally he came to the foot of his father's bed and dropped over it like, it seemed to that sufferer's prejudiced eye, some hideous animal gaping over a fence.

'I say, guv'nor.'

'Well, Frederick?'

'Narrow squeak, that, you know.'

'Pah!'

'Do you wish to thank your brave preserver?'

Lord Emsworth plucked at the coverlet.

'If that young man comes near me,' he said, 'I will not be answerable for the consequences.'

'Eh?' Freddie stared. 'Don't you like him?'

'Like him! I think he is the most appalling young man I ever met.'

It is customary when making statements of this kind to except present company, but so deeply did Lord Emsworth feel on the subject that he omitted to do so. Freddie, having announced that he was dashed, removed himself from the bed-rail and, wandering once more about the room, fidgeted with a toothbrush, a soap-dish, a shoe, a volume on spring bulbs, and a collar-stud.

'I say, guv'nor.'

'Well, Frederick?'

'That's all very well, you know, guv'nor,' said the Hon. Freddie, returning to his post and seeming to draw moral support from the feel of the bed-rail, 'but after what's happened it looks to me as if you were jolly well bound to lend your countenance to the union, if you know what I mean.'

'Union? What are you talking about? What union?'

'Gertrude and old Beefers.'

'Who the devil is old Beefers?'

'Oh, I forgot to tell you about that. This bird Popjoy's name isn't Popjoy. It's Bingham. Old Beefy Bingham. You know, the fellow Aunt Georgie doesn't want to marry Gertrude.'

'Eh?'

'Throw your mind back. They pushed her off to Blandings to keep her out of his way. And I had the idea of sending him down here *incog.* to ingratiate himself with you. The scheme being that, when you had learned to love him, you would slip him a vacant vicarage, thus enabling them to get married. Beefers is a parson, you know.'

Lord Emsworth did not speak. It was not so much the shock of this revelation that kept him dumb as the astounding discovery that any man could really want to marry Gertrude, and any girl this Popjoy. Like many a thinker before him, he was feeling that there is really no limit to the eccentricity of human tastes. The thing made his head swim.

But when it had ceased swimming he perceived that this was but one aspect of the affair. Before him stood the man who had inflicted Popjoy on him, and with something of King Lear in his demeanour Lord Emsworth rose slowly from the pillows. Words trembled on his lips, but he rejected them as not strong enough and sought in his mind for others.

'You know, guv'nor,' proceeded Freddie, 'there's nothing to prevent you doing the square thing and linking two young hearts in the bonds of the Love God, if you want to. I mean to say, old Braithwaite at Much Matchingham has been ordered to the south of France by his doctor, so there's a living going that you've got to slip to somebody.'

Lord Emsworth sank back on the pillows.

'Much Matchingham!'

'Oh, dash it, you must know Much Matchingham, guv'nor. It's just round the corner. Where old Parsloe lives.'

'Much Matchingham!'

Lord Emsworth was blinking, as if his eyes had seen a dazzling light. How wrong, he felt, how wickedly mistaken and lacking in faith he had been when he had said to himself in his folly that Providence offers no method of retaliation to the just whose pig-men have been persuaded by Humanity's dregs to leave their employment and seek advanced wages elsewhere. Conscience could not bring remorse to Sir Gregory Parsloe-Parsloe, and the law, in its present imperfect state, was powerless to punish. But there was still a way. With this young man Popjoy – or Bingham – or whatever his name was, permanently established not a hundred yards from his park gates, would Sir Gregory Parsloe-Parsloe ever draw another really care-free breath? From his brief, but sufficient, acquaintance with the young man Bingham – or Popjoy – Lord Emsworth thought not.

The punishment was severe, but who could say that Sir Gregory had not earned it?

'A most admirable idea,' said Lord Emsworth cordially. 'Certainly I will give your friend the living of Much Matchingham.'

'You will?'

'Most decidedly.'

'At-a-boy, guv'nor!' said Freddie. 'Came the Dawn!'

# THE GO-GETTER

On the usually unruffled brow of the Hon. Freddie Threepwood, as he paced the gardens of Blandings Castle, there was the slight but well-marked frown of one whose mind is not at rest. It was high summer and the gardens were at their loveliest, but he appeared to find no solace in their splendour. Calceolarias, which would have drawn senile yips of ecstasy from his father, Lord Emsworth, left him cold. He eyed the lobelias with an unseeing stare, as if he were cutting an undesirable acquaintance in the paddock at Ascot.

What was troubling this young man was the continued sales-resistance of his Aunt Georgiana. Ever since his marriage to the only daughter of Donaldson's Dog-Biscuits, of Long Island City, N.Y., Freddie Threepwood had thrown himself heart and soul into the promotion of the firm's wares. And, sent home to England to look about for likely prospects, he had seen in Georgiana, Lady Alcester, as has been already related, a customer who approximated to the ideal. The owner of four Pekinese, two Poms, a Yorkshire terrier, five Sealyhams, a Borzoi and an Airedale, she was a woman who stood for something in dog-loving circles. To secure her patronage would be a big thing for him. It would stamp him as a live wire and a go-getter. It would please his father-in-law hugely. And the proprietor of Donaldson's Dog-Joy was a man who, when even slightly pleased, had a habit of spraying five thousand dollar cheques like a geyser.

And so far, despite all his eloquence, callously oblivious of the ties of kinship and the sacred obligations they involve, Lady Alcester had refused to sign on the dotted line, preferring to poison her menagerie with some degraded garbage called, if he recollected rightly, Peterson's Pup-Food.

A bitter snort escaped Freddie. It was still echoing through the gardens, when he found that he was no longer alone. He had been joined by his cousin Gertrude.

'What ho!' said Freddie amiably. He was fond of Gertrude, and did not hold it against her that she had a mother who was incapable of spotting a good dog-biscuit when she saw one. Between him and Gertrude there had long existed a firm alliance. It was to him that

Gertrude had turned for assistance when the family were trying to stop her getting engaged to good old Beefy Bingham: and he had supplied assistance in such good measure that the engagement was now an accepted fact and running along nicely.

'Freddie,' said Gertrude, 'may I borrow your car?'

'Certainly. Most decidedly. Going over to see old Beefers?'

'No,' said Gertrude, and a closer observer than her cousin might have noted in her manner a touch of awkwardness. 'Mr Watkins wants me to drive him to Shrewsbury.'

'Oh? Well, carry on, as far as I'm concerned. You haven't seen your mother anywhere, have you?'

'I think she's sitting on the lawn.'

'Ah! Is she? Right ho. Thanks.'

Freddie moved off in the direction indicated, and presently came in sight of his relative, seated as described. The Airedale was lying at her feet. One of the Pekes occupied her lap. And she was gazing into the middle distance in a preoccupied manner, as if she, like her nephew, had a weight on her mind.

Nor would one who drew this inference from her demeanour have been mistaken. Lady Alcester was feeling disturbed.

A woman who stands *in loco parentis* to fourteen dogs must of necessity have her cares, but it was not the dumb friends that were worrying Lady Alcester now. What was troubling her was the disquieting behaviour of her daughter Gertrude.

Engaged to the Rev. Rupert Bingham, Gertrude seemed to her of late to have become infatuated with Orlo Watkins, the Crooning Tenor, one of those gifted young men whom Lady Constance Keeble, the châtelaine of Blandings, was so fond of inviting down for lengthy visits in the summertime.

On the subject of the Rev. Rupert Bingham, Lady Alcester's views had recently undergone a complete change. In the beginning, the prospect of having him for a son-in-law had saddened and distressed her. Then, suddenly discovering that he was the nephew and heir of as opulent a shipping magnate as ever broke bread at the Adelphi Hotel, Liverpool, she had soared from the depths to the heights. She was now strongly pro-Bingham. She smiled upon him freely. Upon his appointment to the vacant Vicarage of Much Matchingham, the village nearest to Market Blandings, she had brought Gertrude to the Castle so that the young people should see one another frequently.

And, instead of seeing her betrothed frequently, Gertrude seemed to prefer to moon about with this Orlo Watkins, this Crooning Tenor. For days they had been inseparable.

Now, everybody knows what Crooning Tenors are. Dangerous devils. They sit at the piano and gaze into a girl's eyes and sing in a voice that sounds like gas escaping from a pipe about Love and the Moonlight and You: and, before you know where you are, the girl has scrapped the deserving young clergyman with prospects to whom she is affianced and is off and away with a man whose only means of livelihood consists of intermittent engagements with the British Broadcasting Corporation.

If a mother is not entitled to shudder at a prospect like that, it would be interesting to know what she is entitled to shudder at.

Lady Alcester, then, proceeded to shudder: and was still shuddering when the drowsy summer peace was broken by a hideous uproar. The Peke and the Airedale had given tongue simultaneously, and, glancing up, Lady Alcester perceived her nephew Frederick approaching.

And what made her shudder again was the fact that in Freddie's eye she noted with concern the familiar go-getter gleam, the old dog-biscuit glitter.

However, as it had sometimes been her experience, when cornered by her nephew, that she could stem the flood by talking promptly on other subjects, she made a gallant effort to do so now.

'Have you seen Gertrude, Freddie?' she asked.

'Yes. She borrowed my car to go to Shrewsbury.'

'Alone?'

'No. Accompanied by Watkins. The Yowler.'

A further spasm shook Lady Alcester.

'Freddie,' she said, 'I'm terribly worried.'

'Worried?'

'About Gertrude.'

Freddie dismissed Gertrude with a gesture.

'No need to worry about her,' he said. 'What you want to worry about is these dogs of yours. Notice how they barked at me? Nerves. They're a mass of nerves. And why? Improper feeding. As long as you mistakenly insist on giving them Peterson's Pup-Food – lacking, as it is, in many of the essential vitamins – so long will they continue to fly off the handle every time they see a human being on the horizon. Now, pursuant on what we were talking about this morning, Aunt Georgiana, there is a little demonstration I would like . . .'

'Can't you give her a hint, Freddie?'

'Who?'

'Gertrude.'

'Yes, I suppose I could give her a hint. What about?'

'She is seeing far too much of this man Watkins.'

'Well, so am I, for the matter of that. So is everybody who sees him more than once.'

'She seems quite to have forgotten that she is engaged to Rupert Bingham.'

'Rupert Bingham, did you say?' said Freddie with sudden animation. 'I'll tell you something about Rupert Bingham. He has a dog named Bottles who has been fed from early youth on Donaldson's Dog-Joy, and I wish you could see him. Thanks to the bone-forming properties of Donaldson's Dog-Joy, he glows with health. A fine, upstanding dog, with eyes sparkling with the joy of living and both feet on the ground. A credit to his master.'

'Never mind about Rupert's dog!'

'You've got to mind about Rupert's dog. You can't afford to ignore him. He is a dog to be reckoned with. A dog that counts. And all through Donaldson's Dog-Joy.'

'I don't want to talk about Donaldson's Dog-Joy.'

'I do. I want to give you a demonstration. You may not know it, Aunt Georgiana, but over in America the way we advertise this product, so rich in bone-forming vitamins, is as follows: We instruct our demonstrator to stand out in plain view before the many-headed and, when the audience is of sufficient size, to take a biscuit and break off a piece and chew it. By this means we prove that Donaldson's Dog-Joy is so superbly wholesome as actually to be fit for human consumption. Our demonstrator not only eats the biscuit – he enjoys it. He rolls it round his tongue. He chews it and mixes it with his saliva . . .'

'Freddie, please!'

'With his saliva,' repeated Freddie firmly. 'And so does the dog. He masticates the biscuit. He enjoys it. He becomes a bigger and better dog. I will now eat a Donaldson's Dog-Biscuit.'

And before his aunt's nauseated gaze he proceeded to attempt this gruesome feat.

It was an impressive demonstration, but it failed in one particular. To have rendered it perfect, he should not have choked. Want of experience caused the disaster. Long years of training go to the making of the seasoned demonstrators of Donaldson's Dog-Joy. They start in a small way with carpet-tacks and work up through the flat-irons and patent breakfast cereals till they are ready for the big effort. Freddie was a novice. Endeavouring to roll the morsel round his tongue, he allowed it to escape into his windpipe.

The sensation of having swallowed a mixture of bricks and sawdust was succeeded by a long and painful coughing fit. And when at length the sufferer's eyes cleared, no human form met their gaze. There was the Castle. There was the lawn. There were the gardens. But Lady Alcester had disappeared.

However, it is a well-established fact that good men, like Donaldson's Dog-Biscuits, are hard to keep down. Some fifty minutes later, as the Rev. Rupert Bingham sat in his study at Matchingham Vicarage, the parlourmaid announced a visitor. The Hon. Freddie Threepwood limped in, looking shop-soiled.

'What ho, Beefers,' he said. 'I just came to ask if I could borrow Bottles.'

He bent to where the animal lay on the hearth-rug and prodded it civilly in the lower ribs. Bottles waved a long tail in brief acknowledgement. He was a fine dog, though of uncertain breed. His mother had been a popular local belle with a good deal of sex-appeal, and the question of his paternity was one that would have set a Genealogical College pursing its lips perplexedly.

'Oh, hullo, Freddie,' said the Rev. Rupert.

The young Pastor of Souls spoke in an absent voice. He was frowning. It is a singular fact – and one that just goes to show what sort of a world this is – that of the four foreheads introduced so far to the reader of this chronicle, three have been corrugated with care. And, if girls had consciences, Gertrude's would have been corrugated, too – giving us a full hand.

'Take a chair,' said the Rev. Rupert.

'I'll take a sofa,' said Freddie, doing so. 'Feeling a bit used up. I had to hoof it all the way over.'

'What's happened to your car?'

'Gertrude took it to drive Watkins to Shrewsbury.'

The Rev. Rupert sat for a while in thought. His face, which was large and red, had a drawn look. Even the massive body which had so nearly won him a Rowing Blue at Oxford gave the illusion of having shrunk. So marked was his distress that even Freddie noticed it.

'Something up, Beefers?' he inquired.

For answer the Rev. Rupert Bingham extended a ham-like hand which held a letter. It was written in a sprawling, girlish handwriting.

'Read that.'

'From Gertrude?'

'Yes. It came this morning. Well?'

Freddie completed his perusal and handed the document back. He was concerned.

'I think it's the bird,' he said.

'So do I.'

'It's long,' said Freddie, 'and it's rambling. It is full of stuff about "Are we sure?" and "Do we know our own minds?" and "Wouldn't it be better, perhaps?" But I think it is the bird.'

'I can't understand it.'

Freddie sat up.

'I can,' he said. 'Now I see what Aunt Georgiana was drooling about. Her fears were well founded. The snake Watkins has stolen Gertrude from you.'

'You think Gertrude's in love with Watkins?'

'I do. And I'll tell you why. He's a yowler, and girls always fall for yowlers. They have a glamour.'

'I've never noticed Watkins's glamour. He has always struck me as a bit of a weed.'

'Weed he may be, Beefers, but, none the less, he knows how to do his stuff. I don't know why it should be, but there is a certain type of tenor voice which acts on girls like catnip on a cat.'

The Rev. Rupert breathed heavily.

'I see,' he said.

'The whole trouble is, Beefers,' proceeded Freddie, 'that Watkins is romantic and you're not. Your best friend couldn't call you romantic. Solid worth, yes. Romance, no.'

'So it doesn't seem as if there was much to be done about it?'

Freddie reflected.

'Couldn't you manage to show yourself in a romantic light?'

'How?'

'Well – stop a runaway horse.'

'Where's the horse?'

'M'yes,' said Freddie. 'That's by way of being the difficulty, isn't it? The horse – where is it?'

There was silence for some moments.

'Well, be that as it may,' said Freddie. 'Can I borrow Bottles?'

'What for?'

'Purposes of demonstration. I wish to exhibit him to my Aunt Georgiana, so that she may see for herself to what heights of robustness a dog can rise when fed sedulously on Donaldson's Dog-Joy. I'm having a lot of trouble with that woman, Beefers. I try all the artifices which win to success in salesmanship, and they don't. But I have a feeling that if she could see Bottles and poke him in the ribs and note the firm, muscular flesh, she might drop. At any rate, it's worth trying. I'll take him along, may I?'

'All right.'

'Thanks. And, in regard to your little trouble, I'll be giving it my best attention. You're looking in after dinner tonight?'

'I suppose so,' said the Rev. Rupert moodily.

The information that her impressionable daughter had gone off to roam the countryside in a two-seater car with the perilous Watkins had come as a grievous blow to Lady Alcester. As she sat on the terrace, an hour after Freddie had begun the weary homeward trek from Matchingham Vicarage, her heart was sorely laden.

The Airedale had wandered away upon some private ends, but the Peke lay slumbering in her lap. She envied it its calm detachment. To her the future looked black and the air seemed heavy with doom.

Only one thing mitigated her depression. Her nephew Frederick had disappeared. Other prominent local pests were present, such as flies and gnats, but not Frederick. The grounds of Blandings Castle appeared to be quite free from him.

And then even this poor consolation was taken from the stricken woman. Limping a little, as if his shoes hurt him, the Hon. Freddie came round the corner of the shrubbery, headed in her direction. He was accompanied by something having the outward aspect of a dog.

'What ho, Aunt Georgiana!'

'Well, Freddie?' sighed Lady Alcester resignedly.

The Peke, opening one eye, surveyed the young man for a moment, seemed to be debating within itself the advisability of barking, came apparently to the conclusion that it was too hot, and went to sleep again.

'This is Bottles,' said Freddie.

'Who?'

'Bottles. The animal I touched on some little time back. Note the well-muscled frame.'

'I never saw such a mongrel in my life.'

'Kind hearts are more than coronets,' said Freddie. 'The point at issue is not this dog's pedigree, which, I concede, is not all Burke and Debrett, but his physique. Reared exclusively on a diet of Donaldson's Dog-Joy, he goes his way with his chin up, frank and fearless. I should like you, if you don't mind, to come along to the stables and watch him among the rats. It will give you some idea.'

He would have spoken further, but at this point something occurred, as had happened during his previous sales-talk, to mar the effect of Freddie's oratory.

The dog Bottles, during this conversation, had been roaming to and fro in the inquisitive manner customary with dogs who find themselves in strange territory. He had sniffed at trees. He had rolled on the turf. Now, returning to the centre of things, he observed for the first time that on the lap of the woman seated in the chair there lay a peculiar something.

What it was Bottles did not know. It appeared to be alive. A keen desire came upon him to solve this mystery. To keep the records straight, he advanced to the chair, thrust an inquiring nose against the object, and inhaled sharply.

The next moment, to his intense surprise, the thing had gone off like a bomb, had sprung to the ground, and was moving rapidly towards him.

Bottles did not hesitate. A rough-and-tumble with one of his peers he enjoyed. He, as it were, rolled it round his tongue and mixed it with his saliva. But this was different. He had never met a Pekinese before, and no one would have been more surprised than himself if he had been informed that this curious, fluffy thing was a dog. Himself he regarded it as an Act of God, and, thoroughly unnerved, he raced three times round the lawn and tried to climb a tree. Failing in this endeavour, he fitted his ample tail if possible more firmly into its groove and vanished from the scene.

The astonishment of the Hon. Freddie Threepwood was only equalled by his chagrin. Lady Alcester had begun now to express her opinion of the incident, and her sneers, her jeers, her unveiled innuendoes were hard to bear. If, she said, the patrons of Donaldson's Dog-

Joy allowed themselves to be chased off the map in this fashion by Pekinese, she was glad she had never been weak enough to be persuaded to try it.

'It's lucky,' said Lady Alcester in her hard, scoffing way, 'that Susan wasn't a rat. I suppose a rat would have given that mongrel of yours heart failure.'

'Bottles,' said Freddie stiffly, 'is particularly sound on rats. I think, in common fairness, you ought to step to the stables and give him a chance of showing himself in a true light.'

'I have seen quite enough, thank you.'

'You won't come to the stables and watch him dealing with rats?'

'I will not.'

'In that case,' said Freddie sombrely, 'there is nothing more to be said. I suppose I may as well take him back to the Vicarage.'

'What Vicarage?'

'Matchingham Vicarage.'

'Was that Rupert's dog?'

'Of course it was.'

'Then have you seen Rupert?'

'Of course I have.'

'Did you warn him? About Mr Watkins?'

'It was too late to warn him. He had had a letter from Gertrude, giving him the raspberry.'

'What!'

'Well, she said Was he sure and Did they know their own minds, but you can take it from me that it was tantamount to the raspberry. Returning, however, to the topic of Bottles, Aunt Georgiana, I think you ought to take into consideration the fact that, in his recent encounter with the above Peke, he was undergoing a totally new experience and naturally did not appear at his best. I repeat once more that you should see him among the rats.'

'Oh, Freddie!'

'Hullo?'

'How can you babble about this wretched dog when Gertrude's whole future is at stake? It is simply vital that somehow she be cured of this dreadful infatuation . . .'

'Well, I'll have a word with her if you like, but, if you ask me, I think the evil has spread too far. Watkins has yowled himself into her very soul. However, I'll do my best. Excuse me, Aunt Georgiana.'

From a neighbouring bush the honest face of Bottles was protruding. He seemed to be seeking assurance that the All Clear had been blown.

It was at the hour of the ante-dinner cocktail that Freddie found his first opportunity of having the promised word with Gertrude. Your true salesman and go-getter is never beaten, and a sudden and brilliant idea for accomplishing the conversion of his Aunt Georgiana had come to him as he brushed his hair. He descended to the drawing-room with a certain jauntiness, and was reminded by the sight of Gertrude of his mission. The girl was seated at the piano, playing dreamy chords.

'I say,' said Freddie, 'a word with you, young Gertrude. What is all this bilge I hear about you and Beefers?'

The girl flushed.

'Have you seen Rupert?'

'I was closeted with him this afternoon. He told me all.'

'Oh?'

'He's feeling pretty low.'

'Oh?'

'Yes,' said Freddie, 'pretty low the poor old chap is feeling, and I don't blame him with the girl he's engaged to rushing about the place getting infatuated with tenors. I never heard of such a thing, dash it! What do you see in this Watkins? Wherein lies his attraction? Certainly not in his ties. They're awful. And the same applies to his entire outfit. He looks as if he had bought his clothes off the peg at a second-hand gents' costumiers. And, as if that were not enough, he wears short, but distinct, side-whiskers. You aren't going to tell me that you're seriously considering chucking a sterling egg like old Beefers in favour of a whiskered warbler?'

There was a pause. Gertrude played more dreamy chords.

'I'm not going to discuss it,' she said. 'It's nothing to do with you.'

'Pardon me!' said Freddie. 'Excuse me! If you will throw your mind back to the time when Beefers was conducting his wooing, you may remember that I was the fellow who worked the whole thing. But for my resource and ingenuity you and the old bounder would never have got engaged. I regard myself, therefore, in the light of a guardian angel or something; and as such am entitled to probe the matter to its depths. Of course,' said Freddie, 'I know exactly how you're feeling. I see where you have made your fatal bloomer. This Watkins has cast his glamorous spell about you, and you're looking on Beefers as a piece of unromantic cheese. But mark this, girl . . .'

'I wish you wouldn't call me "girl".'

'Mark this, old prune,' amended Freddie. 'And mark it well. Beefers is tried, true and trusted. A man to be relied on. Whereas Watkins, if I have read those whiskers aright, is the sort of fellow who will jolly well let you down in a crisis. And then, when it's too late, you'll come moaning to me, weeping salt tears and saying, "Ah, why did I not know in time?" And I shall reply, "You unhappy little fathead . . .!"'

'Oh, go and sell your dog-biscuits, Freddie!'

Gertrude resumed her playing. Her mouth was set in an obstinate line. Freddie eyed her with disapproval.

'It's some taint in the blood,' he said. 'Inherited from female parent. Like your bally mother, you are constitutionally incapable of seeing reason. Pig-headed, both of you. Sell my dog-biscuits, you say? Ha! As if I hadn't boosted them to Aunt Georgiana till my lips cracked. And with what result? So far, none. But wait till tonight.'

'It is tonight.'

'I mean, wait till later on tonight. Watch my little experiment.'

'What little experiment?'

'Ah!'

'What do you mean, "Ah"?'

'Just "Ah!"' said Freddie.

The hour of the after-dinner coffee found Blandings Castle apparently an abode of peace. The superficial observer, peeping into the amber drawing-room through the French windows that led to the terrace, would have said that all was well with the inmates of this stately home of England. Lord Emsworth sat in a corner absorbed in a volume dealing with the treatment of pigs in sickness and in health. His sister, Lady Constance Keeble, was sewing. His other sister, Lady Alcester, was gazing at Gertrude. Gertrude was gazing at Orlo Watkins. And Orlo Watkins was gazing at the ceiling and singing in that crooning voice of his a song of Roses.

The Hon. Freddie Threepwood was not present. And that fact alone, if one may go by the views of his father, Lord Emsworth, should have been enough to make a success of any party.

And yet beneath this surface of cosy peace troubled currents were running. Lady Alcester, gazing at Gertrude, found herself a prey to gloom. She did not like the way Gertrude was gazing at Orlo Watkins.

Gertrude, for her part, as the result of her recent conversation with the Hon. Freddie, was experiencing twinges of remorse and doubt. Lady Constance was still ruffled from the effect of Lady Alcester's sisterly frankness that evening on the subject of the imbecility of hostesses who deliberately let Crooning Tenors loose in castles. And Lord Emsworth was in that state of peevish exasperation which comes to dreamy old gentlemen who, wishing to read of Pigs, find their concentration impaired by voices singing of Roses.

Only Orlo Watkins was happy. And presently he, too, was to join the ranks of gloom. For just as he started to let himself go and handle this song as a song should be handled, there came from the other side of the door the sound of eager barking. A dog seemed to be without. And, apart from the fact that he disliked and feared all dogs, a tenor resents competition.

The next moment the door had opened, and the Hon. Freddie Threepwood appeared. He carried a small sack, and was accompanied by Bottles, the latter's manner noticeably lacking in repose.

On the face of the Hon. Freddie, as he advanced into the room, there was that set, grim expression which is always seen on the faces of those who are about to put their fortune to the test, to win or lose it all. The Old Guard at Waterloo looked much the same. For Freddie had decided to stake all on a single throw.

Many young men in his position, thwarted by an aunt who resolutely declined to amble across to the stables and watch a dog redeem himself among the rats, would have resigned themselves sullenly to defeat. But Freddie was made of finer stuff.

'Aunt Georgiana,' he said, holding up the sack, at which Bottles was making agitated leaps, 'you refused to come to the stables this afternoon to watch this Donaldson's Dog-Joy-fed animal in action, so you have left me no alternative but to play the fixture on your own ground.'

Lord Emsworth glanced up from his book.

'Frederick, stop gibbering. And take that dog out of here.'

Lady Constance glanced up from her sewing.

'Frederick, if you are coming in, come in and sit down. And take that dog out of here.'

Lady Alcester, glancing up from Gertrude, exhibited in even smaller degree the kindly cordiality which might have been expected from an aunt.

'Oh, do go away, Freddie! You're a perfect nuisance. And take that dog out of here.'

The Hon. Freddie, with a noble look of disdain, ignored them all.

'I have here, Aunt Georgiana,' he said, 'a few simple rats. If you will kindly step out on to the terrace I shall be delighted to give a demonstration which should, I think, convince even your stubborn mind.'

The announcement was variously received by the various members of the company. Lady Alcester screamed. Lady Constance sprang for the bell. Lord Emsworth snorted. Orlo Watkins blanched and retired behind Gertrude. And Gertrude, watching him blench, seeing him retire, tightened her lips. A country-bred girl, she was on terms of easy familiarity with rats, and this evidence of alarm in one whom she had set on a pedestal disquieted her.

The door opened and Beach entered. He had come in pursuance of his regular duties to remove the coffee cups, but arriving, found other tasks assigned to him.

'Beach!' The voice was that of Lady Constance. 'Take away those rats.'

'Rats, m'lady?'

'Take that sack away from Mr Frederick!'

Beach understood. If he was surprised at the presence of the younger son of the house in the amber drawing-room with a sack of rats in his hand, he gave no indication of the fact. With a murmured apology, he secured the sack and started to withdraw. It was not, strictly, his place to carry rats, but a good butler is always ready to give and take. Only so can the amenities of a large country house be preserved.

'And don't drop the dashed things,' urged Lord Emsworth.

'Very good, m'lord.'

The Hon. Freddie had flung himself into a chair, and was sitting with his chin cupped in his hands, a bleak look on his face. To an ardent young go-getter these tyrannous actions in restraint of trade are hard to bear.

Lord Emsworth returned to his book.

Lady Constance returned to her sewing.

Lady Alcester returned to her thoughts.

At the piano Orlo Watkins was endeavouring to justify the motives which had led him a few moments before to retire prudently behind Gertrude.

'I hate rats,' he said. 'They jar upon me.'

'Oh?' said Gertrude.

'I'm not afraid of them, of course, but they give me the creeps.'

'Oh?' said Gertrude.

There was an odd look in her eyes. Of what was she thinking, this idealistic girl? Was it of the evening, a few short weeks before, when, suddenly encountering a beastly bat in the gloaming, she had found in the Rev. Rupert Bingham a sturdy and intrepid protector? Was she picturing the Rev. Rupert as she had seen him then – gallant, fearless, cleaving the air with long sweeps of his clerical hat, encouraging her the while with word and gesture?

Apparently so, for a moment later she spoke.

'How are you on bats?'

'Rats?'

'Bats.'

'Oh, bats?'

'Are you afraid of bats?'

'I don't like bats,' admitted Orlo Watkins.

Then, dismissing the subject, he reseated himself at the piano and sang of June and the scent of unseen flowers.

Of all the little group in the amber drawing-room, only one member has now been left unaccounted for.

An animal of slow thought-processes, the dog Bottles had not at first observed what was happening to the sack. At the moment of its transference from the custody of Freddie to that of Beach, he had been engaged in sniffing at the leg of a chair. It was only as the door began to close that he became aware of the bereavement that threatened him. He bounded forward with a passionate cry, but it was too late. He found himself faced by unyielding wood. And when he started to scratch vehemently on this wood, a sharp pain assailed him. A book on the treatment of Pigs in sickness and in health, superbly aimed, had struck him in the small of the back. Then, for a space, he, like the Hon. Freddie Threepwood, his social sponsor, sat down and mourned.

'Take that beastly, blasted, infernal dog out of here,' cried Lord Emsworth.

Freddie rose listlessly.

'It's old Beefers' dog,' he said. 'Beefers will be here at any moment. We can hand the whole conduct of the affair over to him.'

Gertrude started.

'Is Rupert coming here tonight?'

'Said he would,' responded Freddie, and passed from the scene. He had had sufficient of his flesh and blood and was indisposed to linger. It was his intention to pop down to Market Blandings in his two-seater, soothe his wounded sensibilities, so far as they were capable of being soothed, with a visit to the local motion-picture house, look in at the Emsworth Arms for a spot of beer, and then home to bed, to forget.

Gertrude had fallen into a reverie. Her fair young face was overcast. A feeling of embarrassment had come upon her. When she had written that letter and posted it on the previous night, she had not foreseen that the Rev. Rupert would be calling so soon.

'I didn't know Rupert was coming tonight,' she said.

'Oh, yes,' said Lady Alcester brightly.

'Like a lingering tune, my whole life through, 'twill haunt me for EV-ah, that night in June with you-oo,' sang Orlo Watkins.

And Gertrude, looking at him, was aware for the first time of a curious sensation of not being completely in harmony with this young whiskered man. She wished he would stop singing. He prevented her thinking.

Bottles, meanwhile, had resumed his explorations. Dogs are philosophers. They soon forget. They do not waste time regretting the might-have-beens. Adjusting himself with composure to the changed conditions, Bottles moved to and fro in a spirit of affable inquiry. He looked at Lord Emsworth, considered the idea of seeing how he smelt, thought better of it, and advanced towards the French windows. Something was rustling in the bushes outside, and it seemed to him that this might as well be looked into before he went and breathed on Lady Constance's leg.

He had almost reached his objective, when Lady Alcester's Airedale, who had absented himself from the room some time before in order to do a bit of bone-burying, came bustling in, ready, his business completed, to resume the social whirl.

Seeing Bottles, he stopped abruptly.

Both then began a slow and cautious forward movement, of a crab-like kind. Arriving at close quarters, they stopped again. Their nostrils twitched a little. They rolled their eyes. And to the ears of those present there came, faintly at first, a low, throaty sound, like the far-off gargling of an octogenarian with bronchial trouble.

This rose to a sudden crescendo. And the next moment hostilities had begun.

In underrating Bottles's qualities and scoffing at him as a fighting force, Lady Alcester had made an error. Capable though he was of pusillanimity in the presence of female Pekinese, there was nothing of the weakling about this sterling animal. He had cleaned up every dog in Much Matchingham and was spoken of on all sides – from the Blue Boar in the High Street to the distant Cow and Caterpillar on the Shrewsbury Road – as an ornament to the Vicarage and a credit to his master's Cloth.

On the present occasion, moreover, he was strengthened by the fact that he felt he had right on his side. In spite of a certain coldness on the part of the Castle circle and a soreness about the ribs where the book on Pigs and their treatment had found its billet, there seems to be no doubt that Bottles had by this time become thoroughly convinced that this drawing-room was his official home. And, feeling that all these delightful people were relying on him to look after their interests and keep alien and subversive influences at a distance, he advanced with a bright willingness to the task of ejecting this intruder.

Nor was the Airedale disposed to hold back. He, too, was no stranger to the ring. In Hyde Park, where, when at his London residence, he took his daily airing, he had met all comers and acquitted himself well. Dogs from Mayfair, dogs from Bayswater, dogs from as far afield as the Brompton Road and West Kensington had had experience of the stuff of which he was made. Bottles reminded him a little of an animal from Pont Street, over whom he had once obtained a decision on the banks of the Serpentine; and he joined battle with an easy confidence.

The reactions of a country-house party to an after-dinner dog-fight in the drawing-room always vary considerably according to the individual natures of its members. Lady Alcester, whose long association with the species had made her a sort of honorary dog herself, remained tranquil. She surveyed the proceedings with unruffled equanimity through a tortoiseshell-rimmed lorgnette. Her chief emotion was one of surprise at the fact that Bottles was unquestionably getting the better of the exchanges. She liked his footwork. Impressed, she was obliged to admit that, if this was the sort of battler it turned out, there must be something in Donaldson's Dog-Joy after all.

The rest of the audience were unable to imitate her nonchalance. The two principals were giving that odd illusion, customary on these occasions, of being all over the place at the same time: and the demeanour of those in the ring-side seats was frankly alarmed. Lady Constance had backed against the wall, from which position she threw a futile cushion. Lord Emsworth, in his corner, was hunting feebly for ammunition and wishing that he had not dropped the pince-nez, without which he was no sort of use in a crisis.

And Gertrude? Gertrude was staring at Orlo Watkins, who, with a resource and presence of mind unusual in one so young, had just climbed on top of a high cabinet containing china.

His feet were on a level with her eyes, and she saw that they were feet of clay.

And it was at this moment, when a girl stood face to face with her soul, that the door opened.

'Mr Bingham,' announced Beach.

Men of the physique of the Rev. Rupert Bingham are not as a rule quick thinkers. From earliest youth, the Rev. Rupert had run to brawn rather than brain. But even the dullest-witted person could have told, on crossing that threshold, that there was a dog-fight going on. Beefy Bingham saw it in a flash, and he acted promptly.

There are numerous methods of stopping these painful affairs. Some advocate squirting water, others prefer to sprinkle pepper. Good results may be obtained, so one school of thought claims, by holding a lighted match under the nearest nose. Beefy Bingham was impatient of these subtleties.

To Beefy all this was old stuff. Ever since he had been given his Cure of Souls, half his time, it sometimes seemed to him, had been spent in hauling Bottles away from the throats of the dogs of his little flock. Experience had given him a technique. He placed one massive hand on the neck of the Airedale, the other on the neck of Bottles, and pulled. There was a rending sound, and they came apart.

'Rupert!' cried Gertrude.

Gazing at him, she was reminded of the heroes of old. And few could have denied that he made a strangely impressive figure, this large young man, standing there with bulging eyes and a gyrating dog in each hand. He looked like a statue of Right triumphing over Wrong. You couldn't place it exactly, because it was so long since you had read the book, but he reminded you of something out of *Pilgrim's Progress*.

So, at least, thought Gertrude. To Gertrude it was as if the scales had fallen from her eyes and she had wakened from some fevered dream. Could it be she, she was asking herself, who had turned from this noble youth and strayed towards one who, though on the evidence he seemed to have a future before him as an Alpine climber, was otherwise so contemptible?

'Rupert!' said Gertrude.

Beefy Bingham had now completed his masterly campaign. He had thrown Bottles out of the window and shut it behind him. He had dropped the Airedale to the carpet, where it now sat, licking itself in a ruminative way. He had produced a handkerchief and was passing it over his vermilion brow.

'Oh, Rupert!' said Gertrude, and flung herself into his arms.

The Rev. Rupert said nothing. On such occasions your knowledge-able Vicar does not waste words.

Nor did Orlo Watkins speak. He had melted away. Perhaps, perched on his eyrie, he had seen in Gertrude's eyes the look which, when seen in the eyes of a girl by any interested party, automatically induces the latter to go to his room and start packing, in readiness for the telegram which he will receive on the morrow, summoning him back to London on urgent business. At any rate, he had melted.

It was late that night when the Hon. Freddie Threepwood returned to the home of his fathers. Moodily undressing, he was surprised to hear a knock on the door.

His Aunt Georgiana entered. On her face was the unmistakable look of a mother whose daughter has seen the light and will shortly be marrying a deserving young clergyman with a bachelor uncle high up in the shipping business.

'Freddie,' said Lady Alcester, 'you know that stuff you're always babbling about – I've forgotten its name . . .'

'Donaldson's Dog-Joy,' said Freddie. 'It may be obtained either in the small (or one-and-threepenny) packets or in the half-crown (or large) size. A guarantee goes with each purchase. Unique in its health-giving properties . . .'

'I'll take two tons to start with,' said Lady Alcester.

# LORD EMSWORTH AND THE GIRL FRIEND

The day was so warm, so fair, so magically a thing of sunshine and blue skies and bird-song that anyone acquainted with Clarence, ninth Earl of Emsworth, and aware of his liking for fine weather, would have pictured him going about the place on this summer morning with a beaming smile and an uplifted heart. Instead of which, humped over the breakfast table, he was directing at a blameless kippered herring a look of such intense bitterness that the fish seemed to sizzle beneath it. For it was August Bank Holiday, and Blandings Castle on August Bank Holiday became, in his lordship's opinion, a miniature Inferno.

This was the day when his park and grounds broke out into a noisome rash of swings, roundabouts, marquees, toy balloons and paper bags; when a tidal wave of the peasantry and its squealing young engulfed those haunts of immemorial peace. On August Bank Holiday he was not allowed to potter pleasantly about his gardens in an old coat: forces beyond his control shoved him into a stiff collar and a top hat and told him to go out and be genial. And in the cool of the quiet evenfall they put him on a platform and made him make a speech. To a man with a day like that in front of him fine weather was a mockery.

His sister, Lady Constance Keeble, looked brightly at him over the coffee-pot.

'What a lovely morning!' she said.

Lord Emsworth's gloom deepened. He chafed at being called upon – by this woman of all others – to behave as if everything was for the jolliest in the jolliest of all possible worlds. But for his sister Constance and her hawk-like vigilance, he might, he thought, have been able at least to dodge the top hat.

'Have you got your speech ready?'

'Yes.'

'Well, mind you learn it by heart this time and don't stammer and dodder as you did last year.'

Lord Emsworth pushed plate and kipper away. He had lost his desire for food.

'And don't forget you have to go to the village this morning to judge the cottage gardens.'

'All right, all right, all right,' said his lordship testily. 'I've not forgotten.'

'I think I will come to the village with you. There are a number of those Fresh Air London children staying there now, and I must warn them to behave properly when they come to the Fête this afternoon. You know what London children are. McAllister says he found one of them in the gardens the other day, picking his flowers.'

At any other time the news of this outrage would, no doubt, have affected Lord Emsworth profoundly. But now, so intense was his self-pity, he did not even shudder. He drank coffee with the air of a man who regretted that it was not hemlock.

'By the way, McAllister was speaking to me again last night about that gravel path through the yew alley. He seems very keen on it.'

'Glug!' said Lord Emsworth – which, as any philologist will tell you, is the sound which peers of the realm make when stricken to the soul while drinking coffee.

Concerning Glasgow, that great commercial and manufacturing city in the county of Lanarkshire in Scotland, much has been written. So lyrically does the *Encyclopaedia Britannica* deal with the place that it covers twenty-seven pages before it can tear itself away and go on to Glass, Glastonbury, Glatz, and Glauber. The only aspect of it, however, which immediately concerns the present historian is the fact that the citizens it breeds are apt to be grim, dour, persevering, tenacious men; men with red whiskers who know what they want and mean to get it. Such a one was Angus McAllister, head-gardener at Blandings Castle.

For years Angus McAllister had set before himself as his earthly goal the construction of a gravel path through the Castle's famous yew alley. For years he had been bringing the project to the notice of his employer, though in anyone less whiskered the latter's unconcealed loathing would have caused embarrassment. And now, it seemed, he was at it again.

'Gravel path!' Lord Emsworth stiffened through the whole length of his stringy body. Nature, he had always maintained, intended a yew alley to be carpeted with a mossy growth. And, whatever Nature felt about it, he personally was dashed if he was going to have men with Clydeside accents and faces like dissipated potatoes coming along and mutilating that lovely expanse of green velvet. 'Gravel path, indeed! Why not asphalt? Why not a few hoardings with advertisements of liver pills and a filling-station? That's what the man would really like.'

Lord Emsworth felt bitter, and when he felt bitter he could be terribly sarcastic.

'Well, I think it is a very good idea,' said his sister. 'One could walk there in wet weather then. Damp moss is ruinous to shoes.'

Lord Emsworth rose. He could bear no more of this. He left the table, the room and the house and, reaching the yew alley some minutes later, was revolted to find it infested by Angus McAllister in person. The head-gardener was standing gazing at the moss like a high priest of some ancient religion about to stick the gaff into the human sacrifice.

'Morning, McAllister,' said Lord Emsworth coldly.

'Good morrrrning, your lorrudsheep.'

There was a pause. Angus McAllister, extending a foot that looked like a violin-case, pressed it on the moss. The meaning of the gesture was plain. It expressed contempt, dislike, a generally anti-moss spirit: and Lord Emsworth, wincing, surveyed the man unpleasantly through his pince-nez. Though not often given to theological speculation, he was wondering why Providence, if obliged to make head-gardeners, had found it necessary to make them so Scotch. In the case of Angus McAllister, why, going a step farther, have made him a human being at all? All the ingredients of a first-class mule simply thrown away. He felt that he might have liked Angus McAllister if he had been a mule.

'I was speaking to her leddyship yesterday.'

'Oh?'

'About the gravel path I was speaking to her leddyship.'

'Oh?'

'Her leddyship likes the notion fine.'

'Indeed! Well . . .'

Lord Emsworth's face had turned a lively pink, and he was about to release the blistering words which were forming themselves in his mind when suddenly he caught the head-gardener's eye and paused. Angus McAllister was looking at him in a peculiar manner, and he knew what that look meant. Just one crack, his eye was saying – in Scotch, of course – just one crack out of you and I tender my resignation. And with a sickening shock it came home to Lord Emsworth how completely he was in this man's clutches.

He shuffled miserably. Yes, he was helpless. Except for that kink about gravel paths, Angus McAllister was a head-gardener in a thousand, and he needed him. He could not do without him. That, unfortunately, had been proved by experiment. Once before, at the time when they were grooming for the Agricultural Show that pumpkin which had subsequently romped home so gallant a winner, he had dared to flout Angus McAllister. And Angus had resigned, and he had been forced to plead – yes, plead – with him to come back. An employer cannot hope to do this sort of thing and still rule with an iron hand. Filled with the coward rage that dares to burn but does not dare to blaze, Lord Emsworth coughed a cough that was undisguisedly a bronchial white flag.

'I'll – er – I'll think it over, McAllister.'

'Mphm.'

'I have to go to the village now. I will see you later.'

'Mphm.'

'Meanwhile, I will – er – think it over.'

'Mphm.'

The task of judging the floral displays in the cottage gardens of the little village of Blandings Parva was one to which Lord Emsworth had looked forward with pleasurable anticipation. It was the sort of job he liked. But now, even though he had managed to give his sister Constance the slip and was free from her threatened society, he approached the task with a downcast spirit. It is always unpleasant for a proud man to realize that he is no longer captain of his soul; that he is to all intents and purposes ground beneath the number twelve heel of a Glaswegian head-gardener; and, brooding on this, he judged the cottage gardens with a distrait eye. It was only when he came to the last on his list that anything like animation crept into his demeanour.

This, he perceived, peering over its rickety fence, was not at all a bad little garden. It demanded closer inspection. He unlatched the gate and pottered in. And a dog, dozing behind a water-butt, opened one eye and looked at him. It was one of those hairy, nondescript dogs, and its gaze was cold, wary and suspicious, like that of a stockbroker who thinks someone is going to play the confidence trick on him.

Lord Emsworth did not observe the animal. He had pottered to a bed of wallflowers and now, stooping, he took a sniff at them.

As sniffs go, it was an innocent sniff, but the dog for some reason appeared to read into it criminality of a high order. All the indignant householder in him woke in a flash. The next moment the world had become full of hideous noises, and Lord Emsworth's preoccupation was swept away in a passionate desire to save his ankles from harm.

As these chronicles of Blandings Castle have already shown, he was not at his best with strange dogs. Beyond saying 'Go away, sir!' and leaping to and fro with an agility surprising in one of his years, he had accomplished little in the direction of a reasoned plan of defence when the cottage door opened and a girl came out.

'Hoy!' cried the girl.

And on the instant, at the mere sound of her voice, the mongrel, suspending hostilities, bounded at the newcomer and writhed on his back at her feet with all four legs in the air. The spectacle reminded Lord Emsworth irresistibly of his own behaviour when in the presence of Angus McAllister.

He blinked at his preserver. She was a small girl, of uncertain age – possibly twelve or thirteen, though a combination of London fogs and early cares had given her face a sort of wizened motherliness which in some odd way caused his lordship from the first to look on her as belonging to his own generation. She was the type of girl you see in back streets carrying a baby nearly as large as herself and still retaining sufficient energy to lead one little brother by the hand and shout recrimination at another in the distance. Her cheeks shone from recent soaping, and she was dressed in a velveteen frock which was obviously the pick of her wardrobe. Her hair, in defiance of the prevailing mode, she wore drawn tightly back into a short pigtail.

'Er – thank you,' said Lord Emsworth.

'Thank you, sir,' said the girl.

For what she was thanking him, his lordship was not able to gather. Later, as their acquaintance ripened, he was to discover that this strange gratitude was a habit with his new friend. She thanked everybody for everything. At the moment, the mannerism surprised him. He continued to blink at her through his pince-nez.

Lack of practice had rendered Lord Emsworth a little rusty in the art of making conversation to members of the other sex. He sought in his mind for topics.

'Fine day.'

'Yes, sir. Thank you, sir.'

'Are you' – Lord Emsworth furtively consulted his list – 'are you the daughter of – ah – Ebenezer Sprockett?' he asked, thinking, as he had often thought before, what ghastly names some of his tenantry possessed.

'No, sir. I'm from London, sir.'

'Ah? London, eh? Pretty warm it must be there.' He paused. Then, remembering a formula of his youth: 'Er – been out much this Season?'

'No, sir.'

'Everybody out of town now, I suppose? What part of London?'

'Drury Line, sir.'

'What's your name? Eh, what?'

'Gladys, sir. Thank you, sir. This is Ern.'

A small boy had wandered out of the cottage, a rather hard-boiled specimen with freckles, bearing surprisingly in his hand a large and beautiful bunch of flowers. Lord Emsworth bowed courteously and, with the addition of this third party to the *tête-à-tête*, felt more at his ease.

'How do you do?' he said. 'What pretty flowers.'

With her brother's advent Gladys, also, had lost diffidence and gained conversational aplomb.

'A treat, ain't they?' she agreed eagerly. 'I got 'em for 'im up at the big 'ahse. Coo! The old josser the plice belongs to didn't arf chase me. 'E found me picking 'em and 'e sharted somefin at me and come runnin' after me, but I copped 'im on the shin wiv a stone and 'e stopped to rub it and I come away.'

Lord Emsworth might have corrected her impression that Blandings Castle and its gardens belonged to Angus McAllister, but his mind was so filled with admiration and gratitude that he refrained from doing so. He looked at the girl almost reverently. Not content with controlling savage dogs with a mere word, this super-woman actually threw stones at Angus McAllister – a thing which he had never been able to nerve himself to do in an association which had lasted nine years – and, what was more, copped him on the shin with them. What nonsense, Lord Emsworth felt, the papers talked about the Modern Girl. If this was a specimen, the Modern Girl was the highest point the sex had yet reached.

'Ern,' said Gladys, changing the subject, 'is wearin' 'air-oil todiy.'

Lord Emsworth had already observed this and had, indeed, been moving to windward as she spoke.

'For the Feet,' explained Gladys.

'For the feet?' It seemed unusual.

'For the Feet in the pork this afternoon.'

'Oh, you are going to the Fête?'

'Yes, sir, thank you, sir.'

For the first time, Lord Emsworth found himself regarding that grisly social event with something approaching favour.

'We must look out for one another there,' he said cordially. 'You will remember me again? I shall be wearing' – he gulped – 'a top hat.'

'Ern's going to wear a stror penamaw that's been give 'im.'

Lord Emsworth regarded the lucky young devil with frank envy. He rather fancied he knew that panama. It had been his constant companion for some six years and then had been torn from him by his sister Constance and handed over to the vicar's wife for her rummage-sale.

He sighed.

'Well, goodbye.'

'Goodbye, sir. Thank you, sir.'

Lord Emsworth walked pensively out of the garden and, turning into the little street, encountered Lady Constance.

'Oh, there you are, Clarence.'

'Yes,' said Lord Emsworth, for such was the case.

'Have you finished judging the gardens?'

'Yes.'

'I am just going into this end cottage here. The vicar tells me there is a little girl from London staying there. I want to warn her to behave this afternoon. I have spoken to the others.'

Lord Emsworth drew himself up. His pince-nez were slightly askew, but despite this his gaze was commanding and impressive.

'Well, mind what you say,' he said authoritatively. 'None of your district-visiting stuff, Constance.'

'What do you mean?'

'You know what I mean. I have the greatest respect for the young lady to whom you refer. She behaved on a certain recent occasion – on two recent occasions – with notable gallantry and resource, and I won't have her bally-ragged. Understand that!'

The technical title of the orgy which broke out annually on the first Monday in August in the park of Blandings Castle was the Blandings Parva School Treat, and it seemed to Lord Emsworth, wanly watching the proceedings from under the shadow of his top hat, that if this was the sort of thing schools looked on as pleasure he and they were mentally poles apart. A function like the Blandings Parva School Treat blurred his conception of Man as Nature's Final Word.

The decent sheep and cattle to whom this park normally belonged had been hustled away into regions unknown, leaving the smooth expanse of turf to children whose vivacity scared Lord Emsworth and adults who appeared to him to have cast aside all dignity and every other noble quality which goes to make a one hundred per cent British citizen. Look at Mrs Rossiter over there, for instance, the wife of Jno. Rossiter, Provisions, Groceries and Homemade Jams. On any other day of the year, when you met her, Mrs Rossiter was a nice, quiet, docile woman who gave at the knees respectfully as you passed. Today, flushed in the face and with her bonnet on one side, she seemed to have gone completely native. She was wandering to and fro drinking lemonade out of a bottle and employing her mouth, when not so occupied, to make a devastating noise with what he believed was termed a squeaker.

The injustice of the thing stung Lord Emsworth. This park was his own private park. What right had people to come and blow squeakers in it? How would Mrs Rossiter like it if one afternoon he suddenly invaded her neat little garden in the High Street and rushed about over her lawn, blowing a squeaker?

And it was always on these occasions so infernally hot. July might have ended in a flurry of snow, but directly the first Monday in August arrived and he had to put on a stiff collar, out came the sun, blazing with tropic fury.

Of course, admitted Lord Emsworth, for he was a fair-minded man, this cut both ways. The hotter the day, the more quickly his collar lost its starch and ceased to spike him like a javelin. This afternoon, for instance, it had resolved itself almost immediately into something which felt like a wet compress. Severe as were his sufferings, he was compelled to recognize that he was that much ahead of the game.

A masterful figure loomed at his side.

'Clarence!'

Lord Emsworth's mental and spiritual state was now such that not even the advent of his sister Constance could add noticeably to his discomfort.

'Clarence, you look a perfect sight.'

'I know I do. Who wouldn't in a rig-out like this? Why in the name of goodness you always insist . . .'

'Please don't be childish, Clarence. I cannot understand the fuss you make about dressing for once in your life like a reasonable English gentleman and not like a tramp.'

'It's this top hat. It's exciting the children.'

'What on earth do you mean, exciting the children?'

'Well, all I can tell you is that just now, as I was passing the place where they're playing football – Football! In weather like this! – a small boy called out something derogatory and threw a portion of a coco-nut at it.'

'If you will identify the child,' said Lady Constance warmly, 'I will have him severely punished.'

'How the dickens,' replied his lordship with equal warmth, 'can I identify the child? They all look alike to me. And if I did identify him, I would shake him by the hand. A boy who throws coco-nuts at top hats is fundamentally sound in his views. And stiff collars . . .'

'Stiff! That's what I came to speak to you about. Are you aware that your collar looks like a rag? Go in and change it at once.'

'But, my dear Constance . . .'

'At once, Clarence. I simply cannot understand a man having so little pride in his appearance. But all your life you have been like that. I remember when we were children . . .'

Lord Emsworth's past was not of such a purity that he was prepared to stand and listen to it being lectured on by a sister with a good memory.

'Oh, all right, all right, all right,' he said. 'I'll change it, I'll change it.'

'Well, hurry. They are just starting tea.'

Lord Emsworth quivered.

'Have I got to go into that tea-tent?'

'Of course you have. Don't be so ridiculous. I do wish you would realize your position. As master of Blandings Castle . . .'

A bitter, mirthless laugh from the poor peon thus ludicrously described drowned the rest of the sentence.

It always seemed to Lord Emsworth, in analysing these entertainments, that the August Bank Holiday Saturnalia at Blandings Castle reached a peak of repulsiveness when tea was served in the big marquee. Tea over, the agony abated, to become acute once more at the moment when he stepped to the edge of the platform and cleared his throat and tried to recollect what the deuce he had planned to say to the goggling audience beneath him. After that, it subsided again and passed until the following August.

Conditions during the tea hour, the marquee having stood all day under a blazing sun, were generally such that Shadrach, Meshach and Abednego, had they been there, could have learned something new about burning fiery furnaces. Lord Emsworth, delayed by the revision of his toilet, made his entry when the meal was half over and was pleased to find that his second collar almost instantaneously began to relax its iron grip. That, however, was the only gleam of happiness which was to be vouchsafed him. Once in the tent, it took his experienced eye but a moment to discern that the present feast was eclipsing in frightfulness all its predecessors.

Young Blandings Parva, in its normal form, tended rather to the stolidly bovine than the riotous. In all villages, of course, there must of necessity be an occasional tough egg – in the case of Blandings Parva the names of Willie Drake and Thomas (Rat-Face) Blenkiron spring to the mind – but it was seldom that the local infants offered anything beyond the power of a curate to control. What was giving the present gathering its striking resemblance to a reunion of *sans-culottes* at the height of the French Revolution was the admixture of the Fresh Air London visitors.

About the London child, reared among the tin cans and cabbage stalks of Drury Lane and Clare Market, there is a breezy insouciance which his country cousin lacks. Years of back-chat with annoyed parents and relatives have cured him of any tendency he may have had towards shyness, with the result that when he requires anything he grabs for it, and when he is amused by any slight peculiarity in the personal appearance of members of the governing classes he finds no difficulty in translating his thoughts into speech. Already, up and down the long tables, the curate's unfortunate squint was coming in for hearty comment, and the front teeth of one of the school-teachers ran it a close second for popularity. Lord Emsworth was not, as a rule, a man of swift inspirations, but it occurred to him at this juncture that it would be a prudent move to take off his top hat before his little guests observed it and appreciated its humorous possibilities.

The action was not, however, necessary. Even as he raised his hand a rock cake, singing through the air like a shell, took it off for him.

Lord Emsworth had had sufficient. Even Constance, unreasonable woman though she was, could hardly expect him to stay and beam genially under conditions like this. All civilized laws had obviously gone by the board and Anarchy reigned in the marquee. The curate was doing his best to form a provisional government consisting of himself and the two school-teachers, but there was only one man who could have coped adequately with the situation and that was King Herod, who – regrettably – was not among those present. Feeling like some aristocrat of the old regime sneaking away from the tumbril, Lord Emsworth edged to the exit and withdrew.

Outside the marquee the world was quieter, but only comparatively so. What Lord Emsworth craved was solitude, and in all the broad park there seemed to be but one spot where it was to be had. This was a red-tiled shed, standing beside a small pond, used at happier times as a lounge or retiring-room for cattle. Hurrying thither, his lordship had begun to revel in the cool, cow-scented dimness of its interior when from one of the dark corners, causing him to start and bite his tongue, there came the sound of a subdued sniff.

He turned. This was persecution. With the whole park to mess about in, why should an infernal child invade this one sanctuary of his? He spoke with angry sharpness. He came of a line of warrior ancestors and his fighting blood was up.

'Who's that?'

'Me, sir. Thank you, sir.'

Only one person of Lord Emsworth's acquaintance was capable of expressing gratitude for having been barked at in such a tone. His wrath died away and remorse took its place. He felt like a man who in error has kicked a favourite dog.

'God bless my soul!' he exclaimed. 'What in the world are you doing in a cow-shed?'

'Please, sir, I was put.'

'Put? How do you mean, put? Why?'

'For pinching things, sir.'

'Eh? What? Pinching things? Most extraordinary. What did you – er – pinch?'

'Two buns, two jem-sengwiches, two apples and a slicer cake.'

The girl had come out of her corner and was standing correctly at attention. Force of habit had caused her to intone the list of the purloined articles in the sing-song voice in which she was wont to recite the multiplication-table at school, but Lord Emsworth could see that she was deeply moved. Tear-stains glistened on her face, and no Emsworth had ever been able to watch unstirred a woman's tears. The ninth Earl was visibly affected.

'Blow your nose,' he said, hospitably extending his handkerchief.

'Yes, sir. Thank you, sir.'

'What did you say you had pinched? Two buns . . .'

'. . . Two jem-sengwiches, two apples and a slicer cake.'

'Did you eat them?'

'No, sir. They wasn't for me. They was for Ern.'

'Ern? Oh, ah, yes. Yes, to be sure. For Ern, eh?'

'Yes, sir.'

'But why the dooce couldn't Ern have – er – pinched them for himself? Strong, able-bodied young feller, I mean.'

Lord Emsworth, a member of the old school, did not like this disposition on the part of the modern young man to shirk the dirty work and let the woman pay.

'Ern wasn't allowed to come to the treat, sir.'

'What! Not allowed? Who said he mustn't?'

'The lidy, sir.'

'What lidy?'

'The one that come in just after you'd gorn this morning.'

A fierce snort escaped Lord Emsworth. Constance! What the devil did Constance mean by taking it upon herself to revise his list of guests without so much as a . . . Constance, eh? He snorted again. One of these days Constance would go too far.

'Monstrous!' he cried.

'Yes, sir.'

'High-handed tyranny, by Gad. Did she give any reason?'

'The lidy didn't like Ern biting 'er in the leg, sir.'

'Ern bit her in the leg?'

'Yes, sir. Plying 'e was a dorg. And the lidy was cross and Ern wasn't allowed to come to the treat, and I told 'im I'd bring 'im back somfing nice.'

Lord Emsworth breathed heavily. He had not supposed that in these degenerate days a family like this existed. The sister copped Angus McAllister on the shin with stones, the brother bit Constance in the leg . . . It was like listening to some grand old saga of the exploits of heroes and demigods.

'I thought if I didn't 'ave nothing myself it would make it all right.'

'Nothing?' Lord Emsworth started. 'Do you mean to tell me you have not had tea?'

'No, sir. Thank you, sir. I thought if I didn't 'ave none, then it would be all right Ern 'aving what I would 'ave 'ad if I 'ad 'ave 'ad.'

His lordship's head, never strong, swam a little. Then it resumed its equilibrium. He caught her drift.

'God bless my soul!' said Lord Emsworth. 'I never heard anything so monstrous and appalling in my life. Come with me immediately.'

'The lidy said I was to stop 'ere, sir.'

Lord Emsworth gave vent to his loudest snort of the afternoon.

'Confound the lidy!'

'Yes, sir. Thank you, sir.'

Five minutes later Beach, the butler, enjoying a siesta in the house-keeper's room, was roused from his slumbers by the unexpected ringing of a bell. Answering its summons, he found his employer in the library, and with him a surprising young person in a velveteen frock, at the sight of whom his eyebrows quivered and, but for his iron self-restraint, would have risen.

'Beach!'

'Your lordship?'

'This young lady would like some tea.'

'Very good, your lordship.'

'Buns, you know. And apples, and jem – I mean jam-sandwiches, and cake, and that sort of thing.'

'Very good, your lordship.'

'And she has a brother, Beach.'

'Indeed, your lordship?'

'She will want to take some stuff away for him.' Lord Emsworth turned to his guest. 'Ernest would like a little chicken, perhaps?'

'Coo!'

'I beg your pardon?'

'Yes, sir. Thank you, sir.'

'And a slice or two of ham?'

'Yes, sir. Thank you, sir.'

'And – he has no gouty tendency?'

'No, sir. Thank you, sir.'

'Capital! Then a bottle of that new lot of port, Beach. It's some stuff they've sent me down to try,' explained his lordship. 'Nothing special, you understand,' he added apologetically, 'but quite drinkable. I should like your brother's opinion of it. See that all that is put together in a parcel, Beach, and leave it on the table in the hall. We will pick it up as we go out.'

A welcome coolness had crept into the evening air by the time Lord Emsworth and his guest came out of the great door of the castle. Gladys, holding her host's hand and clutching the parcel, sighed contentedly. She had done herself well at the tea-table. Life seemed to have nothing more to offer.

Lord Emsworth did not share this view. His spacious mood had not yet exhausted itself.

'Now, is there anything else you can think of that Ernest would like?' he asked. 'If so, do not hesitate to mention it. Beach, can you think of anything?'

The butler, hovering respectfully, was unable to do so.

'No, your lordship. I ventured to add – on my own responsibility, your lordship – some hard-boiled eggs and a pot of jam to the parcel.'

'Excellent! You are sure there is nothing else?'

A wistful look came into Gladys's eyes.

'Could he 'ave some flarze?'

'Certainly,' said Lord Emsworth. 'Certainly, certainly, certainly. By all means. Just what I was about to suggest my – er – what *is* flarze?'

Beach, the linguist, interpreted.

'I think the young lady means flowers, your lordship.'

'Yes, sir. Thank you, sir. Flarze.'

'Oh?' said Lord Emsworth. 'Oh? Flarze?' he said slowly. 'Oh, ah, yes. Yes. I see. H'm!'

He removed his pince-nez, wiped them thoughtfully, replaced them, and gazed with wrinkling forehead at the gardens that stretched gaily out before him. Flarze! It would be idle to deny that those gardens contained flarze in full measure. They were bright with Achillea, Bignonia Radicans, Campanula, Digitalis, Euphorbia, Funkia, Gypsophila, Helianthus, Iris, Liatris, Monarda, Phlox Drummondi, Salvia, Thalictrum, Vinca and Yucca. But the devil of it was that Angus McAllister would have a fit if they were picked. Across the threshold of this Eden the ginger whiskers of Angus McAllister lay like a flaming sword.

As a general rule, the procedure for getting flowers out of Angus McAllister was as follows. You waited till he was in one of his rare moods of complaisance, then you led the conversation gently round to the subject of interior decoration, and then, choosing your moment, you asked if he could possibly spare a few to be put in vases. The last thing you thought of doing was to charge in and start helping yourself.

'I – er . . .' said Lord Emsworth.

He stopped. In a sudden blinding flash of clear vision he had seen himself for what he was – the spineless, unspeakably unworthy descendant of ancestors who, though they may have had their faults, had certainly known how to handle employees. It was 'How now, varlet!' and 'Marry come up, thou malapert knave!' in the days of previous Earls of Emsworth. Of course, they had possessed certain advantages which he lacked. It undoubtedly helped a man in his dealings with the domestic staff to have, as they had had, the rights of the high, the middle and the low justice – which meant, broadly, that if you got annoyed with your head-gardener you could immediately divide him into four head-gardeners with a battle-axe and no questions asked – but even so, he realized that they were better men than he was and that, if he allowed craven fear of Angus McAllister to stand in the way of this delightful girl and her charming brother getting all the flowers they required, he was not worthy to be the last of their line.

Lord Emsworth wrestled with his tremors.

'Certainly, certainly, certainly,' he said, though not without a qualm. 'Take as many as you want.'

And so it came about that Angus McAllister, crouched in his potting-shed like some dangerous beast in its den, beheld a sight which first froze his blood and then sent it boiling through his veins. Flitting to and fro through his sacred gardens, picking his sacred flowers, was a small girl in a velveteen frock. And – which brought apoplexy a step closer – it was the same small girl who two days before had copped him on the shin with a stone. The stillness of the summer evening was shattered by a roar that sounded like boilers exploding, and Angus McAllister came out of the potting-shed at forty-five miles per hour.

Gladys did not linger. She was a London child, trained from infancy to bear herself gallantly in the presence of alarms and excursions, but this excursion had been so sudden that it momentarily broke her nerve. With a horrified yelp she scuttled to where Lord Emsworth stood and, hiding behind him, clutched the tails of his morning-coat.

'Oo-er!' said Gladys.

Lord Emsworth was not feeling so frightfully good himself. We have pictured him a few moments back drawing inspiration from the nobility of his ancestors and saying, in effect, 'That for McAllister!', but truth now compels us to admit that this hardy attitude was largely due to the fact that he believed the head-gardener to be a safe quarter of a mile away among the swings and roundabouts of the Fête. The spectacle of the man charging vengefully down on him with gleaming eyes and bristling whiskers made him feel like a nervous English infantryman at the Battle of Bannockburn. His knees shook and the soul within him quivered.

And then something happened, and the whole aspect of the situation changed.

It was, in itself, quite a trivial thing, but it had an astoundingly stimulating effect on Lord Emsworth's morale. What happened was that Gladys, seeking further protection, slipped at this moment a small, hot hand into his.

It was a mute vote of confidence, and Lord Emsworth intended to be worthy of it.

'He's coming,' whispered his lordship's Inferiority Complex agitatedly.

'What of it?' replied Lord Emsworth stoutly.

'Tick him off,' breathed his lordship's ancestors in his other ear.

'Leave it to me,' replied Lord Emsworth.

He drew himself up and adjusted his pince-nez. He felt filled with a cool masterfulness. If the man tendered his resignation, let him tender his damned resignation.

'Well, McAllister?' said Lord Emsworth coldly.

He removed his top hat and brushed it against his sleeve.

'What is the matter, McAllister?'

He replaced his top hat.

'You appear agitated, McAllister.'

He jerked his head militantly. The hat fell off. He let it lie. Freed from its loathsome weight he felt more masterful than ever. It had just needed that to bring him to the top of his form.

'This young lady,' said Lord Emsworth, 'has my full permission to pick all the flowers she wants, McAllister. If you do not see eye to eye with me in this matter, McAllister, say so and we will discuss what you are going to do about it, McAllister. These gardens, McAllister, belong to me, and if you do not – er – appreciate that fact you will, no doubt, be able to find another employer – ah – more in tune with your views. I value your services highly, McAllister, but I will not be dictated to in my own garden, McAllister. Er – dash it,' added his lordship, spoiling the whole effect.

A long moment followed in which Nature stood still, breathless.

The Achillea stood still. So did the Bignonia Radicans. So did the Campanula, the Digitalis, the Euphorbia, the Funkia, the Gypsophila, the Helianthus, the Iris, the Liatris, the Monarda, the Phlox Drummondi, the Salvia, the Thalictrum, the Vinca and the Yucca. From far off in the direction of the park there sounded the happy howls of children who were probably breaking things, but even these seemed hushed. The evening breeze had died away.

Angus McAllister stood glowering. His attitude was that of one sorely perplexed. So might the early bird have looked if the worm earmarked for its breakfast had suddenly turned and snapped at it. It had never occurred to him that his employer would voluntarily suggest that he sought another position, and now that he had suggested it, Angus McAllister disliked the idea very much. Blandings Castle was in his bones. Elsewhere, he would feel an exile. He fingered his whiskers, but they gave him no comfort.

He made his decision. Better to cease to be a Napoleon than be a Napoleon in exile.

'Mphm,' said Angus McAllister.

'Oh, and by the way, McAllister,' said Lord Emsworth, 'that matter of the gravel path through the yew alley. I've been thinking it over, and I won't have it. Not on any account. Mutilate my beautiful moss with a beastly gravel path? Make an eyesore of the loveliest spot in one of the finest and oldest gardens in the United Kingdom? Certainly not. Most decidedly not. Try to remember, McAllister, as you work in the gardens of Blandings Castle, that you are not back in Glasgow, laying out recreation grounds. That is all, McAllister. Er – dash it – that is all.'

'Mphm,' said Angus McAllister.

He turned. He walked away. The potting-shed swallowed him up. Nature resumed its breathing. The breeze began to blow again. And all over the gardens birds who had stopped on their high note carried on according to plan.

Lord Emsworth took out his handkerchief and dabbed with it at his forehead. He was shaken, but a novel sense of being a man among men thrilled him. It might seem bravado, but he almost wished – yes, dash it, he almost wished – that his sister Constance would come along and start something while he felt like this.

He had his wish.

'Clarence!'

Yes, there she was, hurrying towards him up the garden path. She, like McAllister, seemed agitated. Something was on her mind.

'Clarence!'

'Don't keep saying "Clarence!" as if you were a dashed parrot,' said Lord Emsworth haughtily. 'What the dickens is the matter, Constance?'

'Matter? Do you know what the time is? Do you know that everybody is waiting down there for you to make your speech?'

Lord Emsworth met her eye sternly.

'I do not,' he said. 'And I don't care. I'm not going to make any dashed speech. If you want a speech, let the vicar make it. Or make it yourself. Speech! I never heard such dashed nonsense in my life.' He turned to Gladys. 'Now, my dear,' he said, 'if you will just give me time to get out of these infernal clothes and this ghastly collar and put on something human, we'll go down to the village and have a chat with Ern.'

# THE CRIME WAVE AT BLANDINGS

The day on which Lawlessness reared its ugly head at Blandings Castle was one of singular beauty. The sun shone down from a sky of cornflower blue, and what one would really like would be to describe in leisurely detail the ancient battlements, the smooth green lawns, the rolling parkland, the majestic trees, the well-bred bees and the gentlemanly birds on which it shone.

But those who read thrillers are an impatient race. They chafe at scenic rhapsodies and want to get on to the rough stuff. When, they ask, did the dirty work start? Who were mixed up in it? Was there blood, and, if so, how much? And – most particularly – where was everybody and what was everybody doing at whatever time it was? The chronicler who wishes to grip must supply this information at the earliest possible moment.

The wave of crime, then, which was to rock one of Shropshire's stateliest homes to its foundations broke out towards the middle of a fine summer afternoon, and the persons involved in it were disposed as follows:

Clarence, ninth Earl of Emsworth, the castle's owner and overlord, was down in the potting-shed, in conference with Angus McAllister, his head-gardener, on the subject of sweet peas.

His sister, Lady Constance, was strolling on the terrace with a swarthy young man in spectacles, whose name was Rupert Baxter and who had at one time been Lord Emsworth's private secretary.

Beach, the butler, was in a deck-chair outside the back premises of the house, smoking a cigar and reading Chapter Sixteen of *The Man With The Missing Toe*.

George, Lord Emsworth's grandson, was prowling through the shrubbery with the airgun which was his constant companion.

Jane, his lordship's niece, was in the summer-house by the lake.

And the sun shone serenely down – on, as we say, the lawns, the battlements, the trees, the bees, the best type of bird and the rolling parkland.

Presently Lord Emsworth left the potting-shed and started to wander towards the house. He had never felt happier. All day his mood had been one of perfect contentment and tranquillity, and for once in a way Angus McAllister had done nothing to disturb it. Too often, when you tried to reason with that human mule, he had a way of saying 'Mphm' and looking Scotch and then saying 'Grmph' and looking Scotch again, and after that just fingering his beard and looking Scotch without speaking, which was intensely irritating to a sensitive employer. But this afternoon Hollywood yes-men could have taken his correspondence course, and Lord Emsworth had none of that uneasy feeling, which usually came to him on these occasions, that the moment his back was turned his own sound, statesmanlike policies would be shelved and some sort of sweet pea New Deal put into practice as if he had never spoken a word.

He was humming as he approached the terrace. He had his programme all mapped out. For perhaps an hour, till the day had cooled off a little, he would read a Pig book in the library. After that he would go and take a sniff at a rose or two and possibly do a bit of snailing. These mild pleasures were all his simple soul demanded. He wanted nothing more. Just the quiet life, with nobody to fuss him.

And now that Baxter had left, he reflected buoyantly, nobody did fuss him. There had, he dimly recalled, been some sort of trouble a week or so back – something about some man his niece Jane wanted to marry and his sister Constance didn't want her to marry – but that had apparently all blown over. And even when the thing had been at its height, even when the air had been shrill with women's voices and Connie had kept popping out at him and saying 'Do *listen*, Clarence!' he had always been able to reflect that, though all this was pretty unpleasant, there was nevertheless a bright side. He had ceased to be the employer of Rupert Baxter.

There is a breed of granite-faced, strong-jawed business man to whom Lord Emsworth's attitude towards Rupert Baxter would have seemed frankly inexplicable. To these Titans a private secretary is simply a Hey-you, a Hi-there, a mere puppet to be ordered hither and thither at will. The trouble with Lord Emsworth was that it was he and not his secretary who had been the puppet. Their respective relations had always been those of a mild reigning monarch and the pushing young devil who has taken on the dictatorship. For years, until he had mercifully tendered his resignation to join an American named Jevons, Baxter had worried Lord Emsworth, bossed him, bustled him, had always been after him to do things and remember things and sign things. Never a moment's peace. Yes, it was certainly delightful to think that Baxter had departed for ever. His going had relieved this Garden of Eden of its one resident snake.

Still humming, Lord Emsworth reached the terrace. A moment later, the melody had died on his lips and he was rocking back on his heels as if he had received a solid punch on the nose.

'God bless my soul!' he ejaculated, shaken to the core.

His pince-nez, as always happened when he was emotionally stirred, had leaped from their moorings. He recovered them and put them on again, hoping feebly that the ghastly sight he had seen would prove to have been an optical illusion. But no. However much he blinked, he could not blink away the fact that the man over there talking to his sister Constance was Rupert Baxter in person. He stood gaping at him with a horror which would have been almost excessive if the other had returned from the tomb.

Lady Constance was smiling brightly, as women so often do when they are in the process of slipping something raw over on their nearest and dearest.

'Here is Mr Baxter, Clarence.'

'Ah,' said Lord Emsworth.

'He is touring England on his motor-bicycle, and finding himself in these parts, of course, he looked us up.'

'Ah,' said Lord Emsworth.

He spoke dully, for his soul was heavy with foreboding. It was all very well for Connie to say that Baxter was touring England, thus giving the idea that in about five minutes the man would leap on his motor-bicycle and dash off to some spot a hundred miles away. He knew his sister. She was plotting. Always ardently pro-Baxter, she was going to try to get Blandings Castle's leading incubus back into office again. Lord Emsworth would have been prepared to lay the odds on this in the most liberal spirit. So he said 'Ah.'

The monosyllable, taken in conjunction with the sagging of her brother's jaw and the glare of agony behind his pince-nez, caused Lady Constance's lips to tighten. A disciplinary light came into her fine eyes. She looked like a female lion-tamer about to assert her personality with one of the troupe.

'Clarence!' she said sharply. She turned to her companion. 'Would you excuse me for a moment, Mr Baxter. There is something I want to talk to Lord Emsworth about.'

She drew the pallid peer aside, and spoke with sharp rebuke.

'Just like a stuck pig!'

'Eh?' said Lord Emsworth. His mind had been wandering, as it so often did. The magic word brought it back. 'Pigs? What about pigs?'

'I was saying that you were looking like a stuck pig. You might at least have asked Mr Baxter how he was.'

'I could see how he was. What's he doing here?'

'I told you what he was doing here.'

'But how does he come to be touring England on motor-bicycles? I thought he was working for an American fellow named something or other.'

'He has left Mr Jevons.'

'What!'

'Yes. Mr Jevons had to return to America, and Mr Baxter did not want to leave England.'

Lord Emsworth reeled. Jevons had been his sheet-anchor. He had never met that genial Chicagoan, but he had always thought kindly and gratefully of him, as one does of some great doctor who has succeeded in isolating and confining a disease germ.

'You mean the chap's out of a job?' he cried aghast.

'Yes. And it could not have happened at a more fortunate time, because something has got to be done about George.'

'Who's George?'

'You have a grandson of that name,' explained Lady Constance with the sweet, frozen patience which she so often used when conversing with her brother. 'Your heir, Bosham, if you recollect, has two sons, James and George. George, the younger, is spending his summer holidays here. You may have noticed him about. A boy of twelve with auburn hair and freckles.'

'Oh, George? You mean George? Yes, I know George. He's my grandson. What about him?'

'He is completely out of hand. Only yesterday he broke another window with that airgun of his.'

'He needs a mother's care?' Lord Emsworth was vague, but he had an idea that that was the right thing to say.

'He needs a tutor's care, and I am glad to say that Mr Baxter has very kindly consented to accept the position.'

'What!'

'Yes. It is all settled. His things are at the Emsworth Arms, and I am sending down for them.'

Lord Emsworth sought feverishly for arguments which would quash this frightful scheme.

'But he can't be a tutor if he's galumphing all over England on a motor-bicycle.'

'I had not overlooked that point. He will stop galumphing over England on a motor-bicycle.'

'But –'

'It will be a wonderful solution of a problem which was becoming more difficult every day. Mr Baxter will keep George in order. He is so firm.'

She turned away, and Lord Emsworth resumed his progress towards the library.

It was a black moment for the ninth Earl. His worst fears had been realized. He knew just what all this meant. On one of his rare visits to London he had once heard an extraordinarily vivid phrase which had made a deep impression upon him. He had been taking his after-luncheon coffee at the Senior Conservative Club and some fellows in an adjoining nest of armchairs had started a political discussion, and one of them had said about something or other that, mark his words, it was the 'thin end of the wedge'. He recognized what was happening now as the thin end of the wedge. From Baxter as a temporary tutor to Baxter as a permanent secretary would, he felt, be so short a step that the contemplation of it chilled him to the bone.

A short-sighted man whose pince-nez have gone astray at the very moment when vultures are gnawing at his bosom seldom guides his steps carefully. Anyone watching Lord Emsworth totter blindly across the terrace would have foreseen that he would shortly collide with something, the only point open to speculation being with what he would collide. This proved to be a small boy with ginger hair and freckles who emerged abruptly from the shrubbery carrying an airgun.

'Coo!' said the small boy. 'Sorry, grandpapa.'

Lord Emsworth recovered his pince-nez and, having adjusted them on the old spot, glared balefully.

'George! Why the dooce don't you look where you're going?'

'Sorry, grandpapa.'

'You might have injured me severely.'

'Sorry, grandpapa.'

'Be more careful another time.'

'Okay, big boy.'

'And don't call me "big boy".'

'Right ho, grandpapa. I say,' said George, shelving the topic, 'who's the bird talking to Aunt Connie?'

He pointed – a vulgarism which a good tutor would have corrected – and Lord Emsworth, following the finger, winced as his eye rested once more upon Rupert Baxter. The secretary – already Lord Emsworth had mentally abandoned the qualifying 'ex' – was gazing out over the rolling parkland, and it seemed to his lordship that his gaze was proprietorial. Rupert Baxter, flashing his spectacles over the grounds of Blandings Castle, wore – or so it appeared to Lord Emsworth – the smug air of some ruthless monarch of old surveying conquered territory.

'That is Mr Baxter,' he replied.

'Looks a bit of a blister,' said George critically.

The expression was new to Lord Emsworth, but he recognized it at once as the ideal description of Rupert Baxter. His heart warmed to the little fellow, and he might quite easily at this moment have given him sixpence.

'Do you think so?' he said lovingly.

'What's he doing here?'

Lord Emsworth felt a pang. It seemed brutal to dash the sunshine from the life of this admirable boy. Yet somebody had got to tell him.

'He is going to be your tutor.'

'Tutor?'

The word was a cry of agony forced from the depths of the boy's soul. A stunned sense that all the fundamental decencies of life were being outraged had swept over George. His voice was thick with emotion.

'Tutor?' he cried. '*Tew*-tor? Ter-YEWtor? In the middle of the summer holidays? What have I got to have a tutor for in the middle of the summer holidays? I do call this a bit off. I mean, in the middle of the summer holidays. Why do I want a tutor? I mean to say, in the middle of . . .'

He would have spoken at greater length, for he had much to say on the subject, but at this point Lady Constance's voice, musical but imperious, interrupted his flow of speech.

'Gee-orge.'

'Coo! Right in the middle –'

'Come here, George. I want you to meet Mr Baxter.'

'Cool!' muttered the stricken child again and, frowning darkly, slouched across the terrace. Lord Emsworth proceeded to the library, a tender pity in his heart for this boy who by his crisp summing-up of Rupert Baxter had revealed himself so kindred a spirit. He knew just how George felt. It was not always easy to get anything into Lord Emsworth's head, but he had grasped the substance of his grandson's complaint unerringly. George, about to have a tutor in the middle of the summer holidays, did not want one.

Sighing a little, Lord Emsworth reached the library and found his book.

There were not many books which at a time like this could have diverted Lord Emsworth's mind from what weighed upon it, but this one did. It was Whiffle on *The Care Of The Pig* and, buried in its pages, he forgot everything. The chapter he was reading was that noble one about swill and bran-mash, and it took him completely out of the world, so much so that when some twenty minutes later the door suddenly burst open it was as if a bomb had been exploded under his nose. He dropped Whiffle and sat panting. Then, although his pince-nez had followed routine by flying off, he was able by some subtle instinct to sense that the intruder was his sister Constance, and an observation beginning with the words 'Good God, Connie!' had begun to leave his lips, when she cut him short.

'Clarence,' she said, and it was plain that her nervous system, like his, was much shaken, 'the most dreadful thing has happened!'

'Eh?'

'That man is here.'

'What man?'

'That man of Jane's. The man I told you about.'

'What man did you tell me about?'

Lady Constance seated herself. She would have preferred to have been able to do without tedious explanations, but long association with her brother had taught her that his was a memory that had to be refreshed. She embarked, accordingly, on these explanations, speaking wearily, like a schoolmistress to one of the duller members of her class.

'The man I told you about — certainly not less than a hundred times — was a man Jane met in the spring, when she went to stay with her friends the Leighs in Devonshire. She had a silly flirtation with him, which, of course, she insisted in magnifying into a great romance. She kept saying they were engaged. And he hasn't a penny. Nor prospects. Nor, so I gathered from Jane, a position.'

Lord Emsworth interrupted at this point to put a question.

'Who,' he asked courteously, 'is Jane?'

Lady Constance quivered a little.

'Oh, Clarence! Your niece Jane.'

'Oh, my *niece* Jane? Ah! Yes. Yes, of course. My niece Jane. Yes, of course, to be sure. My –'

'Clarence, please! For pity's sake! Do stop doddering and listen to me. For once in your life I want you to be firm.'

'Be what?'

'Firm. Put your foot down.'

'How do you mean?'

'About Jane. I had been hoping that she had got over this ridiculous infatuation – she has seemed perfectly happy and contented all this time – but no. Apparently they have been corresponding regularly, and now the man is here.'

'Here?'

'Yes.'

'Where?' asked Lord Emsworth, gazing in an interested manner about the room.

'He arrived last night and is staying in the village. I found out by the merest accident. I happened to ask George if he had seen Jane, because I wanted Mr Baxter to meet her, and he said he had met her going towards the lake. So I went down to the lake, and there I discovered her with a young man in a tweed coat and flannel knicker-bockers. They were kissing one another in the summer-house.'

Lord Emsworth clicked his tongue.

'Ought to have been out in the sunshine,' he said, disapprovingly.

Lady Constance raised her foot quickly, but instead of kicking her brother on the shin merely tapped the carpet with it. Blood will tell.

'Jane was defiant. I think she must be off her head. She insisted that she was going to marry this man. And, as I say, not only has he not a penny, but he is apparently out of work.'

'What sort of work does he do?'

'I gather that he has been a land-agent on an estate in Devonshire.'

'It all comes back to me,' said Lord Emsworth. 'I remember now. This must be the man Jane was speaking to me about yesterday. Of course, yes. She asked me to give him Simmons's job. Simmons is retiring next month. Good fellow,' said Lord Emsworth sentimentally. 'Been here for years and years. I shall be sorry to lose him. Bless my soul, it won't seem like the same place without old Simmons. Still,' he said, brightening, for he was a man who could make the best of things, 'no doubt this new chap will turn out all right. Jane seems to think highly of him.'

Lady Constance had risen slowly from her chair. There was incredulous horror on her face.

'Clarence! You are not telling me that you have promised this man Simmons's place?'

'Eh? Yes, I have. Why not?'

'Why not! Do you realize that directly he gets it he will marry Jane?'

'Well, why shouldn't he? Very nice girl. Probably make him a good wife.'

Lady Constance struggled with her feelings for a space.

'Clarence,' she said, 'I am going out now to find Jane. I shall tell her that you have thought it over and changed your mind.'

'What about?'

'Giving this man Simmons's place.'

'But I haven't.'

'Yes, you have.'

And so, Lord Emsworth discovered as he met her eye, he had. It often happened that way after he and Connie had talked a thing over. But he was not pleased about it.

'But, Connie, dash it all —'

'We will not discuss it any more, Clarence.'

Her eye played upon him. Then she moved to the door and was gone. Alone at last, Lord Emsworth took up his Whiffle on *The Care Of The Pig* in the hope that it might, as had happened before, bring calm to the troubled spirit. It did, and he was absorbed in it when the door opened once more.

His niece Jane stood on the threshold.

Lord Emsworth's niece was the third prettiest girl in Shropshire. In her general appearance she resembled a dewy rose, and it might have been thought that Lord Emsworth, who yielded to none in his appreciation of roses, would have felt his heart leap up at the sight of her.

This was not the case. His heart did leap, but not up. He was a man with certain definite views about roses. He preferred them without quite such tight lips and determined chins. And he did not like them to look at him as if he were something slimy and horrible which they had found under a flat stone.

The wretched man was now fully conscious of his position. Under the magic spell of Whiffle he had been able to thrust from his mind for a while the thought of what Jane was going to say when she heard the bad news; but now, as she started to advance slowly into the room in that sinister, purposeful way characteristic of so many of his female relations, he realized what he was in for, and his soul shrank into itself like a salted snail.

Jane, he could not but remember, was the daughter of his sister Charlotte, and many good judges considered Lady Charlotte a tougher egg even than Lady Constance, or her younger sister, Lady Julia. He still quivered at some of the things Charlotte had said to him in her time; and, eyeing Jane apprehensively, he saw no reason for supposing that she had not inherited quite a good deal of the maternal fire.

The girl came straight to the point. Her mother, Lord Emsworth recalled, had always done the same.

'I should like an explanation, Uncle Clarence.'

Lord Emsworth cleared his throat unhappily.

'Explanation, my dear?'

'Explanation was what I said.'

'Oh, explanation? Ah, yes. Er – what about?'

'You know jolly well what about. That agent job. Aunt Constance says you've changed your mind. Have you?'

'Er . . . Ah . . . Well . . .'

'Have you?'

'Ah . . . Well . . . Er . . .'

'Have you?'

'Well . . . Er . . . Ah . . . Yes.'

'Worm!' said Jane. 'Miserable, crawling, cringing, gelatine-backboned worm!'

Lord Emsworth, though he had been expecting something along these lines, quivered as if he had been harpooned.

'That,' he said, attempting a dignity which he was far from feeling, 'is not a very nice thing to say . . .'

'If you only knew the things I would like to say! I'm holding myself in. So you've changed your mind, have you? Ha! Does a sacred promise mean nothing to you, Uncle Clarence? Does a girl's whole life's happiness mean nothing to you? I never would have believed that you could have been such a blighter.'

'I am not a blighter.'

'Yes, you are. You're a life-blighter. You're trying to blight my life. Well, you aren't going to do it. Whatever happens, I mean to marry George.'

Lord Emsworth was genuinely surprised.

'Marry George? But Connie told me you were in love with this fellow you met in Devonshire.'

'His name is George Abercrombie.'

'Oh, ah?' said Lord Emsworth, enlightened. 'Bless my soul, I thought you meant my grandson, George, and it puzzled me. Because you couldn't marry him, of course. He's your brother or cousin or something. Besides, he's too young for you. What would George be? Ten? Eleven?'

He broke off. A reproachful look had hit him like a shell.

'Uncle Clarence!'

'My dear?'

'Is this a time for drivelling?'

'My dear!'

'Well, is it? Look in your heart and ask yourself. Here I am, with everybody spitting on their hands and dashing about trying to ruin my life's whole happiness, and instead of being kind and understanding and sympathetic you start talking rot about young George.'

'I was only saying –'

'I heard what you were saying, and it made me sick. You really must be the most callous man that ever lived. I can't understand you of all people behaving like this, Uncle Clarence. I always thought you were fond of me.'

'I am fond of you.'

'It doesn't look like it. Flinging yourself into this foul conspiracy to wreck my life.'

Lord Emsworth remembered a good one.

'I have your best interests at heart, my dear.'

It did not go very well. A distinct sheet of flame shot from the girl's eyes.

'What do you mean, my best interests? The way Aunt Constance talks, and the way you are backing her up, anyone would think that George was someone in a straw hat and a scarlet cummerbund that I'd picked up on the pier at Blackpool. The Abercrombies are one of the oldest families in Devonshire. They date back to the Conquest, and they practically ran the Crusades. When your ancestors were staying at home on the plea of war work of national importance and wangling jobs at the base, the Abercrombies were out fighting the Paynim.'

'I was at school with a boy named Abercrombie,' said Lord Emsworth musingly.

'I hope he kicked you. No, no, I don't mean that. I'm sorry. The one thing I'm trying to do is to keep this little talk free of – what's the word?'

Lord Emsworth said he did not know.

'Acrimony. I want to be calm and cool and sensible. Honestly, Uncle Clarence, you would love George. You'll be a sap if you give him the bird without seeing him. He's the most wonderful man on earth. He got into the last eight at Wimbledon this year.'

'Did he, indeed? Last eight what?'

'And there isn't anything he doesn't know about running an estate. The very first thing he said when he came into the park was that a lot of the timber wanted seeing to badly.'

'Blast his impertinence,' said Lord Emsworth warmly. 'My timber is in excellent condition.'

'Not if George says it isn't. George knows timber.'

'So do I know timber.'

'Not so well as George does. But never mind about that. Let's get back to this loathsome plot to ruin my life's whole happiness. Why can't you be a sport, Uncle Clarence, and stand up for me? Can't you understand what this means to me? Weren't you ever in love?'

'Certainly I was in love. Dozens of times. I'll tell you a very funny story –'

'I don't want to hear funny stories.'

'No, no. Quite. Exactly.'

'All I want is to hear you saying that you will give George Mr Simmons's job, so that we can get married.'

'But your aunt seems to feel so strongly –'

'I know what she feels strongly. She wants me to marry that ass Roegate.'

'Does she?'

'Yes, and I'm not going to. You can tell her from me that I wouldn't marry Bertie Roegate if he were the only man in the world –'

'There's a song of that name,' said Lord Emsworth, interested. 'They sang it during the War. No, it wasn't "man". It was "girl". "If you were the only . . ." How did it go? Ah, yes. "If you were the only girl in the world and I was the only boy . . ."'

'Uncle Clarence!'

'My dear?'

'Please don't sing. You're not in the tap-room of the Emsworth Arms now.'

'I have never been in the tap-room of the Emsworth Arms.'

'Or at a smoking-concert. Really, you seem to have the most extraordinary idea of the sort of attitude that's fitting when you're talking to a girl whose life's happiness everybody is sprinting about trying to ruin. First you talk about young George, then you start trying to tell funny stories, and now you sing comic songs.'

'It wasn't a comic song.'

'It was, the way you sang it. Well?'

'Eh?'

'Have you decided what you are going to do about this?'

'About what?'

The girl was silent for a moment, during which moment she looked so like her mother that Lord Emsworth shuddered.

'Uncle Clarence,' she said in a low, trembling voice, 'you are not going to pretend that you don't know what we've been talking about all this time? Are you or are you not going to give George that job?'

'Well —'

'Well?'

'Well —'

'We can't stay here for ever, saying "Well" at one another. Are you or are you not?'

'My dear, I don't see how I can. Your aunt seems to feel so very strongly . . .'

He spoke, mumbling, avoiding his companion's eye, and he had paused, searching for words, when from the drive outside there arose a sudden babble of noise. Raised voices were proceeding from the great open spaces. He recognized his sister Constance's penetrating soprano, and mingling with it his grandson George's treble 'Coo'. Competing with both, there came the throaty baritone of Rupert Baxter. Delighted with the opportunity of changing the subject, he hurried to the window.

'Bless my soul! What's all that?'

The battle, whatever it may have been about, had apparently rolled away in some unknown direction, for he could see nothing from the window but Rupert Baxter, who was smoking a cigarette in what seemed a rather overwrought manner. He turned back, and with infinite relief discovered that he was alone. His niece had disappeared. He took up Whiffle on *The Care Of The Pig* and had just started to savour once more the perfect prose of that chapter about swill and bran-mash, when the door opened. Jane was back. She stood on the threshold, eyeing her uncle coldly.

'Reading, Uncle Clarence?'

'Eh? Oh, ah, yes. I was just glancing at Whiffle on *The Care Of The Pig*!'

'So you actually have the heart to read at a time like this? Well, well! Do you ever read Western novels, Uncle Clarence?'

'Eh? Western novels? No. No, never.'

'I'm sorry. I was reading one the other day, and I hoped that you might be able to explain something that puzzled me. What one cowboy said to another cowboy.'

'Oh, yes?'

'This cowboy – the first cowboy – said to the other cowboy – the second cowboy – "Gol dern ye, Hank Spivis, for a sneaking, ornery, low-down, double-crossing, hornswoggling skunk." Can you tell me what a sneaking, ornery, low-down, double-crossing, hornswoggling skunk is, Uncle Clarence?'

'I'm afraid I can't, my dear.'

'I thought you might know.'

'No.'

'Oh.'

She passed from the room, and Lord Emsworth resumed his Whiffle.

But it was not long before the volume was resting on his knee while he stared before him with a sombre gaze. He was reviewing the recent scene and wishing that he had come better out of it. He was a vague man, but not so vague as to be unaware that he might have shown up in a more heroic light.

How long he sat brooding, he could not have said. Some little time, undoubtedly, for the shadows on the terrace had, he observed as he glanced out of the window, lengthened quite a good deal since he had seen them last. He was about to rise and seek consolation from a ramble among the flowers in the garden below, when the door opened – it seemed to Lord Emsworth, who was now feeling a little morbid, that that blasted door had never stopped opening since he had come to the library to be alone – and Beach, the butler, entered.

He was carrying an airgun in one hand and in the other a silver salver with a box of ammunition on it.

Beach was a man who invested all his actions with something of the impressiveness of a high priest conducting an intricate service at some romantic altar. It is not easy to be impressive when you are carrying an airgun in one hand and a silver salver with a box of ammunition on it in the other, but Beach managed it. Many butlers in such a position would have looked like sportsmen setting out for a day with the birds, but Beach still looked like a high priest. He advanced to the table at Lord Emsworth's side and laid his cargo upon it as if the gun and the box of ammunition had been a smoked offering and his lordship a tribal god.

Lord Emsworth eyed his faithful servitor sourly. His manner was that of a tribal god who considers the smoked offering not up to sample.

'What the devil's all this?'

'It is an airgun, m'lord.'

'I can see that, dash it. What are you bringing it here for?'

'Her ladyship instructed me to convey it to your lordship – I gathered for safe keeping, m'lord. The weapon was until recently the property of Master George.'

'Why the dooce are they taking his airgun away from the poor boy?' demanded Lord Emsworth hotly. Ever since the lad had called Rupert Baxter a blister he had been feeling a strong affection for his grandson.

'Her ladyship did not confide in me on that point, m'lord. I was merely instructed to convey the weapon to your lordship.'

At this moment, Lady Constance came sailing in to throw light on the mystery.

'Ah, I see Beach has brought it to you. I want you to lock that gun up somewhere, Clarence. George is not to be allowed to have it any more.'

'Why not?'

'Because he is not to be trusted with it. Do you know what happened? He shot Mr Baxter!'

'What!'

'Yes. Out on the drive just now. I noticed that the boy's manner was sullen when I introduced him to Mr Baxter, and said that he was going to be his tutor. He disappeared into the shrubbery, and just now, as Mr Baxter was standing on the drive, George shot him from behind a bush.'

'Good!' cried Lord Emsworth, then prudently added the word 'gracious'.

There was a pause. Lord Emsworth took up the gun and handled it curiously.

'Bang!' he said, pointing it at a bust of Aristotle which stood on a bracket by the book-shelves.

'Please don't wave the thing about like that, Clarence. It may be loaded.'

'Not if George has just shot Baxter with it. No,' said Lord Emsworth, pulling the trigger, 'it's not loaded.' He mused awhile. An odd, nostalgic feeling was creeping over him. Far-off memories of his boyhood had begun to stir within him. 'Bless my soul,' he said. 'I haven't had one of these things in my hand since I was a child. Did you ever have one of these things, Beach?'

'Yes, m'lord, when a small lad.'

'Bless my soul, I remember my sister Julia borrowing mine to shoot her governess. You remember Julia shooting the governess, Connie?'

'Don't be absurd, Clarence.'

'It's not absurd. She did shoot her. Fortunately women wore bustles in those days. Beach, don't you remember my sister Julia shooting the governess?'

'The incident would, no doubt, have occurred before my arrival at the castle, m'lord.'

'That will do, Beach,' said Lady Constance. 'I do wish, Clarence,' she continued as the door closed, 'that you would not say that sort of thing in front of Beach.'

'Julia did shoot the governess.'

'If she did, there is no need to make your butler a confidant.'

'Now, what was that governess's name? I have an idea it began with –'

'Never mind what her name was or what it began with. Tell me about Jane. I saw her coming out of the library. Had you been speaking to her?'

'Yes. Oh, yes. I spoke to her.'

'I hope you were firm.'

'Oh, very firm. I said "Jane . . ." But listen, Connie, damn it, aren't we being a little hard on the girl? One doesn't want to ruin her whole life's happiness, dash it.'

'I knew she would get round you. But you are not to give way an inch.'

'But this fellow seems to be a most suitable fellow. One of the Abercrombies and all that. Did well in the Crusades.'

'I am not going to have my niece throwing herself away on a man without a penny.'

'She isn't going to marry Roegate, you know. Nothing will induce her. She said she wouldn't marry Roegate if she were the only girl in the world and he was the only boy.'

'I don't care what she said. And I don't want to discuss the matter any longer. I am now going to send George in, for you to give him a good talking-to.'

'I haven't time.'

'You have time.'

'I haven't. I'm going to look at my flowers.'

'You are not. You are going to talk to George. I want you to make him see quite clearly what a wicked thing he has done. Mr Baxter was furious.'

'It all comes back to me,' cried Lord Emsworth, 'Mapleton!'

'What *are* you talking about?'

'Her name was Mapleton. Julia's governess.'

'Do stop about Julia's governess. Will you talk to George?'

'Oh, all right, all right.'

'Good. I'll go and send him to you.'

And presently George entered. For a boy who had just stained the escutcheon of a proud family by shooting tutors with airguns, he seemed remarkably cheerful. His manner was that of one getting together with an old crony for a cosy chat.

'Hullo, grandpapa,' he said breezily.

'Hullo, my boy,' replied Lord Emsworth, with equal affability.

'Aunt Connie said you wanted to see me.'

'Eh? Ah! Oh! Yes.' Lord Emsworth pulled himself together. 'Yes, that's right. Yes, to be sure. Certainly I want to see you. What's all this, my boy, eh? Eh, what? What's all this?'

THE CRIME WAVE AT BLANDINGS

'What's all what, grandpapa?'

'Shooting people and all that sort of thing. Shooting Baxter and all that sort of thing. Mustn't do that, you know. Can't have that. It's very wrong and – er – very dangerous to shoot at people with a dashed great gun. Don't you know that, hey? Might put their eye out, dash it.'

'Oh, I couldn't have hit him in the eye, grandpapa. His back was turned and he was bending over, tying his shoelace.'

Lord Emsworth started.

'What! Did you get Baxter in the seat of the trousers?'

'Yes, grandpapa.'

'Ha, ha . . . I mean, disgraceful . . . I – er – I expect he jumped?'

'Oh, yes, grandpapa. He jumped like billy-o.'

'Did he, indeed? How this reminds me of Julia's governess. Your Aunt Julia once shot her governess under precisely similar conditions. She was tying her shoelace.'

'Coo! Did *she* jump?'

'She certainly did, my boy.'

'Ha, ha!'

'Ha, ha!'

'Ha, ha!'

'Ha, h – . . . Ah . . . Er – well, just so,' said Lord Emsworth, a belated doubt assailing him as to whether this was quite the tone. 'Well, George, I shall of course impound this – er – instrument.'

'Right ho, grandpapa,' said George, with the easy amiability of a boy conscious of having two catapults in his drawer upstairs.

'Can't have you going about the place shooting people.'

'Okay, Chief.'

Lord Emsworth fondled the gun. That nostalgic feeling was growing.

'Do you know, young man, I used to have one of these things when I was a boy.'

'Coo! Were guns invented then?'

'Yes, I had one when I was your age.'

'Ever hit anything, grandpapa?'

Lord Emsworth drew himself up a little haughtily.

'Certainly I did. I hit all sorts of things. Rats and things. I had a very accurate aim. But now I wouldn't even know how to load the dashed affair.'

'This is how you load it, grandpapa. You open it like this and shove the slug in here and snap it together again like that and there you are.'

'Indeed? Really? I see. Yes. Yes, of course, I remember now.'

'You can't kill anything much with it,' said George, with a wistfulness which betrayed an aspiration to higher things. 'Still, it's awfully useful for tickling up cows.'

'And Baxter.'

'Yes.'

'Ha, ha!'

'Ha, ha!'

Once more, Lord Emsworth forced himself to concentrate on the right tone.

'We mustn't laugh about it, my boy. It's no joking matter. It's very wrong to shoot Mr Baxter.'

'But he's a blister.'

'He is a blister,' agreed Lord Emsworth, always fair-minded. 'Nevertheless. . . . Remember, he is your tutor.'

'Well, I don't see why I've got to have a tutor right in the middle of the summer holidays. I sweat like the dickens all through the term at school,' said George, his voice vibrant with self-pity, 'and then plumb spank in the middle of the holidays they slosh a tutor on me. I call it a bit thick.'

Lord Emsworth might have told the little fellow that thicker things than that were going on in Blandings Castle, but he refrained. He dismissed him with a kindly, sympathetic smile and resumed his fondling of the airgun.

Like so many men advancing into the sere and yellow of life, Lord Emsworth had an eccentric memory. It was not to be trusted an inch as far as the events of yesterday or the day before were concerned. Even in the small matter of assisting him to find a hat which he had laid down somewhere five minutes ago it was nearly always useless. But by way of compensation for this it was a perfect encyclopaedia on the remote past. It rendered his boyhood an open book to him.

Lord Emsworth mused on his boyhood. Happy days, happy days. He could recall the exact uncle who had given him the weapon, so similar to this one, with which Julia had shot her governess. He could recall brave, windswept mornings when he had gone prowling through the stable yard in the hope of getting a rat – and many a fine head had he secured. Odd that the passage of time should remove the desire to go and pop at things with an airgun. . . .

Or did it?

With a curious thrill that set his pince-nez rocking gently on his nose, Lord Emsworth suddenly became aware that it did not. All that the passage of time did was to remove the desire to pop temporarily – say for forty years or so. Dormant for a short while – we'll call it fifty years – that desire, he perceived, still lurked unquenched. Little by little it began to stir within him now. Slowly but surely, as he sat there fondling the gun, he was once more becoming a potential popper.

At this point, the gun suddenly went off and broke the bust of Aristotle.

It was enough. The old killer instinct had awakened. Reloading with the swift efficiency of some hunter of the woods, Lord Emsworth went to the window. He was a little uncertain as to what he intended to do when he got there, except that he had a clear determination to loose off at something. There flitted into his mind what his grandson George had said about tickling up cows, and this served to some extent to crystallize his aims. True, cows were not plentiful on the terrace of Blandings Castle. Still, one might have wandered there. You never knew with cows.

There were no cows. Only Rupert Baxter. The ex-secretary was in the act of throwing away a cigarette.

Most men are careless in the matter of throwing away cigarettes. The world is their ashtray. But Rupert Baxter had a tidy soul. He allowed the thing to fall to the ground like any ordinary young man, it is true, but immediately he had done so his better self awakened. He stooped to pick up the object that disfigured the smooth flagged stones, and the invitation of that beckoning trousers' seat would have been too powerful for a stronger man than Lord Emsworth to resist.

He pulled the trigger, and Rupert Baxter sprang into the air with a sharp cry. Lord Emsworth reseated himself and took up Whiffle on *The Care Of The Pig*.

Everyone is interested nowadays in the psychology of the criminal. The chronicler, therefore, feels that he runs no risk of losing his grip on the reader if he pauses at this point to examine and analyse the workings of Lord Emsworth's mind after the perpetration of the black act which has just been recorded.

At first, then, all that he felt as he sat turning the pages of his Whiffle was a sort of soft warm glow, a kind of tremulous joy such as he might have experienced if he had just been receiving the thanks of the nation for some great public service.

It was not merely the fact that he had caused his late employee to skip like the high hills that induced this glow. What pleased him so particularly was that it had been such a magnificent shot. He was a sensitive man, and though in his conversation with his grandson George he had tried to wear the mask, he had not been able completely to hide his annoyance at the boy's careless assumption that in his airgun days he had been an indifferent marksman.

'Did you ever hit anything, grandpapa?' Boys say these things with no wish to wound, but nevertheless they pierce the armour. 'Did you ever hit anything, grandpapa?' forsooth! He would have liked to see George stop putting finger to trigger for forty-seven years and then, first crack out of the box, pick off a medium-sized secretary at a distance like that! In rather a bad light, too.

But after he had sat for a while, silently glowing, his mood underwent a change. A gunman's complacency after getting his man can never remain for long an unmixed complacency. Sooner or later there creeps in the thought of Retribution. It did with Lord Emsworth. Quite suddenly, whispering in his ear, he heard the voice of Conscience say:

'What if your sister Constance learns of this?'

A moment before this voice spoke, Lord Emsworth had been smirking. He now congealed, and the smile passed from his lips like breath off a razor blade, to be succeeded by a tense look of anxiety and alarm.

Nor was this alarm unjustified. When he reflected how scathing and terrible his sister Constance could be when he committed even so venial a misdemeanour as coming down to dinner with a brass paper-fastener in his shirt front instead of the more conventional stud, his imagination boggled at the thought of what she would do in a case like this. He was appalled. Whiffle on *The Care Of The Pig* fell from his nerveless hand, and he sat looking like a dying duck. And Lady Constance, who now entered, noted the expression and was curious as to its cause.

'What is the matter, Clarence?'

'Matter?'

'Why are you looking like a dying duck?'

'I am not looking like a dying duck,' retorted Lord Emsworth with what spirit he could muster.

'Well,' said Lady Constance, waiving the point, 'have you spoken to George?'

'Certainly. Yes, of course I've spoken to George. He was in here just now and I – er – spoke to him.'

'What did you say?'

'I said' – Lord Emsworth wanted to make this very clear – 'I said that I wouldn't even know how to load one of those things.'

'Didn't you give him a good talking-to?'

'Of course I did. A very good talking-to. I said "Er – George, you know how to load those things and I don't, but that's no reason why you should go about shooting Baxter."'

'Was that all you said?'

'No. That was just how I began. I –'

Lord Emsworth paused. He could not have finished the sentence if large rewards had been offered to him to do so. For, as he spoke, Rupert Baxter appeared in the doorway, and he shrank back in his chair like some Big Shot cornered by G-men.

The secretary came forward limping slightly. His eyes behind their spectacles were wild and his manner emotional. Lady Constance gazed at him wonderingly.

'Is something the matter, Mr Baxter?'

'Matter?' Rupert Baxter's voice was taut and he quivered in every limb. He had lost his customary suavity and was plainly in no frame of mind to mince his words. 'Matter? Do you know what has happened? That infernal boy has shot me *again*!'

'What!'

'Only a few minutes ago. Out on the terrace.'

Lord Emsworth shook off his palsy.

'I expect you imagined it,' he said.

'Imagined it!' Rupert Baxter shook from spectacles to shoes. 'I tell you I was on the terrace, stooping to pick up my cigarette, when something hit me on the . . . something hit me.'

'Probably a wasp,' said Lord Emsworth. 'They are very plentiful this year. I wonder,' he said chattily, 'if either of you are aware that wasps serve a very useful purpose. They keep down the leather-jackets, which, as you know, inflict serious injury upon –'

Lady Constance's concern became mixed with perplexity.

'But it could not have been George, Mr Baxter. The moment you told me of what he had done, I confiscated his airgun. Look, there it is on the table now.'

'Right there on the table,' said Lord Emsworth, pointing helpfully. 'If you come over here, you can see it clearly. Must have been a wasp.'

'You have not left the room, Clarence?'

'No. Been here all the time.'

'Then it would have been impossible for George to have shot you, Mr Baxter.'

'Quite,' said Lord Emsworth. 'A wasp, undoubtedly. Unless, as I say, you imagined the whole thing.'

The secretary stiffened.

'I am not subject to hallucinations, Lord Emsworth.'

'But you are, my dear fellow. I expect it comes from exerting your brain too much. You're always getting them.'

'Clarence!'

'Well, he is. You know that as well as I do. Look at that time he went grubbing about in a lot of flower-pots because he thought you had put your necklace there.'

'I did not –'

'You did, my dear fellow. I dare say you've forgotten it, but you did. And then, for some reason best known to yourself, you threw the flower-pots at me through my bedroom window.'

Baxter turned to Lady Constance, flushing darkly. The episode to which his former employer had alluded was one of which he never cared to be reminded.

'Lord Emsworth is referring to the occasion when your diamond necklace was stolen, Lady Constance. I was led to believe that the thief had hidden it in a flower-pot.'

'Of course, Mr Baxter.'

'Well, have it your own way,' said Lord Emsworth agreeably. 'But bless my soul, I shall never forget waking up and finding all those flower-pots pouring in through the window and then looking out and seeing Baxter on the lawn in lemon-coloured pyjamas with a wild glare in his –'

'Clarence!'

'Oh, all right. I merely mentioned it. Hallucinations – he gets them all the time,' he said stoutly, though in an undertone.

Lady Constance was cooing to the secretary like a mother to her child.

'It really is impossible that George should have done this, Mr Baxter. The gun has never left this –'

She broke off. Her handsome face seemed to turn suddenly to stone. When she spoke again the coo had gone out of her voice and it had become metallic.

'Clarence!'

'My dear?'

Lady Constance drew in her breath sharply.

'Mr Baxter, I wonder if you would mind leaving us for a moment. I wish to speak to Lord Emsworth.'

The closing of the door was followed by a silence, followed in its turn by an odd, whining noise like gas escaping from a pipe. It was Lord Emsworth trying to hum carelessly.

'Clarence!'

'Yes? Yes, my dear?'

The stoniness of Lady Constance's expression had become more marked with each succeeding moment. What had caused it in the first place was the recollection, coming to her like a flash, that when she had entered this room she had found her brother looking like a dying duck. Honest men, she felt, do not look like dying ducks. The only man whom an impartial observer could possibly mistake for one of these birds *in extremis* is the man with crime upon his soul.

'Clarence, was it you who shot Mr Baxter?'

Fortunately there had been that in her manner which led Lord Emsworth to expect the question. He was ready for it.

'Me? Who, me? Shoot Baxter? What the dooce would I want to shoot Baxter for?'

'We can go into your motives later. What I am asking you now is – Did you?'

'Of course I didn't.'

'The gun has not left the room.'

'Shoot Baxter, indeed! Never heard anything so dashed absurd in my life.'

'And you have been here all the time.'

'Well, what of it? Suppose I have? Suppose I had wanted to shoot Baxter? Suppose every fibre in my being had egged me on, dash it, to shoot the feller? How could I have done it, not even knowing how to load the contrivance?'

'You used to know how to load an airgun.'

'I used to know a lot of things.'

'It's quite easy to load an airgun. I could do it myself.'

'Well, I didn't.'

'Then how do you account for the fact that Mr Baxter was shot by an airgun which had never left the room you were in?'

Lord Emsworth raised pleading hands to heaven.

'How do you know he was shot with this airgun? God bless my soul, the way women jump to conclusions is enough to ... How do you know there wasn't another airgun? How do you know the place isn't bristling with airguns? How do you know Beach hasn't an airgun? Or anybody?'

'I scarcely imagine that Beach would shoot Mr Baxter.'

'How do you know he wouldn't? He used to have an airgun when he was a small lad. He said so. I'd watch the man closely.'

'Please don't be ridiculous, Clarence.'

'I'm not being half as ridiculous as you are. Saying I shoot people with airguns. Why should I shoot people with airguns? And how do you suppose I could have potted Baxter at that distance?'

'What distance?'

'He was standing on the terrace, wasn't he? He specifically stated that he was standing on the terrace. And I was up here. It would take a most expert marksman to pot the fellow at a distance like that. Who do you think I am? One of those chaps who shoot apples off their sons' heads?'

The reasoning was undeniably specious. It shook Lady Constance. She frowned undecidedly.

'Well, it's very strange that Mr Baxter should be so convinced that he was shot.'

'Nothing strange about it at all. There wouldn't be anything strange if Baxter was convinced that he was a turnip and had been bitten by a white rabbit with pink eyes. You know perfectly well, though you won't admit it, that the fellow's a raving lunatic.'

'Clarence!'

'It's no good saying "Clarence". The fellow's potty to the core, and always has been. Haven't I seen him on the lawn at five o'clock in the morning in lemon-coloured pyjamas, throwing flower-pots in at my window? Pooh! Obviously, the whole thing is the outcome of the man's diseased imagination. Shot, indeed! Never heard such nonsense. And now,' said Lord Emsworth, rising firmly, 'I'm going out to have a look at my roses. I came to this room to enjoy a little quiet reading and meditation, and ever since I got here there's been a constant stream of people in and out, telling me they're going to marry men named Abercrombie and saying they've been shot and saying I shot them and so on and so forth . . . Bless my soul, one might as well try to read and meditate in the middle of Piccadilly Circus. Tchah!' said Lord Emsworth, who had now got near enough to the door to feel safe in uttering this unpleasant exclamation. 'Tchah!' he said, and adding 'Pah!' for good measure made a quick exit.

But even now his troubled spirit was not to know peace. To reach the great outdoors at Blandings Castle, if you start from the library and come down the main staircase, you have to pass through the hall. To the left of this hall there is a small writing-room. And outside this writing-room Lord Emsworth's niece Jane was standing.

'Yoo-hoo,' she cried. 'Uncle Clarence.'

Lord Emsworth was in no mood for yoo-hooing nieces. George Abercrombie might enjoy chatting with this girl. So might Herbert, Lord Roegate. But he wanted solitude. In the course of the afternoon he had had so much female society thrust upon him that if Helen of Troy had appeared in the doorway of the writing-room and yoo-hooed at him, he would merely have accelerated his pace.

He accelerated it now.

'Can't stop, my dear, can't stop.'

'Oh, yes you can, old Sure-shot,' said Jane, and Lord Emsworth found that he could. He stopped so abruptly that he nearly dislocated his spine. His jaw had fallen and his pince-nez were dancing on their string like leaves in the wind.

'Two-Gun Thomas, the Marksman of the Prairie – He never misses. Kindly step this way, Uncle Clarence,' said Jane, 'I would like a word with you.'

Lord Emsworth stepped that way. He followed the girl into the writing-room and closed the door carefully behind him.

'You – you didn't see me?' he quavered.

'I certainly did see you,' said Jane. 'I was an interested eye-witness of the whole thing from start to finish.'

Lord Emsworth tottered to a chair and sank into it, staring glassily at his niece. Any Chicago business man of the modern school would have understood what he was feeling and would have sympathized with him.

The thing that poisons life for gunmen and sometimes makes them wonder moodily if it is worthwhile going on is this tendency of the outside public to butt in at inconvenient moments. Whenever you settle some business dispute with a commercial competitor by means of your sub-machine gun, it always turns out that there was some officious witness passing at the time, and there you are, with a new problem confronting you.

And Lord Emsworth was in worse case than his spiritual brother of Chicago would have been, for the latter could always have solved his perplexities by rubbing out the witness. To him this melancholy pleasure was denied. A prominent Shropshire landowner, with a position to keep up in the county, cannot rub out his nieces. All he can do, when they reveal that they have seen him wallowing in crime, is to stare glassily at them.

'I had a front seat for the entire performance,' proceeded Jane. 'When I left you, I went into the shrubbery to cry my eyes out because of your frightful cruelty and inhumanity. And while I was crying my eyes out, I suddenly saw you creep to the window of the library with a hideous look of low cunning on your face and young George's airgun in your hand. And I was just wondering if I couldn't find a stone and bung it at you, because it seemed to me that something along those lines was what you had been asking for from the start, when you raised the gun and I saw that you were taking aim. The next moment there was a shot, a cry, and Baxter weltering in his blood on the terrace. And as I stood there, a thought floated into my mind. It was – What will Aunt Constance have to say about this when I tell her?'

Lord Emsworth emitted a low, gargling sound, like the death rattle of that dying duck to which his sister had compared him.

'You – you aren't going to tell her?'

'Why not?'

An ague-like convulsion shook Lord Emsworth.

'I implore you not to tell her, my dear. You know what she's like. I should never hear the end of it.'

'She would give you the devil, you think?'

'I do.'

'So do I. And you thoroughly deserve it.'

'My dear!'

'Well, don't you? Look at the way you've been behaving. Working like a beaver to ruin my life's happiness.'

'I don't want to ruin your life's happiness.'

'You don't? Then sit down at this desk and dash off a short letter to George, giving him that job.'

'But –'

'What did you say?'

'I only said, "But –"'

'Don't say it again. What I want from you, Uncle Clarence, is prompt and cheerful service. Are you ready? "Dear Mr Abercrombie . . ."'

'I don't know how to spell it,' said Lord Emsworth, with the air of a man who has found a way out satisfactory to all parties.

'I'll attend to the spelling. A-b, ab; e-r, er; c-r-o-m, crom; b-i-e, bie. The whole constituting the word "Abercrombie", which is the name of the man I love. Got it?'

'Yes,' said Lord Emsworth sepulchrally. 'I've got it.'

'Then carry on. "Dear Mr Abercrombie. Pursuant" – one p, two u's – spread 'em about a bit, an r and s, and an ant – "Pursuant on our recent conversation –"'

'But I've never spoken to the man in my life.'

'It doesn't matter. It's just a form. "Pursuant on our recent conversation, I have much pleasure in offering you the post of land-agent at Blandings Castle, and shall be glad if you will take up your duties immediately. Yours faithfully, Emsworth." E-m-s-w-o-r-t-h.'

Jane took the letter, pressed it lovingly on the blotting-pad and placed it in the recesses of her costume. 'Fine,' she said. 'That's that. Thanks awfully, Uncle Clarence. This has squared you nicely for your recent foul behaviour in trying to ruin my life's happiness. You made a rocky start, but you've come through magnificently at the finish.'

Kissing him affectionately, she passed from the room, and Lord Emsworth, slumped in his chair, tried not to look at the vision of his sister Constance which was rising before his eyes. What Connie was going to say when she learned that in defiance of her direct commands he had given this young man . . .

He mused on Lady Constance, and wondered if there were any other men in the world so sister-pecked as he. It was weak of him, he knew, to curl up into an apologetic ball when assailed by a mere sister. Most men reserved such craven conduct for their wives. But it had always been so, right back to those boyhood days which he remembered so well. And too late to alter it now, he supposed.

The only consolation he was able to enjoy in this dark hour was the

reflection that, though things were bad, they were unquestionably less
bad than they might have been. At the least, his fearful secret was safe.
That rash moment of recovered boyhood would never now be brought
up against him. Connie would never know whose hand it was that had
pulled the fatal trigger. She might suspect, but she could never know.
Nor could Baxter ever know. Baxter would grow into an old, white-
haired, spectacled pantaloon, and always this thing would remain an
insoluble mystery to him.

Dashed lucky, felt Lord Emsworth, that the fellow had not been
listening at the door during the recent conversation . . .

It was at this moment that a sound behind him caused him to turn
and, having turned, to spring from his chair with a convulsive leap
that nearly injured him internally. Over the sill of the open window,
like those of a corpse emerging from the tomb to confront its murderer,
the head and shoulders of Rupert Baxter were slowly rising. The
evening sun fell upon his spectacles, and they seemed to Lord
Emsworth to gleam like the eyes of a dragon.

Rupert Baxter had not been listening at the door. There had been no
necessity for him to do so. Immediately outside the writing-room
window at Blandings Castle there stands a rustic garden seat, and on
this he had been sitting from beginning to end of the interview which
has just been recorded. If he had been actually in the room, he might
have heard a little better, but not much.

When two men stand face to face, one of whom has recently shot the
other with an airgun and the second of whom has just discovered who
it was that did it, it is rarely that conversation flows briskly from the
start. One senses a certain awkwardness – what the French call *gêne*. In
the first half-minute of this encounter the only thing that happened in
a vocal way was that Lord Emsworth cleared his throat, immediately
afterwards becoming silent again. And it is possible that his silence
might have prolonged itself for some considerable time, had not
Baxter made a movement as if about to withdraw. All this while he
had been staring at his former employer, his face an open book in
which it was easy for the least discerning eye to read a number of
disconcerting emotions. He now took a step backwards, and Lord
Emsworth's aphasia left him.

'Baxter!'

There was urgent appeal in the ninth Earl's voice. It was not often that he wanted Rupert Baxter to stop and talk to him, but he was most earnestly desirous of detaining him now. He wished to soothe, to apologize, to explain. He was even prepared, should it be necessary, to offer the man his old post of private secretary as the price of his silence.

'Baxter! My dear fellow!'

A high tenor voice, raised almost to A in Alt by agony of soul, has a compelling quality which it is difficult even for a man in Rupert Baxter's mental condition to resist. Rupert Baxter had not intended to halt his backward movement, but he did so, and Lord Emsworth, reaching the window and thrusting his head out, was relieved to see that he was still within range of the honeyed word.

'Er – Baxter,' he said, 'could you spare me a moment?'

The secretary's spectacles flashed coldly.

'You wish to speak to me, Lord Emsworth?'

'That's exactly it,' assented his lordship, as if he thought it a very happy way of putting the thing. 'Yes, I wish to speak to you.' He paused, and cleared his throat again. 'Tell me, Baxter – tell me, my dear fellow – were you – er – were you sitting on that seat just now?'

'I was.'

'Did you, by any chance, overhear my niece and myself talking?'

'I did.'

'Then I expect – I fancy – perhaps – possibly – no doubt you were surprised at what you heard?'

'I was astounded,' said Rupert Baxter, who was not going to be fobbed off with any weak verbs at a moment like this.

Lord Emsworth cleared his throat for the third time.

'I want to tell you all about that,' he said.

'Oh?' said Rupert Baxter.

'Yes. I – ah – welcome this opportunity of telling you all about it,' said Lord Emsworth, though with less pleasure in his voice than might have been expected from a man welcoming an opportunity of telling somebody all about something. 'I fancy that my niece's remarks may – er – possibly have misled you.'

'Not at all.'

'They may have put you on the wrong track.'

'On the contrary.'

'But, if I remember correctly, she gave the impression – by what she said – my niece gave the impression by what she said – anybody

overhearing what my niece said would have received the impression
that I took deliberate aim at you with the gun.'

'Precisely.'

'She was quite mistaken,' said Lord Emsworth warmly. 'She has got
hold of the wrong end of the stick completely. Girls say such dashed
silly things . . . cause a lot of trouble . . . upset people. They ought to
be more careful. What actually happened, my dear fellow, was that I
was glancing out of the library window . . . with the gun in my hand
. . . and without knowing it I must have placed my finger on the
trigger . . . for suddenly . . . without the slightest warning . . . you
could have knocked me down with a feather . . . the dashed thing went
off. By accident.'

'Indeed?'

'Purely by accident. I should not like you to think that I was aiming
at you.'

'Indeed?'

'And I should not like you to tell – er – anybody about the
unfortunate occurrence in a way that would give her . . . I mean them
. . . the impression that I aimed at you.'

'Indeed?'

Lord Emsworth could not persuade himself that his companion's
manner was encouraging. He had a feeling that he was not making head-
way.

'That's how it was,' he said, after a pause.

'I see.'

'Pure accident. Nobody more surprised than myself.'

'I see.'

So did Lord Emsworth. He saw that the time had come to play his
last card. It was no moment for shrinking back and counting the cost.
He must proceed to that last fearful extremity which he had contem-
plated.

'Tell me, Baxter,' he said, 'are you doing anything just now, Baxter?'

'Yes,' replied the other, with no trace of hesitation. 'I am going to
look for Lady Constance.'

A convulsive gulp prevented Lord Emsworth from speaking for an
instant.

'I mean,' he quavered, when the spasm had spent itself, 'I gathered
from my sister that you were at liberty at the moment – that you had
left that fellow what's-his-name – the American fellow – and I was

hoping, my dear Baxter,' said Lord Emsworth, speaking thickly, as if the words choked him, 'that I might be able to persuade you to take up – to resume – in fact, I was going to ask you if you would care to become my secretary again.'

He paused and, reaching for his handkerchief, feebly mopped his brow. The dreadful speech was out, and its emergence had left him feeling spent and weak.

'You were?' cried Rupert Baxter.

'I was,' said Lord Emsworth hollowly.

A great change for the better had come over Rupert Baxter. It was as if those words had been a magic formula, filling with sweetness and light one who until that moment had been more like a spectacled thunder-cloud than anything human. He ceased to lower darkly. His air of being on the point of shooting out forked lightning left him. He even went so far as to smile. And if the smile was a smile that made Lord Emsworth feel as if his vital organs were being churned up with an egg-whisk, that was not his fault. He was trying to smile sunnily.

'Thank you,' he said. 'I shall be delighted.'

Lord Emsworth did not speak.

'I was always happy at the Castle.'

Lord Emsworth did not speak.

'Thank you very much,' said Rupert Baxter. 'What a beautiful evening.'

He passed from view, and Lord Emsworth examined the evening. As Baxter had said, it was beautiful, but it did not bring the balm which beautiful evenings usually brought to him. A blight seemed to hang over it. The setting sun shone bravely on the formal garden over which he looked, but it was the lengthening shadows rather than the sunshine that impressed themselves upon Lord Emsworth.

His heart was bowed down with weight of woe. Oh, says the poet, what a tangled web we weave when first we practise to deceive, and it was precisely the same, Lord Emsworth realized, when first we practise to shoot airguns. Just one careless, offhand pop at a bending Baxter, and what a harvest, what a retribution! As a result of that single idle shot he had been compelled to augment his personal staff with a land-agent, which would infuriate his sister Constance, and a private secretary, which would make his life once again the inferno it had been in the old, bad Baxter days. He could scarcely have got himself into more trouble if he had gone blazing away with a machine gun.

It was with a slow and distrait shuffle that he eventually took himself from the writing-room and proceeded with his interrupted plan of going and sniffing at his roses. And so preoccupied was his mood that Beach, his faithful butler, who came to him after he had been smiling at them for perhaps half an hour, was obliged to speak twice before he could induce him to remove his nose from a Gloire de Dijon.

'Eh?'

'A note for you, m'lord.'

'A note? Who from?'

'Mr Baxter, m'lord.'

If Lord Emsworth had been less careworn, he might have noticed that the butler's voice had not its customary fruity ring. It had a dullness, a lack of tone. It was the voice of a butler who has lost the bluebird. But, being in the depths and so in no frame of mind to analyse the voice-production of butlers, he merely took the envelope from its salver and opened it listlessly, wondering what Baxter was sending him notes about.

The communication was so brief that he was enabled to discover this at a glance.

LORD EMSWORTH,

After what has occurred, I must reconsider my decision to accept the post of secretary which you offered me.

I am leaving the Castle immediately.

R. BAXTER

Simply that, and nothing more.

Lord Emsworth stared at the thing. It is not enough to say that he was bewildered. He was nonplussed. If the Gloire de Dijon at which he had recently been sniffing had snapped at his nose and bitten the tip off, he could scarcely have been more taken aback. He could make nothing of this.

As in a dream, he became aware that Beach was speaking.

'Eh?'

'My month's notice, m'lord.'

'Your what?'

'My month's notice, m'lord.'

'What about it?'

'I was saying that I wish to give my month's notice, m'lord.'

A weak irritation at all this chattering came upon Lord Emsworth. Here he was, trying to grapple with this frightful thing which had come upon him, and Beach would insist on weakening his concentration by babbling.

'Yes, yes, yes,' he said. 'I see. All right. Yes, yes.'

'Very good, m'lord.'

Left alone, Lord Emsworth faced the facts. He understood now what had happened. The note was no longer mystic. What it meant was that for some reason that trump card of his had proved useless. He had thought to stop Baxter's mouth with bribes, and he had failed. The man had seemed to accept the olive branch, but later there must have come some sharp revulsion of feeling, causing him to change his mind. No doubt a sudden twinge of pain in the wounded area had brought the memory of his wrongs flooding back upon him, so that he found himself preferring vengeance to material prosperity. And now he was going to blow the gaff. Even now the whole facts in the case might have been placed before Lady Constance. And even now, Lord Emsworth felt with a shiver, Connie might be looking for him.

The sight of a female form coming through the rose bushes brought him the sharpest shudder of the day, and for an instant he stood panting like a dog. But it was not his sister Constance. It was his niece Jane.

Jane was in excellent spirits.

'Hullo, Uncle Clarence,' she said. 'Having a look at the roses? I've sent that letter off to George, Uncle Clarence. I got the boy who cleans the knives and boots to take it. Nice chap. His name is Cyril.'

'Jane,' said Lord Emsworth, 'a terrible, a ghastly thing has happened. Baxter was outside the window of the writing-room when we were talking, and he heard everything.'

'Golly! He didn't?'

'He did. Every word. And he means to tell your aunt.'

'How do you know?'

'Read this.'

Jane took the note.

'H'm,' she said, having scanned it. 'Well, it looks to me, Uncle Clarence, as if there was only one thing for you to do. You must assert yourself.'

'Assert myself?'

'You know what I mean. Get tough. When Aunt Constance comes trying to bully you, stick your elbows out and put your head on one side and talk back at her out of the corner of your mouth.'

'But what shall I say?'

'Good heavens, there are a hundred things you can say. "Oh, yeah?" "Is zat so?" "Hey, just a minute", "Listen baby", "Scram" . . .'

'Scram?'

'It means "Get the hell outa here".'

'But I can't tell Connie to get the hell outa here.'

'Why not? Aren't you master in your own house?'

'No,' said Lord Emsworth.

Jane reflected.

'Then I'll tell you what to do. Deny the whole thing.'

'Could I, do you think?'

'Of course you could. And then Aunt Constance will ask me, and I'll deny the whole thing. Categorically. We'll both deny it categorically. She'll have to believe us. We'll be two to one. Don't you worry, Uncle Clarence. Everything'll be all right.'

She spoke with the easy optimism of Youth, and when she passed on a few moments later seemed to be feeling that she was leaving an uncle with his mind at rest. Lord Emsworth could hear her singing a gay song.

He felt no disposition to join in the chorus. He could not bring himself to share her sunny outlook. He looked into the future and still found it dark.

There was only one way of taking his mind off this dark future, only one means of achieving a momentary forgetfulness of what lay in store. Five minutes later, Lord Emsworth was in the library, reading Whiffle on *The Care Of The Pig*.

But there is a point beyond which the magic of the noblest writer ceases to function. Whiffle was good – no question about that – but he was not good enough to purge from the mind such a load of care as was weighing upon Lord Emsworth's. To expect him to do so was trying him too high. It was like asking Whiffle to divert and entertain a man stretched upon the rack.

Lord Emsworth was already beginning to find a difficulty in concentrating on that perfect prose, when any chance he might have had of doing so was removed. Lady Constance appeared in the doorway.

'Oh, here you are, Clarence,' said Lady Constance.

'Yes,' said Lord Emsworth in a low, strained voice.

A close observer would have noted about Lady Constance's manner, as she came into the room, something a little nervous and apprehensive, something almost diffident, but to Lord Emsworth, who was not a close observer, she seemed pretty much as usual, and he remained gazing at her like a man confronted with a ticking bomb. A dazed sensation had come upon him. It was in an almost detached way that he found himself speculating as to which of his crimes was about to be brought up for discussion. Had she met Jane and learned of the fatal letter? Or had she come straight from an interview with Rupert Baxter in which that injured man had told all?

He was so certain that it must be one of these two topics that she had come to broach that her manner as she opened the conversation filled him with amazement. Not only did it lack ferocity, it was absolutely chummy. It was as if a lion had come into the library and started bleating like a lamb.

'All alone, Clarence?'

Lord Emsworth hitched up his lower jaw, and said Yes, he was all alone.

'What are you doing? Reading?'

Lord Emsworth said Yes, he was reading.

'I'm not disturbing you, am I?'

Lord Emsworth, though astonishment nearly robbed him of speech, contrived to say that she was not disturbing him. Lady Constance walked to the window and looked out.

'What a lovely evening.'

'Yes.'

'I wonder you aren't out of doors.'

'I was out of doors. I came in.'

'Yes. I saw you in the rose garden.' Lady Constance traced a pattern on the window-sill with her finger. 'You were speaking to Beach.'

'Yes.'

'Yes, I saw Beach come up and speak to you.'

There was a pause. Lord Emsworth was about to break in by asking his visitor if she felt quite well, when Lady Constance spoke again. That apprehension in her manner, that nervousness, was now well marked. She traced another pattern on the window-sill.

'Was it important?'

'Was what important?'

'I mean, did he want anything?'

'Who?'

'Beach.'

'Beach?'

'Yes. I was wondering what he wanted to see you about.'

Quite suddenly there flashed upon Lord Emsworth the recollection that Beach had done more than merely hand him Baxter's note. With it – dash it, yes, it all came back to him – with it he had given his month's notice. And it just showed, Lord Emsworth felt, what a morass of trouble he was engulfed in that the fact of this superb butler handing in his resignation had made almost no impression on him. If such a thing had happened only as recently as yesterday, it would have constituted a major crisis. He would have felt that the foundations of his world were rocking. And he had scarcely listened. 'Yes, yes,' he had said, if he remembered correctly. 'Yes, yes, yes. All right.' Or words to that effect.

Bending his mind now on the disaster, Lord Emsworth sat stunned. He was appalled. Almost since the beginning of time, this super-butler had been at the Castle, and now he was about to melt away like snow in the sunshine – or as much like snow in the sunshine as was within the scope of a man who weighed sixteen stone in the buff. It was frightful. The thing was a nightmare. He couldn't get on without Beach. Life without Beach would be insupportable.

He gave tongue, his voice sharp and anguished.

'Connie! Do you know what's happened? Beach has given notice!'

'What!'

'Yes! His month's notice. He's given it. Beach has. And not a word of explanation. No reason. No –'

Lord Emsworth broke off. His face suddenly hardened. What seemed the only possible solution of the mystery had struck him. Connie was at the bottom of this. Connie must have been coming the *grande dame* on the butler, wounding his sensibilities.

Yes, that must be it. It was just the sort of thing she would do. If he had caught her being the Old English Aristocrat once, he had caught her a hundred times. That way of hers of pursing the lips and raising the eyebrows and generally doing the daughter-of-a-hundred-earls stuff. Naturally no butler would stand it.

'Connie,' he cried, adjusting his pince-nez and staring keenly and accusingly, 'what have you been doing to Beach?'

Something that was almost a sob burst from Lady Constance's lips. Her lovely complexion had paled, and in some odd way she seemed to have shrunk.

'I shot him,' she whispered.

Lord Emsworth was a little hard of hearing.

'You did what?'

'I shot him.'

'Shot him?'

'Yes.'

'You mean, *shot* him?'

'Yes, yes, yes! I shot him with George's airgun.'

A whistling sigh escaped Lord Emsworth. He leaned back in his chair, and the library seemed to be dancing old country dances before his eyes. To say that he felt weak with relief would be to understate the effect of this extraordinary communication. His relief was so intense that he felt absolutely boneless. Not once but many times during the past quarter of an hour he had said to himself that only a miracle could save him from the consequences of his sins, and now the miracle had happened. No one was more alive than he to the fact that women are abundantly possessed of crust, but after this surely even Connie could not have the crust to reproach him for what he had done.

'Shot him?' he said, recovering speech.

A fleeting touch of the old imperiousness returned to Lady Constance.

'Do stop saying "Shot him?" Clarence! Isn't it bad enough to have done a perfectly mad thing, without having to listen to you talking like a parrot? Oh, dear! Oh, dear!'

'But what did you do it for?'

'I don't know. I tell you I don't know. Something seemed suddenly to come over me. It was as if I had been bewitched. After you went out, I thought I would take the gun to Beach –'

'Why?'

'I ... I ... Well, I thought it would be safer with him than lying about in the library. So I took it down to his pantry. And all the way there I kept remembering what a wonderful shot I had been as a child –'

'What?' Lord Emsworth could not let this pass. 'What do you mean, you were a wonderful shot as a child? You've never shot in your life.'

'I have. Clarence, you were talking about Julia shooting Miss Mapleton. It wasn't Julia – it was I. She had made me stay in and do my rivers of Europe over again, so I shot her. I was a splendid shot in those days.'

'I bet you weren't as good as me,' said Lord Emsworth, piqued. 'I used to shoot rats.'

'So used I to shoot rats.'

'How many rats did you ever shoot?'

'Oh, Clarence, Clarence! Never mind about the rats.'

'No,' said Lord Emsworth, called to order. 'No, dash it. Never mind the rats. Tell me about this Beach business.'

'Well, when I got to the pantry, it was empty, and I saw Beach outside by the laurel bush, reading in a deck-chair –'

'How far away?'

'I don't know. What does it matter? About six feet, I suppose.'

'Six feet? Ha!'

'And I shot him. I couldn't resist it. It was like some horrible obsession. There was a sort of hideous picture in my mind of how he would jump. So I shot him.'

'How do you know you did? I expect you missed him.'

'No. Because he sprang up. And then he saw me at the window and came in, and I said, "Oh, Beach, I want you to take this airgun and keep it," and he said, "Very good, m'lady."'

'He didn't say anything about you shooting him?'

'No. And I have been hoping and hoping that he had not realized what had happened. I have been in an agony of suspense. But now you tell me that he has given his notice, so he must have done. Clarence,' cried Lady Constance, clasping her hands like a persecuted heroine, 'you see the awful position, don't you? If he leaves us he will spread the story all over the county and people will think I'm mad. I shall never be able to live it down. You must persuade him to withdraw his notice. Offer him double wages. Offer him anything. He must not be allowed to leave. If he does, I shall never . . . S'h!'

'What do you mean, S' . . . Oh, ah,' said Lord Emsworth, at last observing that the door was opening.

It was his niece Jane who entered.

'Oh, hullo, Aunt Constance,' she said. 'I was wondering if you were in here. Mr Baxter's looking for you.'

Lady Constance was *distraite*.

'Mr Baxter?'

'Yes. I heard him asking Beach where you were. I think he wants to see you about something,' said Jane.

She directed at Lord Emsworth a swift glance, accompanied by a fleeting wink. 'Remember!' said the glance. 'Categorically!' said the wink.

Footsteps sounded outside. Rupert Baxter strode into the room.

At an earlier point in this chronicle, we have compared the aspect of Rupert Baxter, when burning with resentment, to a thunder-cloud, and it is possible that the reader may have formed a mental picture of just an ordinary thunder-cloud, the kind that rumbles a bit but does not really amount to anything very much. It was not this kind of cloud that the secretary resembled now, but one of those which burst over cities in the Tropics, inundating countrysides while thousands flee. He moved darkly towards Lady Constance, his hands outstretched. Lord Emsworth he ignored.

'I have come to say goodbye, Lady Constance,' he said.

There were not many statements that could have roused Lady Constance from her preoccupation, but this one did. She ceased to be the sportswoman brooding on memories of shikari, and stared aghast.

'Goodbye?'

'Goodbye.'

'But, Mr Baxter, you are not leaving us?'

'Precisely.'

For the first time, Rupert Baxter deigned to recognize that the ninth Earl was present.

'I am not prepared,' he said bitterly, 'to remain in a house where my chief duty appears to be to act as a target for Lord Emsworth and his airgun.'

'What!'

'Exactly.'

In the silence which followed these words, Jane once more gave her uncle that glance of encouragement and stimulation – that glance which said 'Be firm!' To her astonishment, she perceived that it was not needed. Lord Emsworth was firm already. His face was calm, his eye steady, and his pince-nez were not even quivering.

'The fellow's potty,' said Lord Emsworth in a clear resonant voice. 'Absolutely potty. Always told you he was. Target for my airgun? Pooh! Pah! What's he talking about?'

Rupert Baxter quivered. His spectacles flashed fire.

'Do you deny that you shot me, Lord Emsworth?'

'Certainly I do.'

'Perhaps you will deny admitting to this lady here in the writing-room that you shot me?'

'Certainly I do.'

'Did you tell me that you had shot Mr Baxter, Uncle Clarence?' said Jane. 'I didn't hear you.'

'Of course I didn't.'

'I thought you hadn't. I should have remembered it.'

Rupert Baxter's hands shot ceilingwards, as if he were calling upon heaven to see justice done.

'You admitted it to me personally. You begged me not to tell anyone. You tried to put matters right by engaging me as your secretary, and I accepted the position. At this time I was perfectly willing to forget the entire affair. But when, not half an hour later . . .'

Lord Emsworth raised his eyebrows. Jane raised hers.

'How very extraordinary,' said Jane.

'Most,' said Lord Emsworth.

He removed his pince-nez and began to polish them, speaking soothingly the while. But his manner, though soothing, was very resolute.

'Baxter, my dear fellow,' he said, 'there's only one explanation of all this. It's just what I was telling you. You've been having these hallucinations of yours again. I never said a word to you about shooting you. I never said a word to my niece about shooting you. Why should I, when I hadn't? And as for what you say about engaging you as my secretary, the absurdity of the thing is manifest on the very face of it. There is nothing on earth that would induce me to have you as my secretary. I don't want to hurt your feelings, but I'd rather be dead in a ditch. Now, listen, my dear Baxter, I'll tell you what to do. You just jump on that motor-bicycle of yours and go on touring England where you left off. And soon you will find that the fresh air will do wonders for that pottiness of yours. In a day or two you won't know . . .'

Rupert Baxter turned and stalked from the room.

'Mr Baxter!' cried Lady Constance.

Her intention of going after the fellow and pleading with him to continue inflicting his beastly presence on the quiet home life of Blandings Castle was so plain that Lord Emsworth did not hesitate.

'Connie!'

'But, Clarence!'

'Constance, you will remain where you are. You will not stir a step.'

'But, Clarence!'

'Not a dashed step. You hear me? Let him scram!'

Lady Constance halted, irresolute. Then suddenly she met the full force of the pince-nez and it was as if she – like Rupert Baxter – had been struck by a bullet. She collapsed into a chair and sat there twisting her rings forlornly.

'Oh, and, by the way, Connie,' said Lord Emsworth, 'I've been meaning to tell you. I've given that fellow Abercrombie that job he was asking for. I thought it all over carefully, and decided to drop him a line saying that pursuant on our recent conversation I was offering him Simmons's place. I've been making inquiries, and I find he's a capital fellow.'

'He's a baa-lamb,' said Jane.

'You hear? Jane says he's a baa-lamb. Just the sort of chap we want about the place.'

'So now we're going to get married.'

'So now they're going to get married. An excellent match, don't you think, Connie?'

Lady Constance did not speak. Lord Emsworth raised his voice a little.

'DON'T YOU, CONNIE?'

Lady Constance leaped in her seat as if she had heard the Last Trump.

'Very,' she said. 'Oh, very.'

'Right,' said Lord Emsworth. 'And now I'll go and talk to Beach.'

In the pantry, gazing sadly out on the stable yard, Beach the butler sat sipping a glass of port. In moments of mental stress, port was to Beach what Whiffle was to his employer, or, as we must now ruefully put it, his late employer. He flew to it when Life had got him down, and never before had Life got him down as it had now.

Sitting there in his pantry, that pantry which so soon would know him no more, Beach was in the depths. He mourned like some fallen monarch about to say goodbye to all his greatness and pass into exile. The die was cast. The end had come. Eighteen years, eighteen happy years, he had been in service at Blandings Castle, and now he must go forth, never to return. Little wonder that he sipped port. A weaker man would have swigged brandy.

Something tempestuous burst open the door, and he perceived that his privacy had been invaded by Lord Emsworth. He rose, and stood staring. In all the eighteen years during which he had held office, his employer had never before paid a visit to the pantry.

But it was not simply the other's presence that caused his gooseberry eyes to dilate to their full width, remarkable though that was. The mystery went deeper than that. For this was a strange, unfamiliar Lord Emsworth, a Lord Emsworth who glared where once he had blinked, who spurned the floor like a mettlesome charger, who banged tables and spilled port.

'Beach,' thundered this changeling, 'what the dooce is all this dashed nonsense?'

'M'lord?'

'You know what I mean. About leaving me. Have you gone off your head?'

A sigh shook the butler's massive frame.

'I fear that in the circumstances it is inevitable, m'lord.'

'Why? What are you talking about? Don't be an ass, Beach. Inevitable, indeed! Never heard such nonsense in my life. Why is it inevitable? Look me in the face and answer me that.'

'I feel it is better to tender my resignation than to be dismissed, m'lord.'

It was Lord Emsworth's turn to stare.

'Dismissed?'

'Yes, m'lord.'

'Beach, you're tight.'

'No, m'lord. Has not Mr Baxter spoken to you, m'lord?'

'Of course he's spoken to me. He's been gassing away half the afternoon. What's that got to do with it?'

Another sigh, seeming to start at the soles of his flat feet, set the butler's waistcoat rippling like corn in the wind.

'I see that Mr Baxter has not yet informed you, m'lord. I assumed that he would have done so before this. But it is a mere matter of time, I fear, before he makes his report.'

'Informed me of what?'

'I regret to say, m'lord, that in a moment of uncontrollable impulse I shot Mr Baxter.'

Lord Emsworth's pince-nez flew from his nose. Without them he could see only indistinctly, but he continued to stare at the butler, and in his eyes there appeared an expression which was a blend of several emotions. Amazement would have been chief of these, had it not been exceeded by affection. He did not speak, but his eyes said 'My brother!'

'With Master George's airgun, m'lord, which her ladyship left in my custody. I regret to say, m'lord, that upon receipt of the weapon I went out into the grounds and came upon Mr Baxter walking near the shrubbery. I tried to resist the temptation, m'lord, but it was too keen. I was seized with an urge which I have not experienced since I was a small lad, and, in short, I –'

'Plugged him?'

'Yes, m'lord.'

Lord Emsworth could put two and two together.

'So that's what he was talking about in the library. That's what made him change his mind and send me that note . . . How far was he away when you shot him?'

'A matter of a few feet, m'lord. I endeavoured to conceal myself behind a tree, but he turned very sharply, and I was so convinced that he had detected me that I felt I had no alternative but to resign my situation before he could make his report to you, m'lord.'

'And I thought you were leaving because my sister Connie shot you!'

'Her ladyship did not shoot me, m'lord. It is true that the weapon exploded accidentally in her ladyship's hand, but the bullet passed me harmlessly.'

Lord Emsworth snorted.

'And she said she was a good shot! Can't even hit a sitting butler at six feet. Listen to me, Beach. I want no more of this nonsense of you resigning. Bless my soul, how do you suppose I could get on without you? How long have you been here?'

'Eighteen years, m'lord.'

'Eighteen years! And you talk of resigning! Of all the dashed absurd ideas!'

'But I fear, m'lord, when her ladyship learns –'

'Her ladyship won't learn. Baxter won't tell her. Baxter's gone.'

'Gone, m'lord?'

'Gone for ever.'

'But I understood, m'lord –'

'Never mind what you understood. He's gone. A few feet away, did you say?'

'M'lord?'

'Did you say Baxter was only a few feet away when you got him?'

'Yes, m'lord.'

'Ah!' said Lord Emsworth.

He took the gun absently from the table and absently slipped a slug into the breech. He was feeling pleased and proud, as champions do whose pre-eminence is undisputed. Connie had missed a mark like Beach – practically a haystack – at six feet. Beach had plugged Baxter – true – and so had young George – but only with the muzzle of the gun almost touching the fellow. It had been left for him, Clarence, ninth Earl of Emsworth, to do the real shooting . . .

A damping thought came to diminish his complacency. It was as if a voice had whispered in his ear the word 'Fluke!' His jaw dropped a little, and he stood for a while, brooding. He felt flattened and discouraged.

Had it been merely a fluke, that superb shot from the library window? Had he been mistaken in supposing that the ancient skill still lingered? Would he – which was what the voice was hinting – under similar conditions miss nine times out of ten?

A stuttering, sputtering noise broke in upon his reverie. He raised his eyes to the window. Out in the stable yard, Rupert Baxter was starting up his motor-bicycle.

'Mr Baxter, m'lord.'

'I see him.'

An overwhelming desire came upon Lord Emsworth to put this thing to the test, to silence for ever that taunting voice.

'How far away would you say he was, Beach?'

'Fully twenty yards, m'lord.'

'Watch!' said Lord Emsworth.

Into the sputtering of the bicycle there cut a soft pop. It was followed by a sharp howl. Rupert Baxter, who had been leaning on the handle-bars, rose six inches with his hand to his thigh.

'There!' said Lord Emsworth.

Baxter had ceased to rub his thigh. He was a man of intelligence, and he realized that anyone on the premises of Blandings Castle who wasted time hanging about and rubbing thighs was simply asking for it. To one trapped in this inferno of Blandings Castle instant flight was the only way of winning to safety. The sputtering rose to a crescendo, diminished, died away altogether. Rupert Baxter had gone on, touring England.

Lord Emsworth was still gazing out of the window, raptly, as if looking at the X which marked the spot. For a long moment Beach stood staring reverently at his turned back. Then, as if performing some symbolic rite in keeping with the dignity of the scene, he reached for his glass of port and raised it in a silent toast.

Peace reigned in the butler's pantry. The sweet air of the summer evening poured in through the open window. It was as if Nature had blown the All Clear.

Blandings Castle was itself again.

# BIRTH OF A SALESMAN

The day was so fair, the breeze so gentle, the sky so blue and the sun so sunny that Lord Emsworth, that vague and woollen-headed peer, who liked fine weather, should have been gay and carefree, especially as he was looking at flowers, a thing which always gave him pleasure. But on his face, as he poked it over the hedge beyond which the flowers lay, a close observer would have noted a peevish frown. He was thinking of his younger son Freddie.

Coming to America to attend the wedding of one of his nieces to a local millionaire of the name of Tipton Plimsoll, Lord Emsworth had found himself, in the matter of board and lodging, confronted with a difficult choice. The British Government, notoriously slow men with a dollar, having refused to allow him to take out of England a sum sufficient to enable him to live in a New York hotel, he could become the guest of the bridegroom's aunt, who was acting as M.C. of the nuptials, or he could dig in with Freddie in the Long Island suburb where the latter had made his home. Warned by his spies that Miss Plimsoll maintained in her establishment no fewer than six Pekinese dogs, a breed of animal which always made straight for his ankles, he had decided on Freddie and was conscious now of having done the wrong thing. Pekes chew the body, but Freddie seared the soul.

The flowers grew in the garden of a large white house at the end of the road, and Lord Emsworth had been goggling at them for some forty minutes, for he was a man who liked to take his time over these things, when his reverie was interrupted by the tooting of a horn and the sound of a discordant voice singing 'Buttons and Bows'. Freddie's car drew up, with Freddie at the wheel.

'Oh, there you are, guv'nor,' said Freddie.

'Yes,' said Lord Emsworth, who was. 'I was looking at the flowers. A nice display. An attractive garden.'

'Where every prospect pleases and only man is vile,' said Freddie austerely. 'Keep away from the owner of that joint, guv'nor. He lowers the tone of the neighbourhood.'

'Indeed? Why is that?'

'Not one of the better element. His wife's away, and he throws

parties. I've forgotten his name ... Griggs or Follansbee or something
... but we call him the Timber Wolf. He's something in the lumber
business.'

'And he throws parties?'

'Repeatedly. You might say incessantly. Entertains blondes in
droves. All wrong. My wife's away, but do you find me festooned in
blondes? No. I pine for her return. Well, I must be oozing along. I'm
late.'

'You are off somewhere?'

Freddie clicked his tongue.

'I told you yesterday, guv'nor, and I told you twice this morning,
that I was giving a prospect lunch today at the golf club. I explained
that I couldn't ask you to join us at the trough, because I shall be
handing this bird a sales talk throughout the meal. You'll find your
rations laid out on a tray. A cold collation today, because it's Thursday
and on Thursdays the domestic staff downs tools.'

He drove on, all briskness and efficiency, and Lord Emsworth tut-
tutted an irritable tut-tut.

There, he was telling himself, you had in a nutshell what made
Freddie such a nerve-rasping companion. He threw his weight about.
He behaved as if he were the Spirit of Modern Commerce. He was like
something out of one of those advertisements which show the employee
who has taken the correspondence course in Confidence and Self-
Reliance looking his boss in the eye and making him wilt.

Freddie worked for Donaldson's Inc., dealers in dog-biscuits of
Long Island City, and had been doing so now for three years. And in
those three years some miracle had transformed him from a vapid
young London lizard into a go-getter, a live wire and a man who
thought on his feet and did it now. Every night since Lord Emsworth
had come to enjoy his hospitality, if enjoy is the word, he had spoken
lyrically and at length of his success in promoting the interests of
Donaldson's Dog-Joy ('Get your dog thinking the Donaldson
way'), making no secret of his view that it had been a lucky day for
the dear old firm when it had put him on the payroll. As a salesman he
was good, a fellow who cooked with gas and did not spare himself,
and he admitted it.

All of which might have been music to Lord Emsworth's ears, for a
younger son earning his living in America is unquestionably a vast
improvement on a younger son messing about and getting into debt in

England, had it not been for one circumstance. He could not rid himself of a growing conviction that after years of regarding this child of his as a drone and a wastrel, the child was now regarding him as one. A world's worker himself, Freddie eyed with scorn one who, like Lord Emsworth, neither toiled nor spun. He patronized Lord Emsworth. He had never actually called Lord Emsworth a spiv, but he made it plain that it was in this category that he had mentally pencilled in the author of his being. And if there is one thing that pierces the armour of an English father of the upper classes, it is to be looked down on by his younger son. Little wonder that Lord Emsworth, as he toddled along the road, was gritting his teeth. A weaker man would have gnashed them.

His gloom was not lightened by the sight of the cold collation which leered at him on his return to the house. There was the tray of which Freddie had spoken, and on it a plate on which, like corpses after a battle, lay a slice of vermilion ham, a slice of sepia corned beef, a circle of mauve liverwurst and, of all revolting things, a large green pickle. It seemed to Lord Emsworth that Freddie's domestic staff was temperamentally incapable of distinguishing between the needs of an old gentleman who had to be careful what he ate and those of a flock of buzzards taking pot luck in the Florida Everglades.

For some moments he stood gaping at this unpleasant picture in still life; then there stole into his mind the thought that there might be eggs in the ice-box. He went thither and tested his theory and it was proved correct.

'Ha!' said Lord Emsworth. He remembered how he had frequently scrambled eggs at school.

But his school days lay half a century behind him, and time in its march robs us of our boyhood gifts. Since the era when he had worn Eton collars and ink spots on his face, he had lost the knack, and it all too speedily became apparent that Operation Eggs was not going to be the walkover he had anticipated. Came a moment when he would have been hard put to it to say whether he was scrambling the eggs or the eggs were scrambling him. And he had paused to clarify his thoughts on this point, when there was a ring at the front door bell. Deeply encrusted in yolk, he shuffled off to answer the summons.

A girl was standing in the porch. He inspected her through his pince-nez with the vacant stare on which the female members of his family had so often commented adversely. She seemed to him, as he drank her slowly in, a nice sort of girl. A man with a great many nieces who were always bursting in on him and ballyragging him when he wanted to read his pig book, he had come to fear and distrust the younger members of the opposite sex, but this one's looks he liked immediately. About her there was none of that haughty beauty and stormy emotion in which his nieces specialized. She was small and friendly and companionable.

'Good morning,' he said.

'Good morning. Would you like a richly bound encyclopaedia of Sport?'

'Not in the least,' said Lord Emsworth cordially. 'Can you scramble eggs?'

'Why, sure.'

'Then come in,' said Lord Emsworth. 'Come in. And if you will excuse me leaving you, I will go and change my clothes.'

Women are admittedly wonderful. It did not take Lord Emsworth long to remove his best suit, which he had been wearing in deference to the wishes of Freddie, who was a purist on dress, and don the older and shabbier one which made him look like a minor employee in some shady firm of private detectives, but, brief though the interval had been, the girl had succeeded in bringing order out of chaos. Not only had she quelled what had threatened to become an ugly revolt among the eggs, but she had found bacon and coffee and produced toast. What was virtually a banquet was set out in the living-room, and Lord Emsworth was about to square his elbows and have at it, when he detected an omission.

'Where is your plate?' he asked.

'Mine?' The girl seemed surprised. 'Am I in on this?'

'Most certainly.'

'That's mighty nice of you. I'm starving.'

'These eggs,' said Lord Emsworth some moments later, speaking thickly through a mouthful of them, 'are delicious. Salt?'

'Thanks.'

'Pepper? Mustard? Tell me,' said Lord Emsworth, for it was a matter that had been perplexing him a good deal, 'why do you go about the countryside offering people richly bound encyclopaedias of Sport? Deuced civil of you, of course,' he added hastily, lest she might think that he was criticizing, 'but why do you?'

'I'm selling them.'

'Selling them?'

'Yes.'

A bright light shone upon Lord Emsworth. It had been well said of him that he had an I.Q. some thirty points lower than that of a not too agile-minded jelly-fish, but he had grasped her point. She was selling them.

'Of course, yes. Quite. I see what you mean. You're *selling* them.'

'That's right. They set you back five dollars and I get forty per cent. Only I don't.'

'Why not?'

'Because people won't buy them.'

'No?'

'No, sir.'

'Don't people want richly bound encyclopaedias of Sport?'

'If they do, they keep it from me.'

'Dear, dear.' Lord Emsworth swallowed a piece of bacon emotionally. His heart was bleeding for this poor child. 'That must be trying for you.'

'It is.'

'But why do you have to sell the bally things?'

'Well, it's like this. I'm going to have a baby.'

'Good God!'

'Oh, not immediately. Next January. Well, that sort of thing costs money. Am I right or wrong?'

'Right, most decidedly,' said Lord Emsworth, who had never been a young mother himself but knew the ropes. 'I remember my poor wife complaining of the expense when my son Frederick was born. "Oh dear, oh dear, oh dear," I remember her saying. She was alive at the time,' explained Lord Emsworth.

'Ed works in a garage.'

'Does he? I don't think I have met him. Who is Ed?'

'My husband.'

'Oh, your husband? You mean your husband. Works in a garage, does he?'

'That's right. And the take-home pay doesn't leave much over for extras.'

'Like babies?'

'Like babies. So I got this job. I didn't tell Ed, of course. He'd have a fit.'

'He is subject to fits?'

'He wants me to lie down and rest.'

'I think he's right.'

'Oh, he's right, all right, but how can I? I've got to hustle out and sell richly bound encyclopaedias.'

'Of Sport?'

'Of Sport. And it's tough going. You do become discouraged. Besides getting blisters on the feet. I wish you could see my feet right now.'

On the point of saying that he would be delighted, Lord Emsworth paused. He had had a bright idea and it had taken his breath away. This always happened when he had bright ideas. He had had one in the Spring of 1921 and another in the Summer of 1933, and those had taken his breath away, too.

'I will sell your richly bound encyclopaedias of Sport,' he said.

'You?'

The bright idea which had taken Lord Emsworth's breath away was that if he went out and sold richly bound encyclopaedias of Sport, admitted by all the cognoscenti to be very difficult to dispose of, it would rid him once and for all of the inferiority complex which so oppressed him when in the society of his son Freddie. The brassiest of young men cannot pull that Spirit of Modern Commerce stuff on a father if the father is practically a Spirit of Modern Commerce himself.

'Precisely,' he said.

'But you couldn't.'

Lord Emsworth bridled. A wave of confidence and self-reliance was surging through him.

'Who says I couldn't? My son Frederick sells things, and I resent the suggestion that I am incapable of doing anything that Frederick can do.' He wondered if it would be possible to explain to her what a turnip-headed young ass Frederick was, then gave up the attempt as hopeless. 'Leave this to me,' he said. 'Lie down on that sofa and get a nice rest.'

'But –'

'Don't argue,' said Lord Emsworth dangerously, becoming the dominant male. 'Lie down on that sofa.'

Two minutes later, he was making his way down the road, still awash with that wave of confidence and self-reliance. His objective was the large white house where the flowers were. He was remembering what Freddie had said about its owner. The man, according to Freddie, threw parties and entertained blondes in his wife's absence. And while we may look askance from the moral standpoint at one who does this, we have to admit that it suggests the possession of sporting blood. That reckless, raffish type probably buys its encyclopaedias of Sport by the gross.

But one of the things that make life so difficult is that waves of confidence and self-reliance do not last. They surge, but they recede, leaving us with dubious minds and cooling feet. Lord Emsworth had started out in uplifted mood, but as he reached the gate of the white house the glow began to fade.

It was not that he had forgotten the technique of the thing. Freddie had explained it too often for him to do that. You rapped on the door. You said 'I wonder if I could interest you in a good dog biscuit?' And then by sheer personal magnetism you cast a spell on the householder so that he became wax in your hands. All perfectly simple and straightforward. And yet, having opened the gate and advanced a few feet into the driveway, Lord Emsworth paused. He removed his pince-nez, polished them, replaced them on his nose, blinked, swallowed once or twice and ran a finger over his chin. The first fine frenzy had abated. He was feeling like a nervous man who in an impulsive moment has volunteered to go over Niagara Falls in a barrel.

He was still standing in the driveway, letting 'I dare not' wait upon 'I would', as cats do in adages, when the air became full of tooting horns and grinding brakes and screaming voices.

'God bless my soul,' said Lord Emsworth, coming out of his coma.

The car which had so nearly caused a vacancy in the House of Lords was bursting with blondes. There was a blonde at the wheel, another at her side, further blondes in the rear seats and on the lap of the blonde beside the blonde at the wheel a blonde Pekinese dog. They were all shouting, and the Pekinese dog was hurling abuse in Chinese.

'God bless my soul,' said Lord Emsworth. 'I beg your pardon. I really must apologize. I was plunged in thought.'

'Oh, was that what you were plunged in?' said the blonde at the wheel, mollified by his suavity. Speak civilly to blondes, and they will speak civilly to you.

'I was thinking of dog biscuits. Of dog biscuits. Of . . . er . . . in short . . . dog biscuits. I wonder,' said Lord Emsworth, striking while the iron was hot, 'if I could interest you in a good dog biscuit?'

The blonde at the wheel weighed the question.

'Not me,' she said. 'I never touch 'em.'

'Nor me,' said a blonde at the back. 'Doctor's orders.'

'And if you're thinking of making a quick sale to Eisenhower here,' said the blonde beside the driver, kissing the Pekinese on the tip of its nose, a feat of daring at which Lord Emsworth marvelled, 'he only eats chicken.'

Lord Emsworth corrected himself.

'When I said dog biscuit,' he explained, 'I meant a richly bound encyclopaedia of Sport.'

The blondes exchanged glances.

'Look,' said the one at the wheel. 'If you don't know the difference between a dog biscuit and a richly bound encyclopaedia of Sport, seems to me you'd be doing better in some other line of business.'

'Much better,' said the blonde beside her.

'A whole lot better,' agreed the blonde at the back.

'No future in it, the way you're going,' said the blonde at the wheel, summing up. 'That's the first thing you want to get straight on, the difference between dog biscuits and richly bound encyclopaedias of Sport. It's a thing that's cropping up all the time. There *is* a difference. I couldn't explain it to you offhand, but you go off into a corner somewheres and mull it over quietly and you'll find it'll suddenly come to you.'

'Like a flash,' said the blonde at the back.

'Like a stroke of lightning or sump'n,' assented the blonde at the wheel. 'You'll be amazed how you ever came to mix them up. Well, goodbye. Been nice seeing you.'

The car moved on toward the house, and Lord Emsworth, closing his burning ears to the happy laughter proceeding from its interior, tottered out into the road. His spirit was broken. It was his intention to return home and stay there. And he had started on his way when there came stealing into his mind a disturbing thought.

That girl. That nice young Mrs Ed who was going to have a fit in January . . . or, rather, a baby. (It was her husband, he recalled, who had the fits.) She was staking everything on his salesmanship. Could he fail her? Could he betray her simple trust?

The obvious answer was 'Yes, certainly', but the inherited chivalry of a long line of ancestors, all of whom had been noted for doing the square thing by damsels in distress, caused Lord Emsworth to shrink from making it. In the old days when knighthood was in flower and somebody was needed to rescue a suffering female from a dragon or a two-headed giant, the cry was always 'Let Emsworth do it!', and the Emsworth of the period had donned his suit of mail, stropped his sword, parked his chewing gum under the round table and snapped into it. A pretty state of things if the twentieth-century holder of the name were to allow himself to be intimidated by blondes.

Blushing hotly, Lord Emsworth turned and made for the gate again.

In the living-room of the white house, cool in the shade of the tree which stood outside its window, there had begun to burgeon one of those regrettable neo-Babylonian orgies which are so frequent when blondes and men who are something in the lumber business get together. Cocktails were circulating, and the blonde who had been at the wheel of the car was being the life and soul of the party with her imitation of the man outside who had been unable to get himself straightened out in the matter of dog biscuits and richly bound encyclopaedias. Her 'Lord Emsworth' was a nice bit of impressionistic work, clever but not flattering.

She was giving a second encore when her performance was interrupted by a shrill yapping from without, and the blonde who had sat beside her knitted her brow in motherly concern.

'Somebody's teasing Eisenhower,' she said.

'Probably found a cat,' said the timber wolf. 'Tell me more. What sort of a character was this character?'

'Tall,' said a blonde.

'Old,' said another blonde.

'Skinny,' said a third blonde.

And a fourth blonde added that he had worn pince-nez.

A sudden gravity fell upon the timber wolf. He was remembering that on several occasions these last few days he had seen just such a man peering over his hedge in a furtive and menacing manner, like Sherlock Holmes on the trail. This very morning he had seen him. He had been standing there outside the hedge, motionless . . . watching . . . watching . . .

The fly in the ointment of men who throw parties for blondes when their wives are away, the thing that acts as a skeleton at the feast and induces goose pimples when the revelry is at its height, is the fact that they can never wholly dismiss the possibility that these wives, though they ought to be ashamed of themselves for entertaining unworthy suspicions, may have engaged firms of private detectives to detect them privately and report on their activities. It was this thought that now came whistling like an east wind through the mind of the timber wolf, whose name, just to keep the record straight, was not Griggs or Follansbee but Spenlow (George).

And as he quivered beneath its impact, one of his guests, who had hitherto taken no part in the conversation, spoke as follows:

'Oo, look! Eisenhower's got him up a tree!'

And George Spenlow, following her pointing finger, saw that she was correct. There the fellow was, roosting in the branches and adjusting his pince-nez as if the better to view the scene within. He quivered like a jelly and stared at Lord Emsworth. Lord Emsworth stared at him. Their eyes met.

Much has been written of the language of the eyes, but except between lovers it is never a very satisfactory medium of communication. George Spenlow, trying to read the message in Lord Emsworth's, completely missed the gist.

What Lord Emsworth was trying to convey with the language of the eye was an apology for behaviour which at first sight, he admitted, might seem a little odd. He had rapped on the door, he was endeavouring to explain, but, unable to attract attention to his presence, had worked his way round the house to where he heard voices, not a thought on his mind except a passionate desire to sell richly bound encyclopaedias of Sport, and suddenly something had exploded like a land mine on the ground beside him and, looking down, he had perceived a Pekinese dog advancing on him with bared teeth. This had left him no option but to climb the tree to avoid its slavering jaws. 'Oh, for the wings of a dove!' he had said to himself, and had got moving. He concluded his remarks by smiling a conciliatory smile.

It pierced George Spenlow like a dagger. It seemed to him that this private investigator, elated at having caught him with the goods, was gloating evilly.

He gulped.

'You girls stay here,' he said hoarsely. 'I'll go talk to this fellow.'

He climbed through the window, scooped up the Pekinese, restored it to its proprietress and addressed Lord Emsworth in a quavering voice.

'Now listen,' he said.

These men high up in the lumber business are quick thinkers. George Spenlow had seen the way.

'Now listen,' said George Spenlow.

He had taken Lord Emsworth affectionately by the arm and was walking him up and down the lawn. He was a stout, pink, globular man, so like Lord Emsworth's pig, Empress of Blandings, in appearance that the latter felt a wave of homesickness.

'Now listen,' said George Spenlow. 'I think you and I can get together.'

Lord Emsworth, to show that his heart was in the right place, smiled another conciliatory smile.

'Yes, yes, I know,' said George Spenlow, wincing. 'But I think we can. I'll put my cards on the table. I know all about it. My wife. She gets ideas into her head. She imagines things.'

Lord Emsworth, though fogged, was able to understand this.

'My late wife was like that,' he said.

'All women are like that,' said George Spenlow. 'It's something to do with the bone structure of their heads. They let their imagination run away with them. They entertain unworthy suspicions.'

Here again Lord Emsworth was able to follow him. He said he had noticed the same thing in his sister Constance, and George Spenlow began to feel encouraged.

'Sure. Sisters, wives, late wives . . . they're all the same, and it doesn't do to let them get away with it. So here's what. What you tell her is that you found me enjoying a quiet home afternoon with a few old college friends . . . Wait, wait,' said George Spenlow urgently. 'Wait while I finish.'

He had observed his guest shake his head. This was because a mosquito had just bitten Lord Emsworth on the ear, but he had no means of divining this. Shakes of the head are as hard to interpret as the language of the eyes.

'Wait while I finish,' said George Spenlow. 'Hear what I was going to say. You're a man of the world. You want to take the broad, sensible outlook. You want to study the situation from every angle and find out what there is in it for you. Now then how much?'

'You mean how many?'

'Eh?'

'How many would you like?'

'How many what?'

'Richly bound encyclopaedias of Sport.'

'Oh yes, yes, yes,' said George Spenlow, enlightened 'Oh, sure sure, sure, sure, sure. I didn't get you for a moment. About how many would you suggest? Fifty?'

Lord Emsworth shook his head again – petulantly, it seemed to George Spenlow. The mosquito had returned.

'Well, naturally,' proceeded George Spenlow, 'when I said fifty, I meant a hundred. I think that's a nice round number.'

'Very nice,' agreed Lord Emsworth. 'Or would you care for a gross?'

'A gross might be better.'

'You can give them to your friends.'

'That's right. On their birthdays.'

'Or at Christmas.'

'Of course. So difficult to think of a suitable Christmas present.'

'Extraordinarily difficult.'

'Shall we say five hundred dollars on account?'

'That would be capital.'

'And remember,' said George Spenlow, with all the emphasis at his disposal. 'Old college friends.'

A passer-by, watching Lord Emsworth as he returned some twenty minutes later to Freddie's dream house down the road, would have said to himself that there went an old gentleman who had found the blue bird, and he would have been right. Lord Emsworth, as he fingered the crisp roll of bills in his trouser pocket, was not actually saying 'Whoopee!' but, it was a very near thing. He was feeling as if a great burden had been removed from his shoulders.

The girl was asleep when he reached the house. Gently, without disturbing her slumbers, Lord Emsworth reached for her bag and deposited the five hundred dollars in it. Then he tiptoed out and set a course for the golf club. He wanted to find his son Freddie.

'Ah, Frederick,' he would say. 'So you sell dog biscuits do you? Pooh! Anyone can sell dog biscuits. Give me something tougher, like richly bound encyclopaedias of Sport. Now, I strolled out just now and sold a gross at the first house I visited. So don't talk to me about dog biscuits. In fact, don't talk to me at all, because I am sick of the sound of your voice. And STOP THAT SINGING!!'

Yes, when Freddie began singing 'Buttons and Bows', that would be the moment to strike.

# STICKY WICKET AT BLANDINGS

It was a beautiful afternoon. The sky was blue, the sun yellow, butterflies flitted, birds tooted, bees buzzed and, to cut a long story short, all Nature smiled. But on Lord Emsworth's younger son Freddie Threepwood, as he sat in his sports model car at the front door of Blandings Castle, a fine Alsatian dog at his side, these excellent weather conditions made little impression. He was thinking of dog biscuits.

Freddie was only an occasional visitor at the castle these days. Some years before, he had married the charming daughter of Mr Donaldson of Donaldson's Dog-Joy, the organization whose aim it is to keep the American dog one hundred per cent red-blooded by supplying it with wholesome and nourishing biscuits, and had gone off to Long Island City, U.S.A., to work for the firm. He was in England now because his father-in-law, anxious to extend Dog-Joy's sphere of influence, had sent him back there to see what he could do in the way of increasing sales in the island kingdom. Aggie, his wife, had accompanied him, but after a week or so had found life at Blandings too quiet for her and had left for the French Riviera. The arrangement was that at the conclusion of his English campaign Freddie should join her there.

He was drying his left ear, on which the Alsatian had just bestowed a moist caress, when there came down the front steps a small, dapper elderly gentleman with a black-rimmed monocle in his eye. This was that notable figure of London's Bohemia, his Uncle Galahad, at whom the world of the theatre, the racecourse and the livelier type of restaurant had been pointing with pride for years. He greeted him cordially. To his sisters Constance, Julia, Dora and Hermione Gally might be a blot on the escutcheon, but in Freddie he excited only admiration. He considered him a man of infinite resource and sagacity, as indeed he was.

'Well, young Freddie,' said Gally. 'Where are you off to with that dog?'

'I'm taking him to the Fanshawes.'

'At Marling Hall? That's where that pretty girl I met you with the other day lives, isn't it?'

'That's right. Valerie Fanshawe. Her father's the local Master of Hounds. And you know what that means.'

'What does it mean?'

'That he's the managing director of more dogs than you could shake a stick at, each dog requiring the daily biscuit. And what could be better for them than Donaldson's Dog-Joy, containing as it does all the essential vitamins?'

'You're going to sell him dog biscuits?'

'I don't see how I can miss. Valerie is the apple of his eye, to whom he can deny nothing. She covets this Alsatian and says if I'll give it to her, she'll see that the old man comes through with a substantial order. I'm about to deliver it F.O.B.'

'But, my good Freddie, that dog is Aggie's dog. She'll go up in flames.'

'Oh, that's all right. I've budgeted for that. I have my story all set and ready. I shall tell her it died and I'll get her another just as good. That'll fix Aggie. But I mustn't sit here chewing the fat with you, I must be up and about and off and away. See you later,' said Freddie, and disappeared in a cloud of smoke.

He left Gally pursing his lips. A lifetime spent in the society of bookies, racecourse touts and skittle sharps had made him singularly broadminded, but he could not regard these tactics with approval. Shaking his head, he went back into the house and in the hall encountered Beach, the castle butler. Beach was wheezing a little, for he had been hurrying, and he was no longer the streamlined young butler he had been when he had first taken office.

'Have I missed Mr Frederick, sir?'

'By a hair's breadth. Why?'

'This telegram has arrived for him, Mr Galahad. I thought it might be important.'

'Most unlikely. Probably somebody just wiring him the result of the four o'clock race somewhere. Give it to me. I'll see that he gets it on his return.'

He continued on his way, feeling now rather at a loose end. A sociable man, he wanted someone to talk to. He could of course go and chat with his sister Lady Constance, who was reading a novel on the terrace, but something told him that there would be little profit and entertainment in this. Most of his conversation consisted of anecdotes of his murky past, and Connie was not a good audience for these. He decided on consideration to look up his brother Clarence, with whom it was always a pleasure to exchange ideas, and found that mild and dreamy peer in the library staring fixedly at nothing.

'Ah, there you are, Clarence,' he said, and Lord Emsworth sat up with a startled 'Eh, what?', his stringy body quivering.

'Oh, it's you, Galahad.'

'None other. What's the matter, Clarence?'

'Matter?'

'There's something on your mind. The symptoms are unmistakable. A man whose soul is at rest does not leap like a nymph surprised while bathing when somebody tells him he's there. Confide in me.'

Lord Emsworth was only too glad to do so. A sympathetic listener was precisely what he wanted.

'It's Connie,' he said. 'Did you hear what she was saying at breakfast?'

'I didn't come down to breakfast.'

'Ah, then you probably missed it. Well, right in the middle of the meal – I was eating a kippered herring at the time – she told me she was going to get rid of Beach.'

'What! Get rid of *Beach*?'

'"He is so slow," she said. "He wheezes. We ought to have a younger, smarter butler." I was appalled. I choked on my kippered herring.'

'I don't blame you. Blandings without Beach is unthinkable. So is Blandings with what she calls a young, smart butler at the helm. Good God! I can picture the sort of fellow she would get, some acrobatic stripling who would turn somersaults and slide down the banisters. You must put your foot down, Clarence.'

'Who, me?' said Lord Emsworth.

The idea seemed to him too bizarre for consideration. He was, as has been said, a mild, dreamy man, his sister Constance a forceful and imperious woman modelled on the lines of the late Cleopatra. Nominally he was the master of the house and as such entitled to exercise the Presidential Veto, but in practice Connie's word was always law. Look at the way she made him wear a top hat at the annual village school treat. He had reasoned and pleaded, pointing out in the clearest possible way that for a purely rural festivity of that sort a simple fishing hat would be far more suitable, but every year when August came around there he was, balancing the beastly thing on his head again and just asking the children in the tea tent to throw rock cakes at it.

'I can't put my foot down with Connie.'

'Well, I can, and I'm going to. Fire Beach, indeed! After eighteen years' devoted service. The idea's monstrous.'

'He would of course receive a pension.'

'It's no good her thinking she can gloss it over with any talk about pensions. Wrap it up as she may, the stark fact remains that she's planning to fire him. She must not be allowed to do this frightful thing. Good heavens, you might just as well fire the Archbishop of Canterbury.'

He would have spoken further, but at this moment there came from the stairs outside the slumping of feet, announcing that Freddie was back from the Fanshawes and on his way to his room. Lord Emsworth winced. Like so many aristocratic fathers, he was allergic to younger sons and since going to live in America Freddie had acquired a brisk, go-getter jumpiness which jarred upon him.

'Frederick,' he said with a shudder, and Gally started.

'I've got a telegram for Freddie,' he said. 'I'd better take it up to him.'

'Do,' said Lord Emsworth. 'And I think I will be going and having a look at my flowers.'

He left the room and making for the rose garden pottered slowly to and fro, sniffing at its contents. It was a procedure which as a rule gave him great pleasure, but today his heavy heart found no solace in the scent of roses. Listlessly he returned to the library and took a favourite pig book from its shelf. But even pig books were no palliative. The thought of Beach fading from the Blandings scene, if a man of his bulk could be said to fade, prohibited concentration.

He had sunk into a sombre reverie, when it was interrupted by the entrance of the subject of his gloomy meditations.

'Pardon me, m'lord,' said Beach. 'Mr Galahad desires me to ask if you would step down to the smoking-room and speak to him.'

'Why can't he come up here?'

'He has sprained his ankle, m'lord. He and Mr Frederick fell downstairs.'

'Oh?' said Lord Emsworth, not particularly interested. Freddie was always doing odd things. So was Galahad. 'How did that happen?'

'Mr Galahad informs me that he handed Mr Frederick a telegram.

Mr Frederick, having opened and perused it, uttered a sharp exclamation, reeled, clutched at Mr Galahad, and they both fell downstairs. Mr Frederick, too, has sprained his ankle. He has retired to bed.'

'Bless my soul. Are they in pain?'

'I gather that the agony has to some extent abated. They have been receiving treatment from the kitchen maid. She is a Brownie.'

'She's a *what*?'

'A Brownie, m'lord. I understand it is a species of female Boy Scout. They are instructed in the fundamentals of first aid.'

'Eh? First aid? Oh, you mean first aid,' said Lord Emsworth, reading between the lines. 'Bandages and that sort of thing, what?'

'Precisely, m'lord.'

By the time Lord Emsworth reached the smoking-room the Brownie had completed her ministrations and gone back to her *Screen Gems*. Gally was lying on a sofa, looking not greatly disturbed by his accident. He was smoking a cigar.

'Beach tells me you had a fall,' said Lord Emsworth.

'A stinker,' Gally assented. 'As who wouldn't when an ass of a nephew grabs him at the top of two flights of stairs.'

'Beach seems to think Frederick's action was caused by some bad news in the telegram which you gave to him.'

'That's right. It was from Aggie.'

'Aggie?'

'His wife.'

'I thought her name was Frances.'

'No, Niagara.'

'What a peculiar name.'

'A gush of sentiment on the part of her parents. They spent the honeymoon at Niagara Falls.'

'Ah yes, I have heard of Niagara Falls. People go over them in barrels, do they not? Now there is a thing I would not care to do myself. Most uncomfortable, I should imagine, though no doubt one would get used to it in time. Why was her telegram so disturbing?'

'Because she says she's coming here and will be with us the day after tomorrow.'

'I see no objection to that.'

'Freddie does, and I'll tell you why. He's gone and given her dog to Valerie Fanshawe.'

'Who is Valerie Fanshawe?'

'The daughter of Colonel Fanshawe of Marling Hall, the tally-ho and view-halloo chap. Haven't you met him?'

'No,' said Lord Emsworth, who never met anyone, if he could help it. 'But why should Frances object to Frederick giving this young woman a dog?'

'I didn't say *a* dog, I said *her* dog. Her personal Alsatian, whom she loves to distraction. However, that could be straightened out, I imagine, with a few kisses and a remorseful word or two if Valerie Fanshawe were a girl with a pasty face and spectacles, but unfortunately she isn't. Her hair is golden, her eyes blue, and years of huntin', shootin', and fishin', not to mention swimmin', tennis-playin' and golfin', have rendered her figure lissom and slender. She looks like something out of a beauty chorus, and as you are probably aware the little woman rarely approves of her mate being on chummy terms with someone of that description. Let Aggie get one glimpse of Valerie Fanshawe and learn that Freddie has been showering dogs on her, and she'll probably divorce him.'

'Surely not?'

'It's on the cards. American wives get divorces at the drop of a hat.'

'Bless my soul. What would Frederick do then?'

'Well, her father obviously wouldn't want him working at his dog biscuit emporium. I suppose he would come and live here.'

'What, at the castle?' cried Lord Emsworth, appalled. 'Good God!'

'So you see how serious the situation is. However, I've been giving it intense thought, turning here a stone, exploring there an avenue, and I am glad to say I have found the solution. We must get that dog back before Aggie arrives.'

'You will ask Rosalie Fanshawe to return it?'

'Not quite that. She would never let it go. It will have to be pinched, and that's where you come in.'

'I?'

'Who else is there? Freddie and I are both lying on beds of pain, unable to move, and we can hardly ask Connie to oblige. You are our only mobile force. Your quick intelligence has probably already told you what you have to do. What do people do when they've got a dog? They instruct the butler to let it out for a run last thing at night.'

'Do they?'

'Invariably. Or bang go their carpets. Every dog has its last-thing-at-night outing, and I think we can safely assume that it will be via the back door.'

'What the back door?'

'Via.'

'Oh, via? Yes, yes, quite.'

'So you must pop over to the Fanshawes – say around ten o'clock – and lurk outside their back door till the animal appears, and bring it back here.'

Lord Emsworth stared, aghast.

'But, Galahad!'

'It's no good saying "But, Galahad!" It's got to be done. You don't want Freddie's whole future to turn blue at the edges and go down the drain, do you? Let alone having him at the castle for the rest of his life. Ah, I see you shudder. I thought you would. And, dash it, it's not much I'm asking of you. Merely to go and stand in a back garden and scoop in a dog. A child could do it. If it wasn't that we want to keep the thing a secret just between ourselves, I'd hand the job over to the Brownie.'

'But what if the dog refuses to accompany me? After all, we've scarcely met.'

'I've thought of that. You must sprinkle your trouser legs with aniseed. Dogs follow aniseed to the ends of the earth.'

'But I have no aniseed.'

'Beach is bound to be able to lay his hands on some. And Beach never asks questions. Unlike Connie's young, smart butler, who would probably be full of them. Oh, Beach,' said Gally, who had pressed the bell. 'Have we aniseed in the house?'

'Yes, Mr Galahad.'

'Bring me a stoup of it, will you?'

'Very good, sir,' said Beach.

If the request surprised him, he did not show it. Your experienced butler never allows himself to look surprised at anything. He brought the aniseed. At the appointed hour Lord Emsworth drove off in Freddie's sports model car, smelling to heaven. And Gally, left alone, lit another cigar and turned his attention to *The Times* crossword puzzle.

He found it, however, difficult to concentrate on it. This was not merely because these crossword puzzles had become so abstruse nowadays and he was basically a Sun-god-Ra and Large-Australian-bird-emu man. Having seen Lord Emsworth off on his journey, doubts and fears were assailing him. He was wishing he could feel more confident of his brother's chances of success in the mission which had been entrusted to him. A lifetime association with him had left him feeling that the head of the family was a frail reed on which to lean in an emergency. His genius for doing the wrong thing was a byword in his circle of acquaintance.

Which, he was asking himself, of the many ways open to him for messing everything up would Lord Emsworth select? Drive the car into a ditch? Go to the wrong house? Or would he forget all about his assignment and sit by the roadside musing on pigs? It was impossible to say, and Gally's emotions were similar to those of a General who, having planned a brilliant piece of strategy, finds himself dubious as to the ability of his troops to carry it out. Generals in such circumstances chew their moustaches in an overwrought sort of way, and Gally would have chewed his, if he had had one.

Heavy breathing sounded outside the door. Beach entered.

'Miss Fanshawe, sir,' he announced.

Gally's acquaintance with Valerie Fanshawe was only a slight one and in the interval since they had last met he had forgotten some of her finer points. Seeing her now, he realized how accurate had been his description of her to Lord Emsworth. In the best and deepest sense of the words she was a dish and a pippin – in short, the very last type of girl to whom a young husband should have given his wife's Alsatian.

'Good evening,' he said. 'You must forgive me for not rising as directed in the books of etiquette. I've sprained my ankle.'

'Oh, I'm sorry,' said Valerie. 'I hope I'm not disturbing you.'

'Not at all.'

'I asked for Mr Threepwood, forgetting there were two of you. I came to see Freddie.'

'He's gone to bed. He has sprained his ankle.'

The girl seemed puzzled.

'Aren't you getting the cast of characters mixed up?' she said. 'It was you who sprained the ankle.'

'Freddie also.'

'What, both of you? What happened?'

'We fell downstairs together.'

'What made you do that?'

'Oh, we thought we would. Can I give Freddie a message?'

'If you wouldn't mind. Tell him that all is well. Did he mention to you that he was trying to sell Father those dog biscuits of his?'

'He did.'

'Well, I approached Father on the subject and he said Oh, all right, he would give them a try. He said he didn't suppose they would actually poison the dumb chums and as I was making such a point of it he'd take a chance.'

'Splendid.'

'And I've brought back the dog.'

It was only the most sensational piece of news that could make Gally's monocle drop from his eye. At these words it fell like a shooting star.

'You've done *what*?' he exclaimed, retrieving the monocle and replacing it in order the better to goggle at her.

'He gave me an Alsatian dog this afternoon, and I've brought it back.'

'You mean you don't want it?'

'I want it all right, but I can't have it. The fathead's first act on clocking in was to make a bee line for Father's spaniel and try to assassinate it, the one thing calculated to get himself socially ostracized. Father thinks the world of that spaniel. "Who let this canine paranoiac into the house?" he thundered, foaming at the mouth. I said I had. "Where did you get the foul creature?" he demanded. "Freddie gave him to me," I said. "Then you can damn well take him back to this Freddie, whoever he is," he –'

'Vociferated?'

'Yes, vociferated. "And let me add," he said, "that I am about to get my gun and count ten, and if the animal's still around when I reach that figure, I shall blow his head off at the roots and the Lord have mercy on his soul." Well, I'm pretty quick and I saw right away that what he was hinting at was that he preferred not to associate with the dog, so I've brought him back. I think he went off to the Servants' Hall to have a bite of supper. I shall miss him, of course. Still, easy come, easy go.'

And so saying Valerie Fanshawe, reverting to the subject of Gally's ankle, expressed a hope that he would not have to have it amputated, and withdrew.

If at this moment somebody had started to amputate Gally's ankle, it is hardly probable that he would have noticed it, so centred were his thoughts on this astounding piece of good luck which had befallen a nephew of whom he had always been fond. If, as he supposed, it was the latter's guardian angel who had engineered the happy ending like a conjuror pulling a rabbit out of a hat, he would have liked to slap him on the back and tell him how greatly his efforts were appreciated. Joy cometh in the morning, he told himself, putting the clock forward a little, and by way of celebrating the occasion he rang for Beach and asked him to bring him a whisky and soda.

It was some considerable time before the order was filled, and Beach was full of apologies for his tardiness.

'I must express my regret for being so long, Mr Galahad. I was detained on the telephone by Colonel Fanshawe.'

'The Fanshawe family seem very much with us tonight. Is there a Mrs Fanshawe?'

'I understand so, Mr Galahad.'

'No doubt she will be dropping in shortly. What did the Colonel want?'

'He was asking for his lordship, but I have been unable to locate him.'

'He's gone for a stroll.'

'Indeed? I was not aware. Colonel Fanshawe wished him to come to Marling Hall tomorrow morning in his capacity of Justice of the Peace. It appears that the butler at Marling Hall apprehended a prowler who was lurking in the vicinity of the back door and has locked him in the cellar. Colonel Fanshawe is hoping that his lordship will give him a sharp sentence.'

For the second time that night Gally's monocle had fallen from the parent eye socket. He had not, as we have seen, been sanguine with regard to the possibility of his brother getting through the evening without mishap, but he had not foreseen anything like this. This was outstanding, even for Clarence.

'Beach,' he said, 'this opens up a new line of thought. You speak of a prowler.'

'Yes, sir.'

'Who was lurking at the Fanshawe back door and is now in the Fanshawe cellar.'

'Yes, sir.'

'Well, here's something for your files. The prowler you have in mind was none other than Clarence, ninth Earl of Emsworth.'

'Sir!'

'I assure you. I sent him to Marling Hall on a secret mission, the nature of which I am not empowered to disclose, and how he managed to get copped we shall never know. Suffice it that he did and is now in the cellar. Wine cellar or coal?'

'Coal, I was given to understand, sir.'

'Our task, then, is to get him out of it. Don't speak. I must think, I must think.'

When an ordinary man is trying to formulate a scheme for extricating his brother from a coal cellar, the procedure is apt to be a lengthy one involving the furrowed brow, the scratched head and the snapped finger, but in the case of a man like Gally this is not so. Only a minimum of time had elapsed before he was able to announce that he had got it.

'Beach!'

'Sir?'

'Go to my bedroom, look in the drawer where the handkerchiefs are, and you will find a small bottle containing white tablets. Bring it to me.'

'Very good, sir. Would this be the bottle to which you refer, sir?' asked Beach, returning a few minutes later.

'That's the one. Now a few necessary facts. Is the butler at the Fanshawes a pal of yours?'

'We are acquainted, sir.'

'Then he won't be surprised if you suddenly pay him a call?'

'I imagine not, Mr Galahad. I sometimes do when I find myself in the neighbourhood of Marling Hall.'

'And on these occasions he sets them up?'

'Sir?'

'You drain a cup or two?'

'Oh yes, sir. I am always offered refreshment.'

'Then it's all over but the cheering. You see this bottle, Beach? It contains what are known as Micky Finns. The name is familiar to you?'

'No, sir.'

'They are a recognized sedative in the United States. When I last went to New York, a great friend of mine, a bartender on Eighth Avenue, happened to speak of them and was shocked to learn that I had none in my possession. They were things, he said, which nobody should be without. He gave me a few, assuring me that sooner or later they were bound to come in useful. Hitherto I have had no occasion to make use of them, but I think you will agree that now is the time for them to come to the aid of the party. You follow me, Beach?'

'No, sir.'

'Come, come. You know my methods, apply them. Slip one of these into this butler's drink, and almost immediately you will see him fold up like a tired lily. Your path thus made straight, you proceed to the cellar, unleash his lordship and bring him home.'

'But, Mr Galahad!'

'Now what?'

'I hardly like –'

'Don't stand there making frivolous objections. If Clarence is not extracted from that cellar before tomorrow morning, his name will be mud. He will become a hissing and a byword.'

'Yes, sir, but –'

'And don't overlook another aspect of the matter. Perform this simple task, and there will be no limit to his gratitude. Purses of gold will change hands. Camels bearing apes, ivory and peacocks, all addressed to you, will shortly be calling at the back door of Blandings Castle. You will clean up to an unimaginable extent.'

It was a powerful plea. Beach's two chins, which had been waggling unhappily, ceased to waggle. A light of resolution came into his eyes. He looked like a butler who has stiffened the sinews and summoned up the blood, as recommended by Henry the Fifth.

'Very good, Mr Galahad,' he said.

Gally resumed his crossword puzzle, more than ever convinced that the compiler of the clues was suffering from softening of the brain, and in due course heavy breathing woke him from the light doze into which he had fallen while endeavouring to read sense into '7 across' and he found that Beach was back from the front. He had the air of one who has recently passed through some great spiritual experience.

'Well?' said Gally. 'All washed up? Everything nice and smooth?'

'Yes, Mr Galahad.'

'You administered the medium dose for an adult?'

'Yes, Mr Galahad.'

'And released his lordship?'

'Yes, Mr Galahad.'

'That's my boy. Where is he?'

'Taking a bath, Mr Galahad. He was somewhat begrimed. Would there be anything further, sir?'

'Not a thing. You can go to bed and sleep peacefully. Good night.'

'Good night, sir.'

It was some minutes later, while Gally was wrestling with '12 down', that he found his privacy invaded by a caller with whom he had not expected to hobnob. It was very seldom that his sister Constance sought his society. Except for shivering austerely whenever they met, she rarely had much to do with him.

'Oh, hullo, Connie,' he said. 'Are you any good at crossword puzzles?'

Lady Constance did not say 'To hell with crossword puzzles,' but it was plain that only her breeding restrained her from doing so. She was in one of those moods of imperious wrath which so often had reduced Lord Emsworth to an apologetic jelly.

'Galahad,' she said. 'Have you seen Beach?'

'Just been chatting with him. Why?'

'I have been ringing for him for half an hour. He really is quite past his duties.'

'Clarence was telling me that that was how you felt about him. He said you were thinking of firing him.'

'I am.'

'I shouldn't.'

'What do you mean?'

'You'll rue the day.'

'I don't understand you.'

'Then let me tell you a little bedtime story.'

'Please do not drivel, Galahad. Really I sometimes think that you have less sense than Clarence.'

'It is a story,' Gally proceeded, ignoring the slur, 'of a feudal devotion to the family interests which it would be hard to overpraise. It shows Beach in so favourable a light that I think you will agree that when you speak of giving him the heave-ho you are talking, if you will forgive me saying so, through the back of your neck.'

'Have you been drinking, Galahad?'

'Only a series of toasts to a butler who will go down in legend and song. Here comes the story.'

He told it well, omitting no detail however slight, and as his narrative unfolded an ashen pallor spread over Lady Constance's face and she began to gulp in a manner which would have interested any doctor specializing in ailments of the thoracic cavity.

'So there you are,' said Gally, concluding. 'Even if you are not touched by his selfless service and lost in admiration of his skill in slipping Micky Finns into people's drinks, you must realize that it would be madness to hand him the pink slip. You can't afford to have him spreading the tale of Clarence's activities all over the county, and you know as well as I do that, if sacked, he will dine out on the thing for months. If I were you, Connie, I would reconsider.'

He eyed the wreck of what had once been a fine upstanding sister with satisfaction. He could read the message of those gulps, and could see that she was reconsidering.

# READ MORE IN PENGUIN

In every corner of the world, on every subject under the sun, Penguin represents quality and variety – the very best in publishing today.

For complete information about books available from Penguin – including Puffins, Penguin Classics and Arkana – and how to order them, write to us at the appropriate address below. Please note that for copyright reasons the selection of books varies from country to country.

**In the United Kingdom**: Please write to *Dept. EP, Penguin Books Ltd, Bath Road, Harmondsworth, West Drayton, Middlesex UB7 0DA*

**In the United States**: Please write to *Consumer Sales, Penguin Putnam Inc., P.O. Box 12289 Dept. B, Newark, New Jersey 07101-5289.* VISA and MasterCard holders call 1-800-788-6262 to order Penguin titles

**In Canada**: Please write to *Penguin Books Canada Ltd, 10 Alcorn Avenue, Suite 300, Toronto, Ontario M4V 3B2*

**In Australia**: Please write to *Penguin Books Australia Ltd, P.O. Box 257, Ringwood, Victoria 3134*

**In New Zealand**: Please write to *Penguin Books (NZ) Ltd, Private Bag 102902, North Shore Mail Centre, Auckland 10*

**In India**: Please write to *Penguin Books India Pvt Ltd, 11 Community Centre, Panchsheel Park, New Delhi 110017*

**In the Netherlands**: Please write to *Penguin Books Netherlands bv, Postbus 3507, NL-1001 AH Amsterdam*

**In Germany**: Please write to *Penguin Books Deutschland GmbH, Metzlerstrasse 26, 60594 Frankfurt am Main*

**In Spain**: Please write to *Penguin Books S. A., Bravo Murillo 19, 1° B, 28015 Madrid*

**In Italy**: Please write to *Penguin Italia s.r.l., Via Benedetto Croce 2, 20094 Corsico, Milano*

**In France**: Please write to *Penguin France, Le Carré Wilson, 62 rue Benjamin Baillaud, 31500 Toulouse*

**In Japan**: Please write to *Penguin Books Japan Ltd, Kaneko Building, 2-3-25 Koraku, Bunkyo-Ku, Tokyo 112*

**In South Africa**: Please write to *Penguin Books South Africa (Pty) Ltd, Private Bag X14, Parkview, 2122 Johannesburg*

# MORE P. G. WODEHOUSE IN PENGUIN

'Witty and effortlessly fluid. His books are laugh-out-loud funny'
Arabella Weir

### The Adventures of Sally

Sally hasn't got the hang of owning a great deal of money yet. Which
is why she agrees to back a show written by her fiancé and staged by
her brother. It seems like a good way of keeping them all happy . . .

### Piccadilly Jim

The life of Jimmy Crocker has been little more than one drunken
brawl after another. His formidable Aunt Nesta has had enough of his
antics and decrees that the young Crocker must be reformed . . .

### Summer Moonshine

The hideous Walsingford Hall belongs to Sir Buckstone, who is in a
little financial difficulty. So for a little monetary help he puts a roof
over the heads of an odd assortment of coves . . .

*also published:*

## THE PSMITH BOOKS

**Psmith Journalist**
**Mike and Psmith**

*and the omnibus:*

**The World of Psmith**
Psmith in the City • Psmith Journalist • Leave it to Psmith

*and:*

| | |
|---|---|
| **Big Money** | **The Luck of the Bodkins** |
| **The Clicking of Cuthbert** | **Money for Nothing** |
| **A Damsel in Distress** | **Pearls, Girls and Monty Bodkin** |
| **French Leave** | **The Small Bachelor** |
| **The Girl in Blue** | **Ukridge** |
| **The Heart of a Goof** | **Uneasy Money** |
| **Hot Water** | **The World of Mr Mulliner** |
| **Laughing Gas** | |

# MORE P. G. WODEHOUSE IN PENGUIN

'P. G. Wodehouse wrote the best English comic novels of the century'
Sebastian Faulks, *Independent on Sunday*

## JEEVES AND WOOSTER

### The Code of the Woosters

Bertie Wooster is in the soup. The problem concerns a cow-creamer,
that should have belonged to Uncle Tom, but was purchased by Sir
Watkyn Bassett. Aunt Dahlia insists that Bertie steal it back, but Sir
Watkyn and his companion Roderick Spode are on to him. Damned
if he does the deed and damned if he doesn't (or rather beaten to a
pulp by Spode), Bertie needs Jeeves's assistance more than ever.

### The Mating Season

Bertie Wooster intends to pay a visit to Deverill Hall to lend a hand
with the village entertainment. He must also ensure that the engagement between Gussie Fink-Nottle and the dreadful Madeline Bassett
remains intact. So Bertie, fearless to the end, poses as Gussie for the
duration. The plot thickens even further, however, when 'Gussie' awakes
the next morning only to be told there is a new guest at Deverill:
someone called Bertie Wooster . . .

*and:*

**Aunts Aren't Gentlemen**
**Carry On, Jeeves**
**The Inimitable Jeeves**
**Jeeves and the Feudal Spirit**
**Jeeves in the Offing**
**Joy in the Morning**

**Much Obliged, Jeeves**
**Right Ho, Jeeves**
**Ring for Jeeves**
**Stiff Upper Lip, Jeeves**
**Thank You, Jeeves**
**Very Good, Jeeves!**

*and the omnibus:*

**Jeeves and Wooster Omnibus**
The Code of the Woosters • The Mating Season • Right Ho, Jeeves

The Inimitable Jeeves, Jeeves in the Offing, Thank You, Jeeves *and*
Very Good, Jeeves!, *all read by Simon Callow, are also available as
Penguin Audiobooks*

# MORE P. G. WODEHOUSE IN PENGUIN

'What can one say about Wodehouse? He exhausts superlatives'
Stephen Fry, *Mail on Sunday*

## SHORT STORIES

### Blandings Castle

'A collection of short snorts between the solid orgies' was how
P. G. Wodehouse regarded these stories, which range from the
Blandings of Lord Emsworth to the Hollywood of the Mulliners.

### Lord Emsworth and Others

Nine delicious stories which include the disgraceful affair of the
crime wave at Blandings, extracts from the unsteady career of Ukridge
and more tales from Mr Mulliner and from the Oldest Member at
the golf club.

### The Man with Two Left Feet

Consider the case of Henry Pitfield Rice, Detective. Or the King of
Coney Island, the Super-Fan, or, of course, Henry Wallace Mills, of
the two left feet. Consider any or all of these twelve vintage cases of
good eggs and decent chaps entangled in snares of young love . . .

### Eggs, Beans and Crumpets

'*Eggs, Beans and Crumpets* was the first Wodehouse I ever read and it
changed my life . . . I devoured it and read, must have been, fifty other
Wodehouse over the next couple of years' Ben Elton, *Booked*

# MORE P. G. WODEHOUSE IN PENGUIN

'The funniest writer ever to put words on paper' Hugh Laurie

## LIFE AT BLANDINGS

*Omnibus editions, also published in separate volumes:*

### Imperial Blandings
Full Moon • Pigs Have Wings • Service with a Smile

Perfect happiness for Lord Emsworth is to listen to the contented night breathing of his medal-winning pig. But so often there is a snake in his Garden of Eden. For Blandings is regarded by his sisters as a suitable repository for young women engaged to impecunious suitors. Worse still a bad baronet and a devious Duke attempt some funny business with the ancestral porker. But usually the Hon. Galahad Threepwood or Lord Ickham can save Lord Emsworth's bacon for him – to *almost* everyone's satisfaction . . .

### Uncle Fred
Uncle Fred in the Springtime • Uncle Dynamite • Cocktail Time

Amid kidnappings, jewel-thefts, *amours* and comedy galore, Frederick, fifth Earl of Ickenham, spreads sweetness and light. Without him, Beefy Bastable, QC, might never have penned his alarming bestseller, *Cocktail Time*; and Lord Emsworth's beloved pig, the Empress, would undoubtedly have been abducted from Blandings. Worst of all, the Earl's myopic nephew Pongo would have breezed past the sweetest girl in the world, and be hitched eternally to the truly ghastly Hermione Bostock.

### Life at Blandings
Something Fresh • Summer Lightning • Heavy Weather

In his inimitable style P. G. Wodehouse entices us into the demesne of Blandings Castle – an apparent paradise where it is eternal high summer. But for Clarence, ninth Earl of Emsworth, there is always something to disturb his tranquil scene, from avoiding his forceful sister, Lady Constance Keeble, to foiling unscrupulous attempts to nobble his beloved pig, the Empress of Blandings, and bailing out Freddie Threepwood from his numerous scrapes.

# MORE P. G. WODEHOUSE IN PENGUIN

'For Wodehouse there has been no fall of Man ... the gardens of Blandings Castle are the original gardens from which we are all exiled'
Evelyn Waugh

### LIFE AT BLANDINGS

The tranquil idyll of life at Blandings is once again shattered by scrapes and skulduggery, mishaps and mix-ups in:

### Galahad at Blandings

A major mix-up at the Castle, in which Gally introduces yet another impostor to Lord Emsworth's residence, and the Empress of Blandings somehow gets drunk in her sty.

### Heavy Weather

Monty Bodkin is hesitating between the Bunch of Grapes and the Drones Club. This is no light decision – it will affect many destinies, including those of the Earl of Emsworth and the Empress; and of the unpleasant Percy Pilbeam. Fate, in playful mood, sent Monty to the Drones Club.

### A Pelican at Blandings

Lovers and thieves gather at Blandings: Lord Emsworth wants them all to go away. To cap it all, the Empress has refused a potato. Galahad, last of the Pelicans, flies to the rescue.

### Sunset at Blandings

This, the last unfinished chronicle of Blandings, includes a treasure trove of detailed notes on the final stages of the plot, enabling us to observe the Master at work.

*also published:*

**Full Moon**
**Pigs Have Wings**
**Service with a Smile**
**Something Fresh**
**Summer Lightning**